JESSICA TURNBULL

Blood and Water

Elemental Dragons Book 1

First edition

ISBN: 9781087190266

Cover art by Deranged Doctor Design - http://www.derangeddoctordesign.com/ Editing by Nicola Hodgson - http://www.root-and-branch-editing.com/

This book was professionally typeset on Reedsy. Find out more at reedsy.com

To my grandfather, Peter Fry.
For always supporting me and encouraging
me to keep writing.

1

Chapter One

Dragons may have been the first to rule the world, but humans have ruled better.

The large, terrifying lizards plagued the Earth with their constant territorial fights. Like most things in nature, they were responsible for their own downfall.

I carefully close the old book in my hands. The cover is faded and worn, and the pages yellow from age, but I don't care. It is the handbook for my next step in life. The chance to be more than just a regular girl. The chance to see my brother again.

Ignoring the roar of the train around me, I flip to my favourite chapter, identified by a folded corner and a faded blue ribbon. This chapter is full of colourful pictures of dragons and people working together. Some of them build houses; others help with shopping. My favourite picture is of a silver dragon soaring through the skies, a middle-aged woman wearing a leather jacket confidently clutching its neck. I hope that my future dragon will be faithful to me, though I know that's a stupid thing to worry about. As long as I treat my companion well, it will be loyal.

Closing the old book carefully as the train shoots around a bend, I glance out of the window, watching nature zoom by. Gnarled trees and pastel flowers dot the landscape. I even catch sight of a fluffy brown rabbit rushing into the undergrowth. The outside world is hidden to us as children. We are hardly ever told what happens out there or what it's like. They don't tell us so that we won't become curious, but it has the opposite effect. At nineteen we leave our town and are released into the wide world, a thought that terrifies me. There's no way of knowing what's on the other side. At fifteen, I only have four years left until I find out.

"Hey, look! I can see the camps on the horizon!"

Someone at the back of the train jumps out of their seat and excitedly taps a window. "Look! One of the Years is practising dragon flying!"

Everyone oohs and aahs at the sight of a royal-blue dragon soaring through the air, its large wings slicing through low clouds. Its companion grips tightly on the reins, almost as if they are scared but trust the dragon's judgement. The dragon is about eight foot tall, its scales covered in emerald-green squiggles, almost like patches of ivy weaving up a tree trunk.

"It's probably one of the older Years. Dragons don't finish growing until Year Three."

I'm nervous.

I'm going to a new area, with new people, new school lessons and I'm going to see my brother for the first time in a year. I'm moving to Aria, one of the best towns in the country. While in a Primary Town you can't visit the people in a Secondary Town, and vice versa. The adults say it's so we don't hurt people if we discover our element early, but I doubt that. I've missed my brother, and my friends too – Marco and Maya the most. It's been hard not having them around every day. But now that I'm moving to a Secondary Town I can see them again and hang around with them.

Hopefully.

That is, if they haven't decided that they don't want to hang around with a First Year, a girl who is younger and less experienced than them.

"Okay, children. Five minutes to go. Make sure you've got your suitcases and books." A tall blonde woman with small grey glasses stands up at the front, clinging to the rail on the ceiling for balance as the train zooms down the tracks. It's Miss Fisher, the Last Year teacher for Primary Town. "The train will stop at the station, and you must immediately enter Camp One. There will be people there to assist you with luggage and directions." She glances out of one of the windows before carrying on. "As soon as you arrive, you will leave your things in your cabin and go to the Square to meet your new teacher." One of the boys at the front sticks his hand up eagerly, making her roll her eyes irritably and pinch the bridge of her nose. "Yes, Brandon. You will be given your dragon egg."

"Yes!" The boy punches the air in excitement.

"I'm going to get an uncommon one!" the girl beside me, Ciara, cries.

"Same! We'll be twins!" Her friend, Naomi, waves her hands in the air excitedly.

Ciara and Naomi have been my only company for the past year, since the others left. We will never officially be friends. They only talk to me because my brother asked them to before he left; he was scared I'd get lonely. I never wanted to hang out with them, but it was either them or be an outcast for a year.

Both are the popular ones of the class, with their pretty faces and high-class tastes. Ciara takes pride in her long blonde hair and petite frame; she's obsessed with her looks. Naomi has tawny brown skin and long caramel-brown hair. She isn't as pretty as her friend but she has the nicer personality when she feels like it.

"Remember though, kids," Miss Fisher shouts above the chatter. "Your dragon egg will depend on how wealthy you are, so don't get your hopes up too high." She glances at me, and I quickly look away, clutching the hand-me-down book about basic dragon knowledge.

"Yeah, Scargirl," Naomi snorts, flicking her fringe out of her face. "Expect to get a crappy one."

Her mention of my cruel nickname makes me flick my hair over one side of my face, where a pink scar lies from my nose all the way to my right eyebrow, cutting through one hazel eye, which, thankfully, I can still see out of.

Obviously this isn't one of Naomi's 'nice' days.

"Just because it's common doesn't mean it's bad," I argue half-heartedly, knowing that I won't be able to convince them otherwise.

"No, it's bad because it takes longer to learn things, duh!" Ciara waves her hand lazily. "Not to mention the damn things are as unruly as hell."

"Whatever. I bet Rocky's doing fine."

Ciara lights up. "Oh yeah! We finally get to see Scargirl's hot brother again!"

Despite a poisonous glance from me, Naomi joins in. "Don't forget Mason and Marco! Bet they've all got girlfriends already."

Ciara nudges me. "Hey, Scarface! Your boyfriend's got a girlfriend. How does that make you feel?"

"Marco is *not* my boyfriend," I scowl, whacking her arm away, though my cheeks redden at the thought.

"Of course he isn't, he's got a girlfriend now!"

I roll my eyes as the two girls explode into bird-like squawks, and open the book at the page I left off. They'll get bored soon, and I won't have to talk to them anymore once I find Rocky and the others; I can hang around with them instead.

I hope.

This page is full of pictures of Avian dragons showing the different tiers: common, uncommon, rare and premier. Your parents' annual salary decides what dragon you get. My family is poor, so I will have a common dragon. Unfortunately, it seems I'm the only one on this train who will receive a common dragon, which might be grounds for teasing. Aria only accepts commoners in special circumstances, so I know I won't be treated well by the other kids or the staff around the Town.

Common dragons come in only three colours, according to the book: white, black and brown. Brown and white are the most common, with only five black common dragons on record. I wonder what colour Rocky got, and what it's like. Would he teach me how to raise my dragon?

Would he even want to see me at all?

The train starts to slow, and my stomach churns. We're here.

"Alright, gather your stuff and get moving!" Miss Fisher shouts over the loud, excited chatter. "Older siblings are waiting for you at the gate, so keep an eye out for them!"

I grab my small black suitcase and clutch my book close to my chest. Looking back at Ciara and Naomi, I'm surprised to see a flicker of nervousness in their usually cool eyes.

Rocky could be there. He might have Maya and Marco there too. Would his dragon be there? What if it eats me?

"There are a lot of dragons at the gate," Ciara mutters, standing on her tiptoes to look over the sea of teenagers.

"I hope they're not hungry," Naomi giggles.

"Yeah, that's how they get rid of the kids they don't want – let the dragons eat them!" Ciara jokes, twirling a strand of blonde hair in her fingers.

"Don't say that!" a small girl with red ribbons in her curly hair shrieks.

"It's a *joke*, Clementine!" Naomi snaps.

Kids start filing off the train, and dragons immediately jump into the air, flying overhead. A grey and black one dives down and lands next to one girl, and a tall girl wades through the crowd and hugs her.

Is Rocky here?

"Scargirl! Keep moving!" Naomi snaps, pushing me forward.

Fresh, cool air blasts my face as I step off the hot, cramped train, but Naomi still clings to the collar of my shirt as she looks around.

"Where is—" A large marble-grey dragon with blue swirls on its face lands next to Naomi, grabbing her arm gently in its teeth.

"Naomi!" Ciara screams.

"Help!" Naomi screeches, desperately trying to tug her arm free.

"Calm down, sis!" A tall boy pushes through the crowd and grabs Naomi's hand.

"Alex!" To my surprise, she throws herself at the boy, hugging him tightly. "I've missed you."

"Hey, I've missed you too."

Something grabs my arm and I whirl around to come face to face with a dark brown dragon that has two small, stubby horns sticking out of its forehead. It looks at me curiously, nostrils flaring, before tugging me gently. Leaving Naomi and Ciara, I pick up my suitcase and walk next to the dragon as the crowd makes room for it to walk through. Its dark amber eyes glow with excitement and its thin tail waves happily. Golden markings in the shape of lightning bolts are wrapped around its tail, almost as if they were birthmarks. I soon realize that it's the owner's element: electricity.

We reach the edge of the crowd and the dragon drops my arm, sniffing the air in confusion. It then swings its head to the left, watching someone excitedly. Following its gaze, I see a tall boy with jet-black hair running towards us.

Rocky.

My big brother came to see me.

"Rocky!" I run and meet him halfway, clinging to his waist. "I didn't know if you'd come!"

"I was always going to come!" He ruffles my hair affectionately. "You know I love you."

His voice is deeper, and he's had a growth spurt since I last saw him. He's probably way over six foot, but he's still got his signature cheesy grin with terrible crooked teeth.

"I love you too. I've missed you so much, and the others."

"I've been worried about you all year," he muttered. "I didn't know if you were alright, if you were doing okay in class, if you'd made any friends…"

Burying my face in his chest, I lie: "I've been fine."

We pull away, but he keeps one arm wrapped around my waist. "Can I take your suitcase?"

"Oh." I look back where I'd dropped it running towards Rocky. The dragon has picked it up by the handle, and is trying to work out how to carry it with the wheels moving in the opposite direction.

"Cerberus!" Rocky calls.

The dragon looks up, and half-waddles, half-clambers over to us, the suitcase knocking against its legs and chest.

"Good girl," Rocky takes the suitcase from the dragon and strokes its snout. "You can pet her; she doesn't bite, only licks."

Cerberus leans towards me expectantly. I hesitantly stroke her cheek, which makes her growl happily. Her scales are surprisingly smooth despite their rough edges, and they are warm to the touch.

"Cerberus is a weird name for a dragon," I comment, grinning as the happy creature presses her snout into my palm.

"I thought she was a guy. Plus, I wanted a cool name. In the end, we just decided to stick to it." We make our way slowly through the gate. "You'll have to start thinking of names. You'll have a baby by the end of the day. As long as it's not a *human* baby, that is."

"Don't be stupid," I tease; "that's next year."

"No, you won't!"

7

It feels good to know that our bond hasn't suffered; that Rocky hasn't changed drastically. I'm happy we can still joke around and wind each other up. Since parents can't visit their kids until they reach Secondary Town, he's become the parental figure in my life. Some people think that our close bond is weird, but I don't care. I look up to him; he's my hero.

"Is it hard?" I blurt out after a few seconds.

"Is what hard, hun?"

"Raising a dragon.... Controlling your element."

"I don't want to lie to you; you'll just suss it out anyway," he grins. "It's hard, yes. Cerberus and I decided to give a light bulb a little extra 'oomph' as practice for an exam. Long story short, we electrocuted three people and nearly burned the cabin down."

"Wow."

"Ironically, we passed." Cerberus bounces beside him proudly as he speaks. "But it's hard controlling your power. And electricity isn't good when you're starting out. Do you know what yours is?"

"Water. I discovered it accidentally in the bath." I smile sheepishly, remembering how one day I managed to raise the water in the tub over my head until it splashed down on the floor.

"Water, huh?"

"Yeah."

"Sounds cool. So, rain just doesn't get you wet?"

"I have to concentrate to make sure the rain drips off me."

"I'll come to you if I ever need a human umbrella."

"Shut up!"

"Your cabin is here; Camp One," He points to a large grey building with a steel door and barred windows. "I know it looks like a prison but it's all safety, promise."

The paintwork on the building is starting to peel off, and the guttering on the roof is dented. A line of white flowers snakes around

8

the building with ivy crawling up to the windows. Four other buildings surround it, all alike. Rusted iron numbers hang above the doors. I'm in cabin three.

"Do you want me to come in with you?"

I don't know many people in my Year, as it's a collection of three different Primary Towns. Only a few people from my town chose to go to this one. I probably won't recognize anyone in my new home.

"Yes, please."

"Cerberus, go and see if any other kids have gathered in the Square. I don't want Haze to be late."

Cerberus nods her small head, accidentally scratching my brother's arm with her horns. She spreads her bat-like wings and leaps upwards, catching a wind current and zooming off.

"Show-off," Rocky mutters, leading me towards the door, his arm still locked around my waist.

He opens the steel door and we peer inside. Several kids have already gathered in the cabin, some talking with older siblings and friends who met them at the gate. Inside, the cabin looks a lot more inviting. The floor and walls are made of a dark cream wood, and bunk beds and drawers line up against the windows. Each bed has a brass plate with the name of a person on it.

"Come on, Adams will be at the back." Rocky ushers me in, and kids immediately turn around to watch us enter.

"Is that the poor girl you were talking about?" one snickers.

"Yep; only girl who's getting a common dragon in First Year," the other pipes up, putting her hand in front of her mouth to hide a laugh.

"I'd hate that. She's gonna stick out in classes!"

Blocking out their mindless gossiping, I head for the back wall, glancing at each nameplate as I pass. Mine is the top bunk at the very back. I'm sharing with a guy called Wes Abbot.

Rocky throws my suitcase on top of my bed, as I couldn't reach without the ladder. "You're the only person in your Year getting a common dragon?"

"Yeah. It's the most exciting thing going on at the moment, apparently," I say sarcastically.

"You don't mind though, do you?" he asks carefully.

"No. Cerberus is great. I don't understand why they're so undesirable."

"When you have money, you want the prettiest, strongest things. Common dragons aren't pretty enough for rich people to want them."

"I don't care. I just want a good companion."

Muffled yaps can be heard from outside. A second later the door swings open, making everyone jump. Cerberus squeezes her shoulders through the door, yelping urgently.

"Fucking hell! Get that unruly thing out of here!" someone up front shouts.

Everyone turns to glare at Rocky and me, muttering about how they're going to hate living with me and my dragon.

My classmates don't like me already. Great.

"Come on, that means introduction will start soon." Rocky grabs my hand and hurries me down the aisle.

Once we close the door behind us, Cerberus bounces in a circle, yapping.

"I'm sorry, Haze. They'll forget about it tomorrow, I promise." Rocky strokes my cheek with his thumb before quickly leading me down a dusty street.

Shops and restaurants line the street on either side, buzzing with activity. Dragons lie around lazily, enjoying the afternoon sunshine. Secondary students and adults laugh in shops, trying on silly items or telling jokes.

"We're actually allowed visitors in Aria," Rocky explains, noticing my fascinated gaze. "Mum has visited me a couple of times."

I struggle to remember the woman who gave birth to me. The strict rules in Primary Towns mean that you don't see your parents while you're there; no letters or anything. I haven't seen my mother since I was six, when I was taken away from her to live in Primary Town.

"How is she?"

"She's fine. She cried when we first met up. She wanted to know everything, you know? What grades we were getting; who we had a crush on; how many fights we had. It was crazy. The next meet-up will be in two weeks. She's dying to see you."

"I'm glad she's okay."

We approach a large tiled area, bare of any shops. Weeds sprang from between the cracks, making the place look older than it probably was. A large hole was blocked off in the middle, surrounded by black scorch marks. Bare earth lay underneath it, yanked out of the ground by something, possibly a dragon or a student with a temper. It's cordoned off by a few wooden poles with yellow tape wrapped around them. A few kids had already gathered. Some older students were hanging around too, there to give support to the younger ones. A short bald man in a black pinstriped suit stood in the middle, his expression locked into a scowl. A large black and red dragon sat next to him, scanning the kids with what I can only call distaste. Its mouth kept opening and closing, almost as if it were baring its teeth.

"Ugh. It's Mr Reedman." Rocky scowls.

"He's not nice, I presume?"

"Not in the slightest. His dragon, Eruption, is a bully too. Nasty piece of work." He turns to Cerberus. "Stay on the outskirts in this meeting. You know how harsh he is with the new kids."

Cerberus narrows her eyes and nods, her gaze locked on Eruption.

"Where are the eggs?" I ask.

"You see that cart over there?" He points to a large wooden cart with a sheet covering its contents and a clipboard pinned to the side.

"How many are in there?"

"There's five cabins that can each house twenty kids, so up to a hundred."

"The eggs must be tiny."

"As soon as they're given to you, they grow to the right size. The egg recognizes the body heat of its owner."

My egg is in there, somewhere. Will it be okay cooped up in that tiny little cart with ninety-nine other eggs?

"How long do they take to hatch?"

"You spend a day looking after it; carrying it around with you everywhere. Then, once it has a good enough memory of you, it hatches. It recognizes you as its parent."

"So, tomorrow?"

"Yep. Exciting, huh?"

"All First Year students remain here. Everyone else must leave!" Mr Reedman booms, glaring at some of the people in the front row.

"I'll be right here when he finishes, okay? I'll even bring Marco if you want."

"Okay."

"Don't be nervous." He kisses my forehead, hugs me and slowly walks away, casting glances behind him. His eyes are reddening, which makes my eyes fill up too.

He'll be waiting for me once I'm done, then we can have a proper catch-up.

"Bye," I mutter, turning back towards Mr Reedman.

"Now, First Years." A dark smile widens on his face. "I will be your Head of Instructors from now until you leave. That's fifteen years old to nineteen years old, for any of you imbeciles out there. There will be no messing around, no slacking and *no* failing."

Mutters rise from the crowd until Eruption opens its mouth and roars at the front row, its sharp teeth glinting in the sunlight. A tall blond man steps out from behind the cart, his eyes scanning the group in front of him. He must be a few years older than me, so I don't know why he's still hanging around.

"This is Raymond Stirling. He is the head of the Cindaraans, which you will learn more about later. See any you like, Raymond?" The man turns to the blond boy, smirking slightly.

"Oh yes." Raymond's eyes lock onto me, making me shuffle uncomfortably. "I'm sure we have a few future Cindaraans here."

I don't know what Cindaraans are, but by the way the two of them keep smirking and eyeing up the crowd, I guess it can't be good. I'll have to avoid them.

Mr Reedman turns to the hulking dragon at the front, stroking one of its horns gently. "This is Eruption. Do behave around him – he holds very deep grudges." He turns towards the cart and tears off the clipboard, making it wobble dangerously.

The poor eggs! Be careful with the little things!

"We'll start with common dragons, shall we?"

I'm in trouble.

"Only one? How unfortunate! Hazel Adams, please step forward!"

The crowd parts, fear on all their faces. No-one wants to be first. Heck, *I* don't even want to be first.

I stop in front of the suited man, trying my hardest to make sure my hands don't shake.

"You poor girl. Not only are you a commoner, but you're also related to Rocky Adams. He got Eruption and I electrocuted, you know."

Oh crap.

"Do you think you're special, Miss Adams?"

My voice doesn't work for a few moments. I'm not a huge fan of public speaking. "N-no, sir." My voice barely comes out as a whisper.

"Good. Now, would you like your egg, Miss Adams?" He walks towards the cart, patting the soft sheet.

"Yes please, sir."

"So polite!" he exclaims sarcastically, before rummaging around in the cart and pulling out a small, cream-coloured egg. "No, not this one..." He puts the egg back and pulls out a small grey spotted one; I recognize it from the book. Common eggs only come in the grey spotted colouring, and are no bigger than a tennis ball until they connect with someone. "Here you are!" he holds out the egg to me, but as I go to take it, he snatches it back. "Go and catch it!"

Before his words can sink in, he throws the egg into the air. An angry roar makes some people behind me scream, and a brown blob catches the egg in mid-air. Cerberus looks down at the bald man, her amber eyes glowing with hatred.

"I thought as much," Mr Reedman mutters. "Miss Adams, you're dismissed. Do you want to be escorted away by Eruption?"

The large dragon rises to his feet, his red eyes locked onto me. Cerberus lands in front of me, blocking my view of the terrifying creature. She is holding the egg gently in her teeth, and nudges it into my hands. For a second I see the outline of the dragon inside, a small lizard creature illuminated orange by the sunlight, before the egg grows to three times its size in my hands.

"Well done. The dragon has connected to you. Now leave, you stupid little child." The bald man turns back to the clipboard. "Let's move onto uncommon dragons now, shall we?"

2

Chapter Two

"Do you think it'll be okay?"

Cerberus looks at the egg, and then nods slowly. She isn't sure either. The two of us lumber along slowly, with me clutching the egg close to my chest as if it would be snatched away and thrown again. I've only been here a few hours and I already know that the next few years are going to be hell.

If my dragon dies, I'm out. When your companion dies you're considered a 'Nothing', as the vast majority of the population has dragons. Most Nothings are lucky to have a job or their own place. Most are left to rot on the streets.

"What right did he have to do that? I've done nothing wrong, and neither has the egg."

Cerberus looks at me apologetically and nuzzles my shoulder. Mr Reedman is holding a grudge against me because I'm related to Rocky, and it was probably an accident.

"Hello, Hazel."

The silky voice makes me jump as Raymond steps in between Cerberus and me, a dark smile on his face.

"Um, hi." I clutch the egg closer to my chest, ready to fight him if he tries to hurt it.

"If your dragon lives, come and see me. The Cindaraans could use someone like you."

"Like me? Why?"

"So they know what a pathetic human being looks like." He twirls his finger, a few clumps of dirt rising into the air around his hands. "I will be seeing you around."

With that, the dirt plummets to the floor and he turns and walks back to the Square, wiping any hint of emotion off his face.

"Where's Rocky? I want Rocky." My eyes sting again, and this time I just let the tears flow. I've already had enough. I just want Rocky to tell me that everything will be okay.

The brown dragon looks mortified and jumps into the air, quickly leaving me alone. I sink to my knees, resting my cheek on the grey egg. Despite all that's going on, I want it to be warm and happy.

After a few minutes, Cerberus returns and the drum of feet tells me that Rocky isn't far behind. "Haze!" He pulls me to my feet and draws me close to him in a hug. "What happened? Are you okay?"

"He threw it!"

"Threw what, Haze?"

"The egg! I don't know if it's okay…"

He pulls away and looks me up and down. "It's grown, right?"

I nod and wipe my nose with my hand. "Yeah."

"Then it's perfectly fine." He smiles slightly, but it doesn't quite reach his eyes.

"Don't lie to me!"

"Shh. I'm not lying. If it wasn't okay, it wouldn't have connected to you." He brushes a few tears from my cheek. "It's fine."

My grip on the egg relaxes a little. He's right. If the dragon wasn't fine, it wouldn't have connected to me in the first place. It feels alright too. There aren't any cracks or signs that the dragon is injured or dead.

"Here, I've brought you something to carry it in." He holds up a small black backpack, worn from years of use. He unzips it and holds it out for me. "Put it in there. It'll still be close to you, but it'll be easier to carry."

Gently I lower the grey egg in and zip it up. "Thanks."

"No problem. Do you want something to eat? You've had a lot of excitement for one day."

"I dunno."

He rolls his green eyes, which are beginning to sparkle with their usual mischief. "Yes, you do. You know where to go, Cerberus."

* * *

Rocky takes me to a small restaurant just outside of the Square. When we passed by, First Years were still receiving their dragons, although they weren't having theirs thrown about like tennis balls. Not many people are around; the restaurant is only just starting to bring out the menus for dinner. Small round wooden tables form the main seating at the front of the restaurant, but two larger tables for bigger parties are pushed up against the wall at the back. A small counter is also at the back, with a door leading into the kitchen. A few potted plants are scattered on each table, and the floor is made of cracked marble.

"I've got a surprise for you," Rocky grins cheekily.

"Hazel!"

I recognize that voice. "Maya!"

Maya has beautiful long black hair and dark skin. She's wearing a tight-fitting blue dress, which is unusual; she didn't like dresses the last time I saw her.

She stands up and we hug silently. I've missed not having my girl best friend around. At least now I can talk to a girl who isn't completely up herself.

Rocky breaks the silence. "Where's Marco? Did he bail?"

Maya pulls away, her hands on her hips. "Did he 'eck. He's in the bathroom. He's so nervous he's practically spent all day pissing."

Hands are clamped around my ears and Rocky hisses: "Don't use that language around her!"

"She's fifteen! She's probably heard it all by now!"

I wriggle out of Rocky's grip. "Marco's nervous?"

Maya smirks. "Yeah. He's scared you've changed and don't like him anymore."

"I was scared about you guys not liking me!"

"You were?" Rocky looks puzzled.

"Yeah, I thought you guys wouldn't want to hang around with me seeing as you're older."

"Don't be stupid!" Maya rolls her eyes. "Rocky was up at three o'clock this morning watching every train that went past and hoping you were on it."

"Really? I was up at three too!"

"You two are sad, sad people." Maya grins, nudging me playfully.

We all sit down and start flicking through the menu, chatting playfully among each other.

"Are you sure Marco hasn't bailed?" Rocky crosses his arms and rolls his eyes. He isn't fond of my best friend.

"I'm pretty sure he's masturbating now," Maya jokes.

I butt into their conversation before Rocky can flip. "Where's the bathroom?"

"It's the door by that plant in the shape of an eagle."

"That's two plants behind one another, you numpty," Rocky grins.

Hauling the backpack over my shoulder, I walk towards the 'eagle' bush and go to open the door when it swings open in front of me.

"Watch where you're going!" a deep voice hisses.

Marco.

He's a little taller than he used to be, and his jet-black hair is long enough to almost fall over his eyes. His face is covered in spots and a few stray hairs, but apart from that he hasn't changed much. His expression softens upon recognising me. Self-consciously, I sweep my dirty blonde fringe over the right side of my face, not wanting him to see the scar and how ugly it's become since he left.

"I've missed you," he says.

"It hasn't been the same without my partner-in-crime." I agree.

He smiles and brushes my hair away from my face. "Hug?"

It almost feels like slipping into a mould when hugging Marco; it's so familiar. Before he left we were inseparable. Teachers at Primary Camp were terrified to split us up when the time came. I'm glad to be around my friends again.

"How was your first day?" he asks, still not willing to let go of me.

"Crap. Mr Reedman threw my dragon in the air and said I was stupid."

"You are stupid."

"Thanks."

"He's always in a bad mood. I think he's got something prickly wedged up his ass."

I sigh. "Wouldn't surprise me."

We finally pull apart, and he goes to open the door again.

"I actually need to go to the toilet." Nudging him playfully, I say: "Sorry to disappoint."

"And here was me thinking that you were trying to pester me," he grins. "See you in a minute."

I quickly went to the bathroom and checked on my dragon so I could re-join the others. Still no sign of anything wrong with it. It's just so tiny and delicate, I'm afraid that even bumping into something would cause a crack. I carefully replace the egg in the backpack and head towards the door. I want to catch up with my friends, and I'm sure they're dying to talk to me too.

"Hey," Marco greets me as I approach, causing Rocky and Maya to stop arguing. He looks uncomfortable, his eyes darting back and forth from Maya to me again. Did something happen?

Placing the backpack on the floor, I smile at him. "Have you ordered yet?"

"No, we can't decide what we want." Rocky flicks through the menu slowly.

"How's the egg? Can I see it?" Maya reaches for the backpack.

"Be careful."

"I will, don't worry. Once the egg is in this state it's near impossible to break it," she says matter-of-factly.

"Watch her drop it and make an omelette," Marco jokes.

"*Thank you*, Marco," Rocky scowls, his green eyes shooting daggers at my uncomfortable friend. "The little thing has been through enough excitement for one day."

"What do you mean?" Marco asks, glancing up from the menu briefly.

"I told you, Mr Reedman threw it in the air." I shuffle uncomfortably.

He pauses. "I thought you were joking! So, he really said you were stupid?"

"He said *what*?" Rocky's hand slams on the table, making me duck my head in embarrassment.

"*Anyway*," I quickly change the topic to avoid further arguments. "What elements are you guys?"

"Fire," Maya says proudly. "It's pretty cool."

"I'm fire and dark. First of my kind, apparently." Marco fiddles with his thumbs.

"Wow, so you're pretty rare, huh?" I tease. "I should sell you to a museum."

"I'm glad your sense of humour hasn't changed," he rolls his eyes. "So, what are you then? You ate worms when you were little; does that make you earth?"

"I did not eat worms."

"You did. Someone was always on worm duty until you were three."

"Sorry to disappoint then, but no. I'm water."

"So, if we need an umbrella, you're it?"

"Hilarious."

We all flick through the menu a bit more, until we decide just to get burgers; no-one is really looking anyway. Maya gives me back the egg after a few minutes, saying that it will be small when it hatches.

"What was life like when we were gone, then? Pretty bleak, I'm guessing," Marco smirks, his brown eyes giving away his teasing.

"It was okay. I only had Ciara and Naomi to talk to though, so that was pretty boring."

"Oh yeah? What did they talk about?" Maya leans on to the table, stretching her arms.

"Boys and sex mostly."

She laughs and turns to Rocky, who looks horrified. "I thought you wanted to leave her with *good* influences?"

"I thought I had!" he cries.

"Now that she's back with us she'll have better influences," she snorts. "Apart from Marco, that is."

"I'm responsible," Marco mutters, though he looks away when Maya turns to glare at him.

"You're sixteen and you've fucked two girls that you had absolutely no interest in. Don't pretend that you're a good influence on poor, innocent little Haze," she mocks, smiling darkly.

Marco continues to play with his thumbs while Rocky and Maya argue over who's better. I place one of my hands over his and squeeze it, which makes a hint of a smile appear on his face.

21

* * *

"Haze, this is Magma. He's a sweetie." Maya pats her dragon's head.

After dinner, it was decided that I would be introduced to everyone's dragons, as I would be seeing them a lot from now on.

Magma is bright red with orange feet, the two colours meaning that he is at least an uncommon dragon. He has bright red markings in the shape of fireballs across his torso, tail and legs, symbolizing Maya's element of fire. Two large horns stick out of his forehead, curved at the base so the tips touch his cheeks. He bows his head in greeting, ignoring Cerberus, who is trying to push past him to get some of the attention.

"Drea is the one at the back," Marco says. "She's in a sulky mood."

Drea is a premier dragon; it's obvious by the hammer-like shape of her tail-tip and the white gemstone in her chest. She is snowy white with red fireballs on her face and dark purple shadows on her stomach, symbolizing fire and dark. Her horns stick out at a perfectly straight point, but are considerably shorter than Magma's.

"Drea's always in a sulky mood. She fits you perfectly," Rocky snorts.

Marco just rolls his eyes in reply.

"So, Haze. Any names for the dragon? It'll be here tomorrow." Maya pats Magma's neck and opens the door to the dragon paddock that the restaurant provides so the dragons can leave.

"I don't really know yet."

"Don't name it something girly," Marco groans.

"Do I look like I'm going to call it Pinkie?"

"She might see the dragon hatch and the name will come to her," Rocky argues. "Like Cerberus and Magma."

"True," Maya sighs. "Just don't give it a stupid name, 'cause then you're stuck with it."

"Anyway, I'll walk you back to your cabin," Rocky says. "I want you to settle in."

"Okay. See you guys tomorrow." Maya and I hug quickly, but Marco is more persistent in wanting a longer hug, which winds Rocky up immensely.

3

Chapter Three

"Will you be okay on your own?"

"Rocky, I'll be fine. Honestly, you're worrying about nothing. I was okay for a year without you; I think I can last a night in a cabin."

The entire walk home Rocky has pestered me about being in a cabin filled with people I don't know. I think he'd like me to stay with him. After today's events, I am nervous about being on my own, but Rocky isn't helping.

"I'll see you tomorrow. Classes don't start until Monday."

"Mine too?"

"Yep. Enjoy tomorrow while you can; school and dragon training are a tough combination." Upon hearing my nervous squeak, he continues: "But I'll be here! And Maya, and..." he pauses and sighs irritably, "*Marco*, if you really *must* hang around with him."

"Okay, I'll hold you to that."

I snuggle into his chest, hugging him tightly while he rubs my back soothingly. "Any problems, you come see me, okay? Don't keep anything from me. We'll find some way of working it out."

"I can't tell you everything," I tease, watching the frown appear on his face.

"Yeah? Like what?"

"Girl problems, for one."

"You can ask me about that, though I'll have no idea what I'm talking about."

Cerberus nudges Rocky's legs playfully, so we pull apart. Patting Cerberus on the head, I take my leave. "G'night."

"Don't go to bed too late, okay?"

I make my way towards the door. "I know."

"Are you sure you don't want me to tuck you in?"

"Rocky, I'm not five! I'll see you tomorrow."

"Okay, okay," he raises his hands in defeat. "Good night."

As soon as I open the door, I'm surprised to see a large group huddled around one of the bunks. Kids are chattering excitedly, oohing and aahing over something on the bed.

"It's so cute!" someone shouts at the front.

"What's its name?" another pipes up, pushing through the crowd to get a closer look.

"I hope mine is that pretty!" a girl on a bed grins from ear to ear.

A short, skinny girl with mid-length ginger hair climbs onto the top bunk. "Enough staring! Me and Laila have to get ready for bed *sometime*, you know!" In her arms lies a small white dragon with purple splotches on its back. A purple gemstone in its chest gives away its status as a premier dragon. "I'm sure all of the rare dragons will hatch during the night!"

I guess premier dragons hatch fastest, which means that my egg will probably be the last one to hatch. *If* it hatches, of course. The poor thing might be dead and I wouldn't know it until Monday morning.

"Yeah! It'll be so cool!"

With an eye roll, I push through the crowd until I reach my bunk at the back. My suitcase still lies in the same position on the bed, which means I should unpack. A wooden door on each side of the bunk bed

25

reads 'Toilets' and 'Stables'. Unfortunately, this means people will be passing back and forth here throughout the night to use the toilet. Great.

"Oh! You must be Hazel. I'm Wes." The boy on the lower bunk gets up and holds his hand out to me, a friendly smile on his face.

He's no taller than I am, of Asian descent with short brown hair and small-framed glasses sitting upon a wonky nose. He looks friendly enough.

"Um, yeah." We shake hands awkwardly, and he quickly brushes his hair back with his hand.

"So, you've got a common dragon, huh?"

"Yeah."

He tilts his head to one side slightly. "Not much of a talker, are you?"

"Not really, no." I smile sheepishly.

"That's fine. Can I see your egg? You're the only person with a common dragon here."

"Uh, sure. Can I see yours?"

"Yeah, course."

Gently, I place the backpack on the floor and lift the egg out, while Wes points to a cream-coloured egg on his pillow. Panic races through my mind as he takes the egg, stroking it curiously. His egg is heavy, and is considerably larger than mine. His dragon is going to be huge.

"Hey, what colour do you think yours will be? White or brown?" he asks.

"I dunno. I only saw it briefly when it connected, but I was more worried about what happened to it than what colour it was."

"Oh... Right. I'm sorry about that. Is it okay?"

"We'll have to wait and find out, I guess."

There's an uncomfortable silence between us before I decide to carry on the conversation. Rocky's nerves will calm considerably if he finds out I've made a friend. "This is an uncommon egg, right? Any ideas about the colour?"

"When it connected, it didn't look like a bright colour," he confesses. "But I don't mind. It's gonna be one of the biggest dragons here!"

"I can tell. It'll be taking up all the room in your bed in no time."

"Yeah, but at least no-one will think twice about messing with me!" He places the egg on the bed carefully. "Here, I'll take that off you."

I'm grateful to have the heavy egg taken off me, and to get mine back unharmed. As I pick it up there's no new movement, but I don't know whether that's normal or not.

"Mine's hatched!" someone screeches by the door.

"Another premier dragon?" Wes sighs. "That's the third one in this cabin."

The small, chubby boy bounces around with a bright yellow and red dragon in his arms, puffing his chest out proudly.

People crowd around him, whispering about how their dragons will look and when it will hatch. Do they have nothing better to do?

"Some people have the attention span of a rock," I mutter under my breath.

"I agree." Wes makes me jump by putting his hand on my shoulder. "You seem nice, though. Quiet, but nice."

"You're okay too."

Ducking his head in embarrassment, he grins. "Thanks."

His hand doesn't move from my shoulder, so I clear my throat awkwardly: "I'm gonna go get ready for bed."

His hand not moving, he grins. I don't think he realizes it's still there. "'Kay. We each have our own stall. You're the first on the register, so you're number one."

"Uh, thanks." I move slowly towards the door, reaching up to drag my suitcase off my bed. "I'll, uh, see you in a minute."

He nods and sits back on his bed, sifting through his suitcase. Quickly I slip into the bathroom, staring at the rows of silver stalls that line the white walls. Wes was right; wooden numbers are nailed to each stall, along with the initials of each person. The door to my stall creaks open when I touch it, so I quickly slip in and close it behind me to prevent myself from making too much noise.

Inside the stall the floor, walls and ceiling are a dull grey colour, with a single light bulb swinging from the ceiling. A toilet, sink and shower cubicle are squeezed into the tiny space; a mirror cabinet is nailed to the wall above the sink with a dirty handprint wiped onto the centre. A large body-length mirror is glued to the back of the door, a dull golden rim around the edges. Finally, next to the toilet is a long white bathtub. It looks new; the taps are almost shiny enough to see my reflection in.

I place the egg in the sink, studying the handprint with distaste. "Well, today could have gone better," I mutter to no-one in particular. "I just wish you hadn't been chucked into the air like a Frisbee." The dragon egg lay unmoving in the sink.

I'm talking to an egg. I've actually lost my mind.

I just hope it hatches. I don't want to be a Nothing. Although having to spend the year with Raymond and his 'Cindaraans' doesn't sound too great either. I'll have to try to avoid them as much as possible, especially if they're all as horrible as Raymond and Mr Reedman.

There's not much point in sitting around moping any longer. I'll just have to see what happens tomorrow.

* * *

Loads of eggs hatched last night, including all of the premier and rare eggs. One or two of the uncommon eggs have started to hatch too, so Wes has been watching his like a hawk since he got up and discovered a small crack in the side. He's not the only one; other kids have been hollering about cracks in their eggs too.

No change in my egg though. It hasn't shown any signs of hatching.

"Hazel! Quick, come watch!" Wes ushers me down with his hand, smiling widely.

Half-heartedly, I trudge down the ladder. As soon as my feet hit the floor, he grabs my arm and pulls me onto his messy bed.

"Its tail poked out the side a minute ago! It's dark brown!" He bounces excitedly as a tiny orange foot breaks a hole through the side of the tough cream shell.

"Can it get out okay?"

"I think it's just in a weird position." His face scrunches up in worry.

"It's probably just woken up," I joke. "Not a morning person."

"Oh? Does it have bed hair like yours?"

Pushing him playfully, I chuckle: "Shut up."

A little squeak later and a brown head breaks through the shell, leaving bits of cream dust on Wes' bed. The minuscule winged lizard blinks up at Wes with bright orange eyes and squeaks, tipping the egg onto its side. Slowly, it hauls itself out of its old home and scrambles towards him. It climbs onto his lap and licks his cheek, its tiny tail lashing side to side in excitement.

"Hello," Wes chuckles, stroking his new companion on its scaly head.

"Boy or girl?" I ask excitedly.

"Girl. She doesn't have a spiky tail."

Well, at least now I know how to tell the difference. I wonder what mine will be like?

"She's huge!"

"Stroke her, it's okay." He holds the brown dragon towards me, her orange feet kicking wildly in the air. I stroke her head gently, and she softens in Wes' grip, making satisfied squeaking noises. "I can't wait to show her off! How's your egg doing?"

"No change."

"Oh. I'm sure it'll hatch soon; it's probably an afternoon person."

"Maybe."

"Don't worry about it too much, just enjoy your day off." He changes the conversation excitedly. "What classes have you signed up for? Apart from English and Maths, obviously."

My heart sinks at the thought of school. The teachers could be as bad as Mr Reedman, or worse, if that's possible. Plus, I'll be in a classroom filled with people I won't know. I'd be lying if I said I wasn't looking forward to new lessons: Dragon Mythology was never an option in Primary Town. I've always been interested in the history of dragons, and how the giant beasts shrunk down to the loyal companions we have today.

"History, Dragon Mythology and Religious Studies."

"Cool! I'm doing Dragon Mythology too, we can pair up!" Jumping to his feet, the strange boy starts rummaging through his suitcase under the bed. After a few moments, he pulls a thick black book out, placing it on my lap.

The book looks expensive, bound in hard black leather with a golden spine. The title is *The History of Dragons: From Dinosaurs to Dogs.*

"What's this?"

"It was on the recommended books list. Didn't you get a list a few weeks before coming here?"

I did remember the long list of books, and the hefty price tag that came with them. "Yeah… I threw it away because I couldn't afford any."

"I was given a fifty pound allowance to buy some. I bought that one because it's really good for the Dragon Mythology course; it's really interesting. If you and I are going to pair up, we've got to be on the same level!" He frowns. "I could only buy two, though. That one, and the core textbook for First Year. Do you not even have that?"

"No. I'll ask my brother if he's got his still."

"Be careful lugging it around; it contains the prospectus for each subject, whether you're learning about it or not." He looks back at the book again. "You can borrow that book, I've already read it."

He's letting *me* borrow it? A girl he met yesterday? "Really?"

He shrugs. "It's fine, so long as you give it back once you're done."

"Thanks."

"What are you doing-"

"Good morning, children." All heads snap towards the door, where Mr Reedman is standing bolt upright, scanning the room slowly. "I hope you have settled in well."

Wes snatches the book out of my hands and shoves it under his pillow, his dragon squeaking in protest.

"I see some dragons have hatched." He stares hard at the ginger girl from last night with her premier dragon, Laila. "Don't forget to register them all at the Square by nine o'clock Monday morning. Any eggs that do not hatch by then are dead." His icy gaze moves onto me, making me drop my eyes to the wooden floorboards. "However, anyone who wishes to register their dragon with me now may do so." He turns to leave. "Oh, before I forget. Dragon starter kits are being sold for forty pounds at Dragons Galore. Make sure to buy one, otherwise you will have no idea how to care for your companion. That is all." Everyone breathes a collective sigh of relief as he leaves; some students follow him out, clutching their dragons close to their chests.

"I'd better register Asteroid." Wes passes the book back to me.

"Asteroid?"

"Yeah. I think it matches her tough appearance." Asteroid jumps into his arms, before perching on his shoulder. "Have you got any names yet?"

"Uh, no. It'll come to me."

"Okay, cool. What are you doing today?"

"Probably go see my brother and my friends. They might have some stuff they can give me from last year."

"Oh. I'll, uh, see you later then."

We smile at each other awkwardly before he takes his leave, Asteroid swaying on his shoulder as he walks.

Forty pounds for a starter kit? Not to mention I need a textbook too!

Clambering halfway up the bunk ladder, I scoop up the egg in one arm and shove it into the backpack. I tuck Wes' book carefully under my pillow, making sure it's fully hidden from view so the others won't get suspicious.

More excited screams fill the cabin as I leave, as a bunch of girls crowd around a hatching egg.

Please hatch. I promise I'll look after you. I'll try to get the best stuff for you!

I squeeze my eyes shut as my stomach churns in worry. It will go when the egg hatches.

If it hatches.

4

Chapter Four

As I near Camp Two, I see Rocky and Marco awkwardly glaring at each other, while Cerberus runs laps around them, her black tongue lolling out of her mouth.

"Hey!" I call to them as I get closer. Cerberus halts her running to bounce over to me, eyes widening excitedly.

Both go in for a hug, but Rocky quickly pushes Marco out of the way. "Nice sleep?"

"Not really. Every time an egg hatched people felt the need to scream about it."

Marco chuckles and slaps me on the back. "That'll be you soon."

"Doubt it."

Rocky finally pulls away so Marco tries to go in for a second hug, only for Rocky to push him away again. "Stop it!" Marco growls, pushing my brother back a few steps.

Please don't argue.

There's always been a rivalry between Marco and Rocky. My brother wants me to be safe and protected, which means no bad influences. Marco is that influence; we'd always wrestle too hard and hurt each other or make the other one cry by taking the teasing too far, so Rocky never approved of our friendship.

"Rocky," I pull on my brother's arm until his angry gaze turns back to me. "Do you still have your stuff from First Year?"

"Like what?"

"Your textbook, and your stuff from starting out with Cerberus."

His gaze hardens in concentration. "I think I've still got the textbook, at the bottom of my drawer. Why, do you want it?"

"Yes, please."

"Sure, follow me." He tells Cerberus to behave before leading me into the cabin.

Inside it is exactly like mine, but black splotches dot the ceiling and walls. They look like burn patches. Rocky walks all the way down to the end to a large set of beige drawers, digging through his clothes until he reaches the bottom; a thick A4-sized textbook in his arms. He throws it onto his bed, huffing with effort.

"Good luck carrying it around."

Marco groans. "I hated that thing. Firstly, carrying it, secondly reading through the boring pages of text. A few more pictures would have brightened it up."

The textbook is a solid red with the words: 'Year One – Core Textbook' printed on the spine in black. Some of the corners of the pages are peeling back, but apart from that it's in good condition.

"Thanks. You wouldn't happen to have your starter kit, would you?"

Rocky shakes his head sadly. "No, Cerberus chewed through all that."

"Great."

"Why? How much is it? I'll get it for you."

"Forty."

"Forty quid?!" His mouth hangs open in shock. "They were twenty-five last year!"

"I don't know what to do," I confess. "It's really important, and there's no way we can afford it."

"Not to mention the two kits after that." Rocky bites his lip.

Three kits? One should really suffice!

Unfortunately, money is what keeps Aria going. Because they have no competitors, they can set the price as high as they want for a profit. It's not fair.

"I'll buy it for you." Marco shuffles his feet uncomfortably when all eyes turn to him. "I missed your fifteenth, so consider it a birthday present."

Marco's father is a plastic surgeon, and his mother is a famous musician, so Marco has grown up surrounded by money all his life. It's no wonder he got a premier dragon.

"Really? You don't-"

"I know, but I will. But, you *have* to hug me-"

I'm in his arms before he can finish his sentence. "Thank you!"

I know Rocky must be seething, but I try to ignore it. He just can't see that Marco is a good friend. Hell, he's buying me a starter kit, and he doesn't even have to.

"Alright," Rocky's voice is filled with venom. "We'll go by the shop as we take the textbook home. No-one will want to carry it around all day."

"Okay." I slip out of Marco's arms and lift the book off the bed. It *is* heavy! And I'm going to have to carry it to school four days a week. Great. "I need a school bag too. Any ideas?"

"There's that clothes shop by Camp Four that sells cheap bags; we'll go there too."

"Let's not waste any time, then." Marco grabs my arm and tugs me towards the door playfully. "All these shops will be sold out by the time we get there!"

* * *

Turns out we were one of the first people there to buy a kit, so Marco bought me one of the best ones. It's a large purple see-through case containing a manual on dragon care, a harness, a small white blanket, a small rechargeable light and a food tray. Doesn't seem worth forty quid. We also went to the clothes shop, Young Flyers. I bought a large grey and white over-the-shoulder bag for school. It should be big enough to lug all my stuff around.

"Which one's your drawer?" Rocky asks, throwing the book upwards so it lands on my bed. We took turns carrying it around, so none of our arms would fall off carrying the unnecessarily heavy book.

"Oh. Wes and I haven't decided yet."

"Wes is the guy you're sharing with?" He glances at the brass plate nailed to the bottom bunk.

"Mm-hm."

"He's not causing you any trouble?"

"No, he's nice."

"Okay, if you're happy."

Marco rolls his eyes, but says nothing, which is probably for the best. While they're both quiet, I take a chance to check on the egg. When I pull it out of the bag, I'm disappointed to find no changes. There's not even a minuscule crack in the tough shell.

"It'll hatch soon, Haze," Marco smiles. "Give it time. You're so impatient."

"I'm *worried*." My stomach churns once more, making me feel like I might be sick. "What if it doesn't hatch?"

"Then breakfast is sorted for a week."

"*Not* appropriate," Rocky scowls at my friend, making him flinch. "Look, Hun. Cerberus was the last egg to hatch in our year, and it looks like yours will be the same. Don't worry yourself sick over it, okay? When that thing hatches as healthy as anything you'll look like a right nutter."

"Okay."

"No, promise me you'll stop worrying. *I'll* worry for you." He holds my hands and stares at me expectantly, his green gaze unwilling to back down.

After a few seconds, I sigh. He's more stubborn than me. I won't win. "Promise. Please don't ever look at me like that again; you look constipated."

Rocky grins, wrapping his arms around my waist. "Okay, deal."

"We should head to the Square," Marco clears his throat uncomfortably. "There were stalls set up. We could get some books, Rocky."

"Oh yeah. I forgot that we need new books for Monday."

"New books?"

"Yeah, we need the Year Two textbook and I need to get a new art pad."

"You've carried on drawing?"

He shrugs. "Never stopped. It's the only class I really like."

"The art teachers love him," Marco says. "They display his art wherever they can."

Rocky shrugs and shuffles his feet, his face heating up in embarrassment.

"Okay. I won't keep you two any longer. Have fun."

* * *

Basically, today was just a lazy day for me after they left. Around nine o'clock, kids started to return from their days out. A few of the richer girls strolled in with their dragons poking their heads out of their designer handbags, like chihuahuas. Wes didn't mind about the drawer; he was just glad to unpack his suitcase fully.

But still no movement from my egg.

Still.

I mean, seriously.

The little bugger is one hell of a sleeper.

"Did you get your starter kit, Hazel?" Wes climbs halfway up the ladder, while Asteroid plods around on my bed aimlessly.

"Yeah, one of my friends bought it for me as a late birthday present."

"That's nice. Who's your friend?"

"Marco White. He's in Year Two."

His eyes grow wide. "Mason White's brother? You know *Mason's brother?*"

Marco's twin brother, Mason, is a budding music artist. Obviously, he's more famous than I first thought.

"It's not a big deal," I shrug. "He doesn't like fuss."

"How do you know each other?"

"From birth. He and Mason had playdates with my brother, Rocky, before I was born. As soon as I came along, we clicked. We've been inseparable ever since."

"Cool. He sounds like a nice guy."

I giggle. "Sometimes he can be a bit grumpy, though."

Asteroid jumps on Wes' hand, chewing and batting at it playfully. Wes carefully pulls his hand away, before sliding it underneath her belly to make her jump up and growl excitedly.

"She's adorable."

Wes looks up for a second and grins. "Yeah. Once your dragon hatches, she'll have a playmate!"

"I hope."

He must have noticed my change in mood, as he quickly changes the subject. "Are you nervous for tomorrow? You know, new classes and stuff."

"Mm-hm." As if on cue, butterflies rise in my stomach. "I might be over-thinking it, though. I promised Rocky I wouldn't worry myself sick."

Wes frowns. "You don't need to worry about it. It won't be half as bad as you think." He smiles slightly and climbs down, Asteroid flinging herself off my bed to follow him.

"I guess," I say to myself.

To distract myself, I check the egg, and I'm surprised to find a little hole in the side. I peer in. It's too dark to see anything, but a rush of excitement hits me.

"Wes! It's hatching!" I scoop the egg up in my arms as I half-scramble, half-fall off the wooden ladder.

My eyes are glued to the egg as the grey shell starts to peel. Little squeaks can be heard from within. The small hole in the side is hit repeatedly from the inside, causing half the egg to crumble in my hands. A small black dragon slithers up my arm, stretching each of its legs individually. It has small, thin wings and a long, spiked tail, giving away his gender as male.

My mouth hangs open in shock. It's a *rare* colour. My book said that only five black ones had been spotted since records began, so the odds of getting this little guy were a billion to one.

"Oh, wow," I breathe, staring at the little creature in my arms.

He looks up at me curiously, his turquoise eyes shining.

"He's awesome!" Wes cries. "You got a black one! What are the chances of *that?*"

Thanks to Wes' shout, kids gather to stare at my new companion, their eyes widening in shock and whispering among each other in disbelief. I don't really pay attention; I'm just happy to see my new friend happy and healthy.

"Can I touch him?" Wes asks.

"Yeah, sure."

The little dragon digs his claws into my arm as Wes strokes him, but soon relaxes his grip as he enjoys the attention.

"Any names in mind?"

I've been thinking about it all day. I want to name him after my element, just to make it a bit more unique. I had loved doing science experiments, and I think something scientific would suit the little guy.

"It's unusual, but I've got one in mind."

"Go on; I'm sure there are weirder names out there."

"Aqueous," I grin. "After my element."

The black dragon snaps his head up at the sound of his name, gazing at me happily. He opens his mouth, but no sound comes out. It almost looks as if he's smiling.

"I think he likes it," I giggle, scratching his scaly chin.

Asteroid lands on my shoulder and leans down to sniff Aqueous, jumping back when he sneezes. He soon apologises by tapping her cheek, which leads to the two trapping each other in a playful headlock, each trying to overpower the other.

"At least they get along," Wes chuckles, pulling Asteroid away when she frees herself from Aqueous' loose grip.

The remains of Aqueous' shell lay scattered across the wooden floor, making me feel a bit embarrassed for letting him hatch in the open. "I'll get this cleared up, then go to bed. I'm tired."

"Same," Wes mouth opens in a large yawns in reply.

Aqueous clings to my shoulder as I lean down and start picking up chunks of the grey shell. "At least we'll get some sleep tonight. No more dragons to hatch."

"And you've cheered up," Wes points out. "Now that Aqueous is here, you can calm down and enjoy yourself."

It's true. The second Aqueous clung to my arm after leaving his shell, a huge weight lifted off my shoulders. "Yep. I feel better about school now, too."

"Good," Wes grins again, his brown eyes sparkling. "Mr Reedman will have to be nice to you now; you've got a really rare and valuable dragon."

"Mm. I'll have to register him before school tomorrow."

"I can go with you, we can walk to school together... If you want."

"Sure. We'll go at ten to nine, so it gives us time to get to school and adjust."

"Cool, it's a plan, then."

5

Chapter Five

Aqueous and I slept soundly all night, although he struggled to get up at eight. In the end, I left him in bed until we had to leave for the Square. He had woken up fully by then, choosing to stay in my bag and poke his head out on the way. He stared at everything and everyone we passed, his mind boggled by what was going on around him. Asteroid also stayed in Wes' backpack, but she had to be convinced. For the first month or so dragons are required to stay in school bags until they are too big, then they must stay under your school desk until they outgrow that as well.

As we approach the Square, Mr Reedman comes into view, holding a clipboard and looking tired of standing around. When his gaze lands on us, Aqueous squeaks in fear and ducks into my school bag.

"Miss Adams," he says coldly, his grumpy expression unchanging. "Have you come to register?"

"Yes."

"I need to see it." He looks down at my bag. "We need to record its appearance."

I don't move; I'm too scared to show him Aqueous.

What will he do once he sees how rare he is?

Will he treat me differently?

What if he takes him away?

"Sometime this week would be good, Miss Adams." The short man taps his foot on the ground impatiently.

Before I can decide what to do, Aqueous pokes his head out of my bag, gazing up at me with worried eyes, as if to say: *what's wrong?*

For a few seconds Mr Reedman looks shocked, his mouth opening in disbelief. However, he quickly composes himself. "I see," he says. "What is its name?"

"Aqueous."

He slowly fills out a form on the clipboard, looking down at Aqueous every so often. "Thank you, Miss Adams. You may leave." He waves his hand once in dismissal.

Wes and I scamper off, thankful to be out of the scary man's presence.

"I didn't expect that!" Wes breathes, casting a look over his shoulder. "He had no idea what to do!"

"At least he registered him. For a second I thought he'd take him away."

"Me too," Wes admits. "But it's all over now. We can go to school now."

Time to enjoy the first day, or absolutely hate it.

* * *

Wes and I approach a group of tall snow-white buildings. English and Maths is taught in one, Art and ICT in another; the school is *huge*. We are herded into a large hall with shiny wooden floors. Loads of kids in our Year have already gathered there, letting their dragons whiz around the room or holding them tightly in their arms.

Shiny golden badges are given to us to show that we are First Years, which is going to be embarrassing to walk around wearing. At least it's only for the first week. We are then separated according to what cabin we're in, and taken to a building with colourful paintings winding up the walls. This will be our base. Every morning at ten to nine we will meet at our base classroom to be registered, then at nine we will be dismissed to go to lessons. As this is the induction day, no Years in the school will have any lessons today, just briefs about what will be happening through the year.

Our base tutor is Mr Gilmore, a new teacher at the school. He's short with a mop of messy brown hair. His dragon is called Thyme, a friendly yellow and orange uncommon dragon with pale pink markings that look like a sun rising on her back, symbolizing the element of light.

"Good morning." Mr Gilmore stands behind a small brown desk, which is littered with paper.

Our base is only small, with a few tables that can fit two people per table. Bunsen burners and other science equipment litter the cupboards and a plastic skeleton leans against the wall at the back. Mr Gilmore seats us in register order so Wes and I sit next to each other.

"Today, I will be giving out maps and lesson timetables. I'll explain school rules on uniform and behaviour. Then you will introduce yourselves and your dragons to your classmates."

Public speaking?

Great, just hit me over the head with a pipe while you're at it.

The lesson timetables are given out. I'll have an hour of Dragon Mythology tomorrow morning as my first lesson, so at least I'll start off with something interesting.

"We're in the same ICT class!" Wes exclaims.

"That's because we're from the same base," I giggle.

"Oh. So, you aren't surprised about being in the same English and Maths classes, then?"

All the core subjects that are compulsory are base classes; the subjects we picked are a mix of all the bases.

"Not really, no." I smile and roll my eyes in fake irritation.

Aqueous squirms in my lap before settling down and resting his head on my stomach. He starts to snore softly, his tail hanging limply between my legs.

"All the dragons are asleep," Wes comments, stroking Asteroid as she sprawls on the wooden table. "I think they're bored."

"You aren't?"

Wes shrugs. "I'd be lying if I said no…"

"Class!" Mr Gilmore only raises his voice slightly, but chatter dies out regardless. "I think this would be a good time to introduce yourselves. Wes Abbot, come up to the front please?"

Wes' eyes bulge slightly, and he looks scared to move. With a tough elbow to the side from me he stands up, waking Asteroid, who lazily clambers onto his shoulder.

"Um, I'm Wes and this is Asteroid," he says quietly, pulling his fingers timidly.

"And what type of dragon is Asteroid?" Mr Gilmore presses.

"Uncommon. I don't know what my element is yet."

Mr Gilmore nods. "Thank you, Wes. Hazel Adams, you're next."

Crap.

As Wes sits down I stand up, clutching Aqueous close to my chest. "This is Aqueous. My name is Hazel."

I'm so awkward it's unbelievable.

"Aqueous is a common dragon, and my element is water."

"Thank you, Hazel. Yvonne Carter is next."

Shakily I sit back down in my seat, Aqueous squeaking in my arms to be released.

That wasn't so bad…

Was it?

It probably was.

"I'm glad that's over," Wes breathes. "You're not good at public speaking either, huh?"

"No. I hate it with a passion."

The other students introduce themselves. I don't listen to most of them, showing off their companions and boasting about their elements. I'm just glad my turn is over. It was embarrassing, but at least I didn't trip up on my words.

"Now that introductions are over, by law I must tell you about our political situation." A few confused murmurs echo around the room, kids gazing quizzically at Mr Gilmore or raising their eyebrows. "Over the course of the year you will have to pick which side you're on." He pauses before continuing. "Choose carefully."

"This is weird," Wes mutters.

"There are two groups: the Cindaraans and the Krystalans. At the moment, the Krystalans are in power and govern the country. They believe that dragons are equal to us, and that companionship is vital for us. The Cindaraans believe that dragons should spend their lives serving us, doing as we say."

So Raymond is leading a political faction here? Maybe that's why he's such an asshole.

"Why?" a kid at the back asks.

"So we can reach our full potential. They would still be our companions, of course, but they would have to earn their keep."

Some kids shrug and murmur. I'm not too sure what to think. They're pretty basic explanations; we don't know what may lie underneath.

"Hazel?" Wes nudges my shoulder.

"Huh?"

"What do you think?"

"I don't know."

He sighs and shrugs. "Me neither."

"Don't worry too much about it; you've got all year," Mr Gilmore says. "Think carefully about what you think would benefit you."

Conversations pop up around the classroom again, and Mr Gilmore allows us to chat for a bit about it.

"I think dragons should pull their weight; some of them are lazy," someone behind me whispers.

"They teach us responsibility; we shouldn't make them work," the person next to them snaps.

"I think we should worry about our own problems."

"I couldn't care less about our problems!"

From the lack of agreement, the class appears to be split between Cindaraans and Krystalans.

Would I be happy if Aqueous had to earn his keep? What would he have to do? How long would he have to work?

My companion has settled back on my lap after the introductions. He is snoring softly once again, his head hanging over my legs floppily. Wes is staring at Asteroid, deep in thought. Aqueous yawns widely, showing off his sharp white teeth before curling up in a tight ball, his feet covering his face.

I don't think I prefer either party, but I'm sure that having to pick between the two will cause arguments for everyone.

One thing is for sure: I don't want to be around Raymond.

* * *

School finished at one. We have four hours of lessons per day for four days of the week: Monday through Thursday. We can then go back to our cabins or go out and have lunch, before returning to the school field at three to attend dragon training.

"Where are you going to get lunch?" Wes asks.

"I dunno. A café, I guess."

"*Haze!*"

I don't get the chance to turn around before my best friend has barrelled into my back, nearly knocking me off balance.

"Marco!" I whack him across the head instinctively. "Be careful!"

"Ow! That was mean!"

"Don't rugby tackle me then!"

"Okay, okay. I'll try to knock you on your ass next time." He chuckles, ruffling my hair playfully and tucking it behind my ears.

Ducking out of his grip and freeing my hair, I mutter: "Whatever."

"Do you want to go to lunch? I've got a good place in mind…"

"Yeah, sure. Is Rocky coming?"

"Yeah, he's in the toilet."

Marco seems to notice Wes for the first time, who is standing beside him awkwardly. Wes smiles slightly, Asteroid staring at Marco quizzically.

"Oh, Marco, this is Wes. Wes, this is Marco." I introduce them awkwardly.

"Hi," Wes mutters.

Marco says nothing, just raises his eyebrows while studying Wes carefully. Asteroid opens her mouth threateningly until Drea plods up behind my best friend, making her cower in surprise.

"Wes, do you wanna come to lunch with us?" I turn towards the quiet boy, anxious about Marco's standoffish behaviour.

His eyes light up and he beams. "Sure."

Aqueous squeaks and emerges from my bag, though quickly retreats upon spotting Drea. Marco doesn't even try to hide his surprise.

"Oh, fuck!" His eyes don't move from where Aqueous' head popped up. "You do realize what dragon you've got, right?"

"I know; he's cool, right?"

"'Cool'? You got an extremely valuable dragon, and it's just 'cool' to you?"

At this moment Cerberus arrives, yapping excitedly and sniffing

Wes curiously. Rocky arrives moments later, a large grin on his face. "Hey guys, guess what I-"

"Hazel's got one of the most valuable dragons as her companion!" Marco exclaims, cutting my brother off.

"Huh? It hatched? Lemme see it!"

Gently, I lift Aqueous out of my school bag, his little legs wriggling. Rocky holds his arms out and takes him, gently scratching his chin. "Aww! He's cute! What have you called him?"

"Aqueous, after my element."

Aqueous squeaks as Cerberus nudges his tail, kicking out with his small legs. Asteroid joins in on the fun, flying around Cerberus' head before landing on her back.

"Hey, Rocky. I've invited Wes to come to lunch with us. That's okay, right?"

"Huh? Sure."

Wes' shoulders relax a bit, and I nudge his arm happily. Marco rolls his eyes, which causes Drea to roll her pale pink eyes in return, making me giggle. They are very alike in their mannerisms and attitudes, it seems. Aqueous wriggles out of Rocky's grip and clings to my arm, unsure what to think of all the attention.

Marco shakes his head in disbelief and mutters: "Let's go to Café Terra, then."

Rocky shrugs. "Fine by me."

* * *

Café Terra is in a small garden, surrounded by colourful flowers and a white picket fence. White metal tables and chairs are the only available seating. I order a sandwich, as I'm not that hungry; the boys order a bit more food because they'd all skipped breakfast this morning. The dragons are given small bowls of chicken to eat. Aqueous seems to really like it, though he struggles to chew it with his small teeth.

"You two excited for dragon training?" Rocky asks.

Wes shrugs. "What's it like?"

"You basically learn about your element. If you don't know it going into the class, you'll definitely know it leaving."

"Cool."

"Dragons also get their first Elemental marking in that class. That's how you know," Marco chips in.

Asteroid jumps on Cerberus, trying unsuccessfully to wrestle the much larger dragon to the floor. The bigger dragon runs around in circles trying to shake the younger dragon off her back.

"Cerberus, be good!" Rocky snaps.

The brown dragon freezes and plonks herself on the floor, a sulky expression on her face.

"Let them play; they're not doing any harm." I reach over and pat the sulky dragon on the head.

"You can say that, but wait until she knocks over some old lady."

"I don't see any old-"

"Don't be cheeky," he sighs.

Marco and I chuckle at my brother's obvious frustration. "It was only a joke!" I manage to get out between laughs.

"Oh wait. Did I tell you about what happened today?" Rocky pipes up, his eyes glowing in excitement.

"Cerberus knocked over an old lady?" I unhelpfully throw out.

"*No.* Ciara Fay asked me out."

For heaven's sake. Ciara? Really?

Really?

"Ciara from our Year?" Wes asks.

"Unfortunately." Aqueous brushes up against my legs as I sigh.

"'Unfortunately'? You don't like her?" Rocky stops eating, eyeing everyone with a confused glance.

Marco rolls his eyes. "Who does? Don't you remember what she was like in Primary Town? A new boyfriend every week? Is that what you're gonna be?"

"No, she said that she's grown up."

"Pfft." The disbelieving noise comes out of my mouth before I can stop it.

Rocky glares at everyone around the table. "Whatever. It's not up to you guys anyway."

Rocky is too sweet for Ciara. The problem is that I don't know her motives. Does she actually want to be with him, or is she just using him as a pawn in one of her stupid games?

She hasn't changed. She's still the snobby, arrogant girl that she was a year ago.

Wes wriggles uncomfortably, but thankfully he changes the subject. "Did you guys have to choose between the two political parties when you were in our Year?"

"They asked you too?" Marco raises an eyebrow. "It's been newly introduced this year, but I didn't think they'd demand a decision from the First Years."

"It's already causing arguments," Rocky points out. "Our Year is starting to split in half over it."

"They've chosen already?" I call Aqueous back when he starts to wander over to another group of people, curious about their companions. Thankfully, he scampers back and tackles Asteroid, who quickly pins him down with one foot.

"It was drummed into us last year. I think most of the teachers here are Cindaraan supporters; that's why they want to know."

"What do you guys think?" Wes murmurs.

Marco flicks his hand in dismissal. "I don't know, and we've got to decide by the end of the month."

Rocky starts playing with his plate, flicking crumbs off the table. "I don't like it. I guarantee it will cause more harm than good."

"That's a given," Marco agrees.

What on earth is going on?

If it's newly introduced, then why do they want us to decide on our political views so quickly? Why does it matter?

6

Chapter Six

"Good afternoon, class," Mr Reedman walks up and down the line of kids, eyeing each of us. "I will be the main dragon training teacher for this year, and I am also your Fire Instructor, for those of you who have the element fire. This lesson, we will be learning about how to control your element, firstly by discovering it. You will go through eight tests to see which one you react best to." He nods to Eruption, who launches into the air and hovers above our heads. "You will not have to do all eight if your element is discovered." He looks behind him, at the row of seven people, each with dragons of differing Elemental markings. "The other instructors will also be assessing which element you react best to." All seven dragons launch into the air, their strong wings beating loudly. "First will be the Light Instructor, Mrs Bennett."

A tall, slim, blonde-haired woman steps forward, a friendly smile on her face. "Spread out, and try not to injure yourselves."

Reluctantly we spread out, but I keep close to Wes, just in case. A pink and brown dragon with pale pink markings on its face flies forward, firing a beam of bright light out of its mouth, making my eyes water for staring at it. Screams fill the air as the dragon flies overhead, but they don't last long. As I open my eyes, a few kids are holding balls of light in their hands, so Mrs Bennett quickly ushers them away. Then I see Aqueous flying above me, his mouth bared threateningly at the remaining seven dragons.

"Come here, it's okay." I hold out my arms to him. After a few moments' hesitation, he falls into them, but his gaze is still locked on the remaining dragons.

The tests for dark, earth and electricity go the same way, with kids who show signs of having that element being taken away. Wes and I are still standing. Ciara left at dark, and Naomi with earth.

"Now it's the fire test." Mr Reedman smiles darkly, gesturing for Eruption to fly forward.

My heart jumps into my throat at seeing the large ball of fire charge in Eruption's mouth. Aqueous wriggles in my grip, growling at the beast.

As Mr Reedman steps away from the terrified children, Eruption lunges forward, a large blaze of fire exploding from his mouth. I close my eyes and wait to feel searing flames, but a strong gust of wind tugs at my clothes instead. My eyes snap open, and I see Eruption being blown back slightly, losing focus on breathing fire. Everyone stands around in a confused silence for a few moments, until an old man steps forward, a large grin on his face.

"That's a strong element you've got there!" The man takes Wes' hand and shakes it. "You used it for the wrong test, but you used it nonetheless!"

Wes did that?

Oh goodness.

He's dead.

"Don't encourage his behaviour!" Mr Reedman snaps, storming up next to the man. "We need to know who has fire!"

The man shakes his hand in dismissal. "We'll leave it until last, to make sure none of the other elements get in the way."

Mr Reedman looks furious, his hands balled into tight fists and his face going a bright red. "Fine! But get this boy out of my sight!"

Wes looks back at me, and I return his confused stare. If that was him, then what made him do it? Fear?

A tall, lanky man with floppy hair steps forward as the old man and Wes back off. He gestures his dragon forward, a dark green one with bright blue swirl markings on its stomach.

"Now, the water test," he says.

Yes! No more tests!

The man steps back, and his dragon surges forward, drenching everyone in cool water. I close my eyes and concentrate hard on letting the water drip off me, which thankfully it does. I'm surprised to feel that Aqueous is completely dry in my arms; the water must have just dripped off him too.

The man steps forward once more and points to all the children that either remained dry or are now holding a ball of water in their hands. "Come with me; my name is Mr Knight."

We form a straight line behind Mr Knight as the other students did with their Element Instructors. There aren't many other kids who have water; including me, there are only seven. The biggest class at the moment appears to be earth, but there are still about forty kids left for the remaining three tests: ice, wind and fire.

After the ice and wind tests, only eight kids left with their Instructors, which means that fire is the biggest class by miles. Mr Reedman looked impressed as all the remaining kids held a ball of fire in their hands. However, he quickly masks that and turns to everyone.

"Now that you know your element, you should see a small marking on your dragon of said element. If you have the marking of a different element as well, please see me at the end to discuss it."

I soon spot a small blue water swirl on Aqueous' cheek. I'm relieved that I don't see two: I don't want to spend more time with Mr Reedman than I have to.

"Your Instructors will now take you to different areas of the field to discuss your lessons. Listen carefully; they will not be repeated."

After all the excitement, kids happily follow their instructors to different areas of the large, overgrown field. Mr Knight takes us to a small pond, and makes us sit in the grass before handing out sheets of paper.

"These," he holds up one sheet, "are your timetables. I will see you Friday through Sunday at nine o'clock for water dragon training. The rest of the week you will have Mr Reedman."

A few groans echo from the small group, making Mr Knight raise an eyebrow. "I know he's not fun, but you'll just have to deal with it," he jokes. "Now, I want to check that everyone is here. Hazel, Jeremy, Yvonne, Polly, Isla, Richard and Lilac." He looks up and does a head count, saying "good" when he realizes everyone is here.

"Now. Shark and I will be teaching you and your dragon how to control your element, water. Is there anyone here who has two?" No-one puts their hand up, so he continues. "You will be taught how to use it, how to control it and how to feel comfortable with it. However, as it is your first day, we will begin on Friday. Does anyone have any questions?"

The short girl next to me with caramel-brown hair, Yvonne, puts her hand up. "Will premier dragons be getting higher training?"

"Yes. Depending on what dragon you've got, the higher the quality of training they will have."

All eyes are on me. Aqueous buries his head into my armpit under their stares.

Mr Knight clears his throat uncomfortably. "Out of interest, how many types of dragon are there here?"

He notes down the status of our dragons. Yvonne has a premier dragon, which is probably why she asked the question. Jeremy and

Lilac have rare dragons, and the rest have uncommon ones, except for me, of course.

"I wouldn't worry too much about higher training at the moment," Mr Knight smiles. "It's all organized on your timetables, and we're only learning the basics for the next month or so." After a long, awkward silence, he clears his throat. "Well," he says. "Class is dismissed. I'll see you all next Friday. Regular dragon training starts next Monday." We get up and turn to leave when he calls us back. "Oh! I almost forgot! You need a mentor for dragon training. By next week you need to have picked someone from one of the higher Years to help you with your training. They don't necessarily have to have the water element; just make sure you've got one for next week."

A mentor?

Who on earth would mentor me?

"Okay, see you next week. Don't overexert yourselves!"

* * *

"Mr Stirling says that he's going to ask his son to mentor me! Won't that be cool?" Wes chirps on about his lesson, a large smile on his face.

"Mm-hm. I still can't believe you blew Eruption out of the air!"

He shrugs. "I didn't want him to hurt Asteroid. Or you, for that matter. He was being very threatening."

Recalling the giant black and red dragon makes me shiver. He knew what he was doing, and I don't think he or Mr Reedman would have cared if someone had been injured.

"Who are you going to ask to mentor you, huh? Your brother?"

"Maybe. But Ciara's probably grabbed him already," I sigh. "I don't know who to ask."

I can't ask Maya, because she's *always* with Mason. We've barely spoken since I arrived because of it. I could ask Marco, but the question is if he'll do it or not – he's lazier than I am.

"I'm sure you'll be fine," Wes smiles.

Marco's my only shot.

"I'll go and find Marco, see if he wants to do it," I say more to reassure myself, but Wes nods anyway.

"I'll see you later. My parents are coming for dinner today; I want to look nice."

"Have fun."

The brown-haired boy waves before haring down the street, Asteroid clinging to his backpack.

It didn't take me long to find Marco; I spotted Drea lazing around in the sun in a large park. A large fancy fountain of a dragon is right in the middle of the large green space, with a few trees dotted here and there. Marco is sat on a bench nearby, talking to someone I don't recognize.

"Hey," I wave as I approach, and Marco straightens up.

"Hey. You okay?" Marco asks as I come closer.

"Yeah, I just need to ask you something."

"You bedding the younger Years now, Marky?" The boy next to him taunts, which makes me recognize him immediately.

Mason.

His brown-blonde hair is no longer long and shaggy, but shorter, with tufts sticking out at weird angles. He's had a growth spurt, but it's clear that his attitude has not sweetened.

I'm ashamed to say that he is good-looking now though. Only a little.

"Fuck off," Marco snaps.

Mason rolls his eyes. "Whatever. Come on Fortune, we're leaving. Later, *Scargirl*."

A white and gold premier dragon follows him out, his head lifted high arrogantly. Red fire markings cover his wings and legs, which means that Mason is fire.

"Good to know he's changed," I mumble sarcastically, covering my face with my fringe as he walks away.

"Hmph," Marco snorts. "What did you want to ask me?" He pats the now empty spot on the bench next to him, and I quickly sit down.

"You know that First Years need mentors for dragon training…?"

"You want me to do it?"

I'm thankful he gets straight to the point as he tucks my fringe behind my ear.

"Yes please. I trust you."

"Why can't Rocky or Maya do it?"

I play with my fingers in embarrassment. "Ciara's probably got Rocky, and every time I see Maya she's too busy to talk. Plus, you know me better than anyone. If anyone's going to mentor me it should be you."

My friend smiles slightly. "Okay, I'll do it. As long as you want me to do it because we're friends, and not because it'll make you look better."

"You know I wouldn't!" I glare at him, offended that he would even imply that I would use him for his money.

He puts his hands up apologetically. "Okay, okay. I was just making sure."

I don't speak for a few seconds, but eventually mutter: "Thanks."

"On the field? If it hasn't changed from last year, that is."

"Nope, still the same place."

He wraps his arm around my waist and pulls his phone out of his pocket, staring at the screen and mumbling something I don't catch.

"Something wrong?"

"Huh?" He narrows his eyes at the screen. "No, nothing. Do you have a phone?"

"No. Do I need one?"

He shakes his head. "Nah. Rocky hasn't got one, and he's doing fine."

He puts the phone back in his pocket. "I only use it to keep in touch with my parents, and that isn't always a good thing."

"How come?"

Mason was always the favourite child, because of his vocal talents. Marco wasn't really given much attention by his parents; I can understand why he isn't totally happy about being in touch with them again.

"They're always nagging me to be more like Mason. I don't want to be like that arrogant prick. How he has any friends is beyond me."

"Maya's interested," I mumble.

Marco snorts. "She fancies him, that's why."

"No! Since when?"

"A while. But he's with Sadie Brookes at the moment. Remember her? She's a right slut now."

It pains me that I have to hear through the grapevine about how Maya's been doing.

"Wasn't she anyway?" I joke half-heartedly.

"She's even worse now. Walks around naked whenever she gets the chance. She had a crush on me for a while."

"Reciprocated?" I ask a little too quickly.

He rests his head on top of mine, so I can rest mine on his shoulder. "No. But..." He pauses and then shakes his head. "Nothing."

"No, tell me. We don't keep things from each other, remember?"

He sighs. "That was a stupid pinky promise."

"It still stands; it's too late to back out now."

"I didn't know you were the secret police," he jabs me in the stomach playfully with his finger. "But, alright. No judging, okay?"

"Okay...?"

"I had sex with her."

I pull away from him in disgust. *"Marco!"*

"You said you wouldn't judge!" he whines.

60

"Why? Why would you do that?" I bury my face in my hands. "I thought Maya was *joking*!"

Marco crosses his arms and scowls, pushing me away with his elbow. "Go away."

"No! I'm sorry, it's just…" I lean against his side, arms around his waist. "I didn't know that you were doing… that." I try to hide the fact that I'm blushing, but if he noticed he doesn't say anything. I always thought that maybe…

His voice tears me away from my straying thoughts. "I'd do it someday."

"But, not with her," I sigh, pushing the image of us to the back of my mind. "She's a waste of time."

"Indeed." He relaxes enough to uncross his arms but still wriggles uncomfortably. "I haven't done it since."

"I thought Maya said there was two girls? Who was the other one?"

He squirms uncomfortably. "She was."

Marco and Maya? I didn't even know they had a thing for each other… I feel a flare of jealousy before I bury it. Marco's an adult; he can do whatever he wants.

"Did you like her?"

"No."

"Did she like you?"

"No."

"Then why-"

"I don't want to talk about." He stiffens, his lips sealed in a thin line. I don't want to push him if he doesn't want to tell me.

"Okay. You don't have to if you don't want to."

We sit in silence for a while, just sitting in the sun and enjoying each other's company. The icy atmosphere soon melted, as neither of us wanted our fights to last long. But, after what he told me today, I now realize that everyone's grown up. A lot.

His stomach starts to growl, making me laugh. "Do you want to go get something to eat? That is, if you're not still full after everything you ate for lunch, fatty."

"Yeah, sure. We can come back and eat it here, if you want."

"Sure. It's still warm out." I stretch my arms before picking Aqueous up; he's has been lying in the grass with his legs in the air and his tongue lolling out.

Drea lumbers along behind us, glaring at anyone who passes by, including Aqueous and me.

"Hey, Haze."

"Yeah?"

"You don't think any different of me, do you?"

How can I?

With my arms held out, I pull him towards me in a hug, and I feel him relax immensely, curling his arms around my waist and resting his chin on my head. "Never. I don't care what you do, I'm always here."

"Thanks. Just, don't tell Maya that you know."

I hesitate for a second, mulling it over. But when I look at the desperation in his eyes, I reluctantly relent. "No problem."

7

Chapter Seven

The next week passes relatively quickly. Most of my school classes are fun, and my teachers are nice too. I haven't made any more friends since Wes, but I have talked to Lilac from water dragon training a few times.

Maya and I have had short conversations as we've passed on the street, but apart from that she's been hanging out with Mason a lot so we haven't had the chance to meet up. I don't think she wants to be friends anymore.

But today I'm excited as it's our first lesson with our mentors, so that means Marco can help me learn and teach me himself. He was on time for once, one of the first mentors there. As soon as I approached him people started hurling abuse at me for even daring to go near someone of his popularity. He quickly shut them up, however, telling them to mind their own business.

My prediction about Ciara and Rocky turned out to be true, but I could see the fury in my brother's eyes when he realized Marco was mentoring me. I looked away when Ciara put her middle finger up at me behind his back.

Grown-up, my ass.

"Welcome to your first dragon training lesson," Mr Reedman booms, quickly silencing all chatter. "Anyone who has not got a mentor should have seen me by now, so I presume the rest of you have got one. In today's lesson, you will teach your dragon how to use the most basic move of your element." He stops and turns towards a short, fat, dark-haired man and a tall, stick-thin woman with black hair.

"That's Sadie's dad," Marco mutters in my ear. "Let's hope he doesn't know who we are."

Mr Reedman continues: "Mr Brookes and Miss Locke will wander around to check how you're all doing. Today will solely be a student–mentor lesson. Now, spread out and begin."

Marco drags me down to the far end of the field, deciding on a relatively flat area. "Here," he says. "The first move is easy; you'll pick it up in no time."

Aqueous yaps in agreement, looking up from attacking a tall clump of grass.

"Tell him to go to the middle," Marco says, taking a step back. "Be firm if you have to."

"Aqueous, go to the middle."

The black dragon looks at me once, huffs as if I'm deliberately trying to annoy him, and continues playing with the grass.

"Aqueous, *now*."

He realizes the fun is over and half-heartedly stands up and lumbers towards the middle, plonking himself on the floor sulkily.

Marco throws a water bottle to me. It slips through my hands clumsily and drops on the floor. He tuts and rolls his eyes. "Use that to train him."

"How?"

"Create a ball of water with it, only a small one."

"Do you know what you're doing?"

He shrugs and winks at me. "I'm winging it."

I pour a bit of the water into my hand, but it falls through my fingers. "I don't..."

"Have you never created a ball of water? Not even for fun?"

"No...? I'm never playing a game with you ever again if that's what you do."

He chuckles and steps around Aqueous, who is now rolling around on the floor, and grabs my hands. "It's easy. Just concentrate on making a ball." He moves around behind me, holding my hands up.

I pour the water again and squeeze my eyes shut, trying not to think about anything. After a few seconds, I feel the water rise from my fingers.

"Still a womanizer I see, Marco."

Crap.

The water sloshes on the ground, which makes Aqueous dive forward and chew the wet grass excitedly. Mr Brookes now stands in front of me, arms crossed, with wet trousers.

"I'm so sorry-" I begin.

"It's no problem. I didn't mean to break your concentration," he says, but his hard gaze is still locked on Marco, who takes a step back and drops my hands. "Control yourself for once, Marco. She's only fifteen."

"She's my *friend*," Marco replies darkly, his hands balling into fists.

"I don't want to know about your personal life." Mr Brookes walks away, careful to step over Aqueous. "Just behave."

Marco sighs irritably and steps towards me again. "Let's try again, shall we?"

He picks up my hands, but this time I feel a burning sensation. With a loud yelp, I jump away from him, staring at my now bright red hands. Aqueous looks up at me, his eyes wide as if to say: *are you alright?*

"I didn't mean to!" Marco protests, grabbing the water bottle and pouring the cool liquid over my throbbing hands. "I'm so sorry, Haze.

Do they hurt?"

"Of course they hurt!" I snap, feeling a stab of guilt at the flash of pain in his eyes.

My companion lands on my shoulder, with his head tilted to one side, watching curiously and wondering what we're doing. He then leans on my arm and opens his mouth, and I gasp as I see a tiny stream of water, no thicker than a pencil, flow out of it. The water is ice cold, and as clear as glass.

"How is he...?"

"The water you touched contained a bit of your elemental powers. Aqueous played with it, and got a new water marking," Marco explains.

Looking carefully at Aqueous, I see matching blue water swirls on both his cheeks, when this morning he only had one. The cool water soothes my hands, which now ache only slightly.

Marco smiles. "Lesson one complete."

* * *

Rocky was not impressed with what happened. It turns out that he was close by, and had seen everything.

Poor Marco barely got a word in to defend himself before Rocky started screaming at him. I'd hoped Marco would keep quiet, but instead the two of them got into a huge row about it.

It was not pretty.

After leaving them to bicker, I decided to have a warm bath after all the excitement of the day. Aqueous always gets really excited about that; he loves splashing about and swimming in the water. I like using my element to make small droplets of water zoom around the room – a trick I learned soon after discovering my element. I have to be careful though; Marco asked me to demonstrate my element a few days ago and the droplets smacked right into him and drenched him.

It was hilarious at the time. One droplet is zooming around Aqueous' head; he bats at it playfully while shooting water at it.

I giggle as my companion covers his chin in bubbles, making it look like he's got a beard. My partner chirps happily, trying to scrape off the bubbles, before getting distracted and mistaking his own tail for a toy. I close my eyes for a while, just enjoying the silence.

Of course, it doesn't last long.

"*Eek!*"

"Get the filthy thing out of here!"

"What if it has *fleas?*"

The screaming and thundering about even makes Aqueous shoot towards the door, scratching to get out and see.

"Hold on, let me put a towel on." Wrapping the white towel around myself that I had left on the toilet earlier, I cautiously open the door.

A beige blur shoots past the door, with a mob of girls behind it. I instantly recognize one of them.

Sadie.

Oh, why.

She has long platinum-blonde hair, most of which is extensions. She's wearing a short, light pink dress, and her face is heavily made up.

Her icy blue eyes land on me, and a dark smile creeps on her face. "Scargirl! I haven't seen you for ages!"

I don't reply, knowing I would only get condescending comments thrown at me.

She turns fully towards me, eyeing me up and down. By this point a crowd has gathered, muttering and pointing in the direction the beige blur went.

"Having a shower, Scargirl?" Sadie says, taking a threatening step towards me.

"Bath," I whisper, not able to tear my eyes away from her icy gaze.

Aqueous growls as she comes within inches of me. The blonde girl's eyes drop and she sneers; "he's puny."

Before I can call my companion back, she kicks him square in the jaw, sending him flying backwards further into the stall.

"Hey! How dare you-" Before I can finish my sentence, she's snatched the towel off me, making me squeak and slam the door shut.

"Wow, Scargirl hasn't developed much, huh?" Sadie jokes, banging heavily on the door just as I lock it. "Her pancake chest was the flattest I've ever seen. Not to mention that hideous scar. Who would want to kiss that?"

My face reddens as the crowd roars in laughter.

"Fucking hell, she wasn't a pretty sight!" someone screams above the noise.

"Doesn't she shave?" Sadie snickers, making everyone laugh again.

They saw me.

The *entire* cabin saw me naked.

How the hell am I going to live this down?

"Now, where'd that little furball go?" Sadie screeches above the crowd, silencing them immediately.

Aqueous crawls towards me, his head ducked in shame. I cuddle him close to me, shivering and crying under the sink.

I'll be teased about this for the rest of my life.

But then I realize in shock: she took my towel.

My clothes are on my bed.

Stupid, idiot! You've set yourself up for more teasing!

My companion nuzzles my chin, looking lost and hopeless. However, he suddenly swings his head round, staring at the bath, his teeth bared and eyes narrowed into tiny slits. A small beige tail sticks out from behind it, swinging back and forth.

What the hell?

I crawl closer to it, realizing that this must be the thing that everyone's after. It tries to squeeze closer behind the bath as I approach, growling desperately. As I reach it, it suddenly jerks itself out of its hiding place and faces me.

It's a tiny beige kitten. It has dazzling blue almond-shaped eyes and a triangular-shaped head. It has an almost unnoticeable light brown face and paws. Its beige fur sticks up in clumps, dirty and tangled. A small, not overly threatening, squeak comes out of its mouth, and it backs off, hackles raised, as Aqueous approaches. The black dragon sniffs the tiny creature, who sniffs him back, but does not drop its attack stance.

"Where the fuck is it?" Sadie shouts.

"Why do you want it so badly?" someone asks.

There's a tense silence before a 'smack' noise and a collective gasp from the crowd.

"Shut up! I didn't give you permission to *speak* to me!" Sadie screeches, before huffing loudly: "The stupid little shit stole some chicken off Exquisite! That scumbag had no right to steal it and take a bite! It's fucking expensive!"

The little kitten flinches with each word, its ears flattened against its tiny head. Aqueous makes a few soft noises, which catches the kitten's attention, who meows back to him. The two then start making noises to each other, almost like they're talking.

"Ugh!" Sadie stomps her feet on the floor repeatedly. "If you see the little shit, you will inform me *straight away*, got it?"

There are a few murmurs of agreement before footsteps signify people leaving, including Sadie, who can be heard by the clipping of her high heels.

"*Mew.*"

The sound of the kitten redirects my attention towards my companion, who is now licking the kitten, trying to untangle its fur.

"Are you two friends?" I wonder out loud.

The black dragon turns to me, turquoise eyes shining. He nods vigorously, while the beige kitten seems unsure.

Slowly I reach out to the kitten, but it backs away. Aqueous nudges it towards me again, seemingly offering words of encouragement. The kitten flinches as I touch it, but quickly relaxes as I scratch its tiny chin. It even lets its guard down and starts purring, rubbing its head into my hand.

I can't just turn it away... Sadie will hurt it.

I cringe as I think about her baring my body to the entire cabin, and my face quickly heats up in embarrassment.

Yes, I'm embarrassed, but I'm also furious with her.

She *kicked* Aqueous.

No hesitation, no remorse. She even looked smug about it.

How dare she? Any ill feelings she has should be directed at me, not Aqueous; he's only trying to protect me.

Then, the details of my predicament come racing back. No clothes, no towels and most people are probably still in the cabin.

I'm going to have to wander out there naked.

"*Mew?*" The kitten nuzzles my hand, trying to get my attention back.

"What the hell am I supposed to do?" I wonder aloud, stroking the kitten once more. "I have nothing to cover myself with... I'm going to have to go out there, and embarrass myself. *Again.*"

Aqueous paws my leg, and the kitten stops purring, instead widening its blue eyes. I would find it more adorable if I weren't so torn up inside.

"Hazel?" Someone knocks on the door lightly, but I that voice.

"Wes, I can't come out right now," I sigh.

"I know... I saw... You know..."

With that comment, I can't stop the tears.

"No, don't cry!" Wes says desperately. "Let me in, I'm sorry!"

"I can't!" I sob, wiping tears off my cheek. "My clothes are on the bed."

"Oh, wait here."

"Where am I going to go, exactly?"

"Oh, yeah, right. Two seconds."

The kitten mews timidly, its large blue eyes wide with fear. It climbs onto my leg and taps my face gently, meowing constantly. Aqueous makes a series of chirping noises, which makes the kitten relax a little.

Wes soon returns, knocking on the door lightly again. "I'm here. I won't look, promise."

With a deep breath I unlock the door and snatch my clothes off him, which he holds behind his back while he faces the other direction. During this, Asteroid squeezes herself through the crack in the door and joins Aqueous and his new friend.

I'm thankful to be able to drain the bath and put my clothes on, even though I'm still damp, while the three new friends play, batting each other lightly on the head and tackling each other. Now that they've bonded with the kitten, what am I supposed to do?

Wes moves away as I open the door, concern on his face. To my surprise, he hugs me awkwardly; it's nice to know he's trying to be supportive.

"It'll blow over soon," he whispers in my ear. "You'll see."

"Sadie won't let it."

"So? Some of the people around here haven't got the longest attention spans, Hazel. They'll find something else to talk about soon."

"*Mew!*"

Wes jerks away and stares at the kitten, who is now rubbing itself against his legs and purring like a lawnmower.

"It must have slipped in while Sadie was preoccupied," I shrug innocently.

Wes sighs and bends down to stroke the kitten, who bats at his glasses playfully. "It's cute! Are you keeping it?"

I shrug again. "And give Sadie more ammunition?"

"But it's getting on with Aqueous and Asteroid so well…" he whines, smiling as Asteroid licks the kitten on the top of the head.

"Wes…"

The kitten bats at his glasses again, pausing its loud purrs to meow loudly.

"Come on…"

With a final sigh, and against my better judgement, I give in. "Fine. But we're sharing it. Responsibilities and all."

"Yes!" Wes punches the air, and Aqueous bounces excitedly.

8

Chapter Eight

When I enter the bedroom, I am met with crude comments from the people gathered in the cabin. They pause in looking under beds and in drawers to hurl abuse at me and laugh. Wes snaps at them and holds the kitten close, boasting that Sadie can't have it now because we're looking after it.

I know he's only trying to help, but I've got to stand up for myself.

I've noticed that, since the 'incident', Wes has been looking at me weirdly. Whenever I turn around he's always… staring. It's unnerving.

No-one has made any stupid comments about the kitten, but I'm sure that's yet to come. Wes and I have arranged to take it to the vet tomorrow, but it specializes in dragon care; we'll have to see if they know anything about cats.

I only slept for a few hours; I couldn't stop cringing about the 'incident'. I was also worrying about school, because news is sure to travel fast.

As soon as I got to school, my prediction came true.

I squirm uncomfortably in my seat as Mr Gilmore gives out the morning announcements. I barely listen because the boys in the back are talking about me, pointing and snickering amongst themselves.

I'd already heard a couple of people whispering about me when I was rushing to the classroom, some making fun of the way I look.

The bell rings, making everyone jump out of their seats and grab their bags. Some kids have even rushed out the door before Mr Gilmore can dismiss them.

"I'll see you all tomorrow," he says, but many people ignore him. "Hazel, come back after school and see me, please."

Oh crap.

Oh crap.

Some kids snigger and start muttering amongst themselves once more, so I rush out the door before I can hear anything.

What if he knows?

Have I done something wrong?

* * *

It became clear that I would find it hard to concentrate in class. In English, the 'popular' kids threw scrunched-up pieces of paper at my head every time the teacher turned towards the board. Either he didn't notice their behaviour or just ignored it.

People shoved crude notes in my locker. One guy even took a naked picture of himself, which I quickly threw away in disgust.

Aqueous scampers ahead of me, eager to see Mr Gilmore so we can get home sooner. He's had to dodge kicks all day; no-one pays attention to my empty threats.

The classroom is empty as I enter, but I decide to wait a few minutes to give him a chance to get here. My mind has been spinning all day trying to work out what he wants to talk to me about: grades, behaviour, attendance or the 'incident'.

"Ah, Hazel." He taps me on the shoulder, making me jump. "Pull a chair up to my desk and sit."

74

Reluctantly, I pull up a chair and sit in front of his desk, which is covered in a mountain of paper and a plugged-in laptop. Aqueous jumps on my lap, interested in a half-eaten sandwich that Mr Gilmore puts down on the table.

"I wanted to talk to you about something," he says, settling down in his seat.

Wordlessly I nod. Aqueous whines on my lap, seemingly thinking the same thing as me.

"There's a school trip coming up."

Oh, thank goodness.

"But, uh…" he squirms uncomfortably. "Students with common dragons aren't allowed to go."

"Why? Am I too poor?" I hiss bluntly.

He takes a deep breath before continuing. "It's a trip to a museum about a mile away from here. They don't allow commoners to enter."

"So, I am too poor? It's a museum! It must only cost a fiver!"

"It's not that; it's a free trip," he explains. "There will be other trips! Camping, visiting an elite dragon training school, skiing-"

"So, the trips that I can go on I can't afford," I conclude.

He doesn't answer for a few seconds. "I'm sorry. On that day, you'll just have a private dragon training session with your mentor."

Aqueous growls, lashing his spiked tail, leaving a small scratch on the side of the desk.

"Fine." I grit my teeth.

"Who is your mentor, out of interest?"

"Marco White."

"Oh." He pauses for a few seconds. "No wonder Mr Knight's wound up."

I narrow my eyes. "Excuse me?"

"Nothing. You can go," he smiles, but it doesn't reach his eyes. "Again, I'm sorry."

75

* * *

"That's not fair!" Wes protests. "Who am I going to talk to all day?"

"I don't care anyway. All the trips that cost money will be too expensive for me to go on, so you'll have to get used to it."

The kitten wriggles in my arms, clinging to my shirt as another large dragon passes. Asteroid chirps at it, offering encouragement. Wes opens the door to the vets, which is just a plain white building with a small wooden sign saying: 'Veterinarians'. Inside it is just as plain: a small white room with a desk and computer. A few wooden chairs are scattered around, and colourful pictures of dragons decorate the walls. A woman at the front desk turns to smile at us as we walk in.

"How can I help?" she says, showing off her pearly white teeth.

"I booked an appointment: Abbot."

She types on the computer, then smiles. "Dr Zhào will see you in a minute."

We settle on the seats, Wes swinging his legs back and forth.

"You booked?" The kitten settles on my lap as it figures out we've stopped moving.

"Yeah, I rang last night," he shrugs sheepishly. "My parents gave me a mobile phone as a late birthday present."

"Cool."

"It's one of the older ones, though; they say I'm not old enough for a touch screen."

The wait is only a few minutes, but Asteroid and Aqueous entertain themselves by playing with colourful blocks that are sprawled across the floor.

"Abbot?" A petite Chinese woman with short black hair ushers us into a room next door.

A metal bench is in the middle of the room, surrounded by cupboards and a weighing scale in the corner. The woman smiles at us once more.

"Which one of you has a sick dragon, huh?"

"Uh, it's not a dragon." Wes carefully takes the kitten from me and places it on the table.

The woman stares at the kitten for a few seconds. "Okay…"

"We were wondering if you knew anything about cats."

"Luckily for you two, I specialize in the care of household pets." She starts examining the kitten, pulling back its ears and checking its eyes. "Where'd you find it?"

"It was hiding in my bathroom." I smile sheepishly.

"His fur is a mess," she mutters.

"'His'? It's a boy?" Wes looks at the kitten excitedly.

"Yes. About three months old. He's obviously been abandoned, seeing as he's comfortable around people," she answers. She picks the kitten up gently, but he squeaks anyway. "I'll be back in a minute."

Wes bounces on the spot excitedly, his eyes shining. "What should we call him?"

I've been so preoccupied that I haven't been thinking of names. With everything that's been going on, I guess I pushed the kitten to the back of my mind. "I dunno. You name him; you seem to have all the ideas."

"*Really?*" He stops bouncing and pauses for a second. "Normie. Normie Abbot-Adams."

"I like it," I elbow his arm playfully. "You had to think hard about that one, huh?"

My friend's face heats up and he shrugs. "It suits him."

After a few minutes, the vet returns with Normie scooped up in a towel. His fur is sopping wet, and his little face is contorted into what I can only describe as a cat's version of a scowl. "All clean now," Dr Zhào smiles.

Normie wriggles in the towel, growling loudly.

"Nothing wrong?" Wes presses.

"Nope. He's perfectly fine, just a bit under-fed." She places Normie on the table, and he quickly jumps out of the towel and shakes himself, before licking his fur vigorously. "Are you planning on keeping him? It's a lot of responsibility."

"We're aware," I reply, not liking her condescending tone.

"Okay. What's his name?" She tries to dry Normie with the towel, ignoring his screams of protest and anger.

"Normie Abbot-Adams," Wes says proudly.

"I'll add him to my register of patients," she smiles. "I'll also give you two a list of what you need to buy for him."

Great.

Looks like I'm not eating for a week.

* * *

Normie pounces on his purple toy mouse once more, batting at it with his back legs.

"See? I told you he needed a toy!" Wes points out.

"Just wait until a piece of thread falls off our clothes; he'll forget all about that mouse in two seconds flat."

Wes snorts in reply. Two days ago, we went out and bought all the things Normie would need, as well as toys. We also have to pay insurance to the vet every month to cover him for any future injuries, as animals other than dragons don't get free service.

The mouse shoots out of his grip when he kicks it too hard, so I bend down to fetch it for him. As soon as I bend down, I feel Wes' stare burning into my back. With a loud sigh, I throw the mouse back to Normie and cross my arms like a sulking toddler.

"Something wrong?" Wes stands up, putting a hand on my shoulder.

"Yes," I mutter bitterly. "Stop staring at my bum!"

His face immediately goes bright red. "I wasn't-"

"Ever since the 'incident' every time I turn around you stare!"

"N-no!" He smoothes his hair down anxiously. "I didn't know you had a tattoo, that's all."

"Don't give me- Wait, what are you talking about?"

He starts to play with his fingers in embarrassment. "That blue swirly tattoo on your, uh, lower back. I've been trying to work out whether it's real."

"*What?*" I storm into my stall in the bathroom and yank my shirt up above my belly button. "Where?"

"On your back!" Wes spins me around until I notice a small blue mark on my back.

The marking starts off like a slim tree trunk, before branching off to the left into a small, perfectly shaped bright blue swirl.

"What is *that?*" I demand, my mouth hanging open from shock.

"You don't... know?" He tilts his head to one side in confusion.

"It'd better be fake!"

"I don't think so," he unhelpfully chips in. "It looks too...vibrant."

Aqueous and Asteroid come in at this point, wondering what all the excitement is about. My eyes snap to Aqueous' markings, and how similar they look to mine.

"Wes, pull your shirt up."

"What? Why...?"

"Just do it."

With a sigh, Wes turns around and lifts his shirt, his mouth instantly dropping open. "Is this a joke?"

Dark grey patches cover his lower back. As I expected, they look almost identical to Asteroid's: grey, cloud-like markings.

"They're Elemental markings!" I exclaim, pointing to Asteroid.

"Only dragons get those!" he protests.

"Obviously not!" I chew my fingernail in thought. "Is there a library around here?"

"Yeah, the one in school, why?"

"There's got to be some information about this! It might be some sort of disease!"

"Let's not jump to conclusions!" my friend hisses. "Let's go there now and try to find out about this."

* * *

We allowed ourselves time to calm down, then headed over to school. The library is huge; the room is lined with shelves upon shelves of colourful books. Tables and computers are set up in a circle around the middle, covered in books and paper. There's an inaccessible balcony above, lined with empty shelves and tall stained glass windows.

The only people in here are a large group sat at a table at the back. My heart sinks upon recognising Marco, Maya, Mason, Ciara, Naomi and Rocky looking through books and laughing amongst each other. However, my heart stops as Sadie joins them, sliding onto Mason's lap.

Why now?

How the hell am I supposed to hide this from them?

My heart starts pumping at the thought of my friends finding out what she did to me. They'll be ashamed of me.

"Plan of action?" I enquire.

"You distract them; I'll try to find some books on it. I'll be back in a minute." With that, Wes disappears into one of the aisles, eyes darting from shelf to shelf for useful books.

"Hazel!" Rocky calls me over, one arm wrapped around Ciara's shoulders.

With a deep breath, I join the group and hide my face behind my messy hair. "Hey, guys."

"Hey." Marco pulls out a chair next to him and pats it for me to sit down.

Slowly I sit down, watching Sadie's joyful expression darken to that of hatred.

"What are you doing here?" my brother grins at me.

"Wes and I are looking for books."

Maya rolls her eyes. "Obviously. What kind?"

"Dragon Mythology." I'm relieved as I come out with a believable answer. "We're really interested in it."

Sadie's stony expression does not falter, which unnerves me even more.

"Are you cold? You're shaking." Marco pulls me close to him, stroking my back and pushing my hair out of the way. "You're really tense too; are you sick?"

"*Sick?*" Rocky cries.

"I'm sure it's nothing," Ciara waves her hand dismissively. "Old Scargirl is probably just trying to get Marco's attention. But, after all, who wouldn't want that?"

Ignoring Ciara, I mutter: "No, I'm fine." My eyes dart back to Sadie for a second, but this time my friend catches it, and narrows his eyes.

"Are you-"

"*Mew!*"

This cannot get *any* worse.

Normie wriggles out of my bag and jumps on the table, promptly followed by Aqueous, who starts tugging his friend's tail anxiously, his turquoise gaze locked on Sadie. He'd begged us to come along, yowling and crying whenever we went too near the door. In the end, I just gave up and put him in my bag to make him happy.

"Aww! Haze! It's so cute!" Maya coos, reaching over to stroke Normie's little head.

Normie confidently struts over to Maya. Ciara and Rocky also coo over him and give him loads of attention. My gaze, however, is locked on Sadie, who now has a dark smile on her face. She winks at me and sticks her tongue out.

"Let me hold it!" she coos in her sweetest voice, reaching out to grab him.

Normie hisses, fluffing up and running into my arms. He growls continuously, his gaze hard but fearful.

"What's up with it?" Marco scratches Normie's chin, which makes him relax a little.

Quickly! Say something!

"He doesn't like being grabbed," I blurt out.

A few eyebrows are raised, but no-one questions me further. Sadie's furious gaze burns into my skin. I'm going to pay for this, for sure.

"How come?" she asks, all sweetness gone.

I shrug. "He's-"

"I've found a book!"

Thank goodness.

Wes sits next to me, proudly holding a fairly old book with no writing on the front. It's just a plain black cover with frayed yellow pages.

"Okay, let's go." I try to get up, but Marco doesn't loosen his grip.

"What's the rush? Stay a while." My best friend raises an eyebrow at me, unnerved by my behaviour.

"No, please go. I can take your spot next to Marco when you get up." Ciara winks at my friend, making Rocky's eyes blaze furiously.

"Not with *her* here." Wes glares at Sadie, his eyes burning.

"Wes, don't-" I begin, only for him to angrily cut me off.

"You're not going to take what she did to you and Aqueous, are you?" he snaps, clenching and unclenching his fists.

"What? What happened? What did you do?" Rocky shoots up, his voice echoing out across the room.

The blonde girl giggles and flips her hair. "Nothing. It was just a bit of fun."

"*Fun?* You embarrassed Hazel in front of everyone! You had no right to kick Aqueous either!" Wes slams the book on the table, making Asteroid jump in front of him protectively.

"*What did you do?*" Rocky shouts, silencing everyone.

Mason slams his hand on the table repeatedly. "*How dare you-*"

"Shh, babe," Sadie coos. "It's fine. I'll tell them."

I crawl onto Marco's lap and bury my face in his chest, trying to hide the tears and the embarrassment. My friend strokes my back and kisses the top of my head, only half-listening to Sadie.

"I was chasing the kitten for stealing Exquisite's food. It ran into the bathroom of her cabin, and she, and others, came to see what the commotion was about," she giggles before collecting herself. "So, I kicked her dragon, and while she was distracted, took her towel. Everyone saw how disgusting she looks with no clothes on."

I freeze in Marco's arms, clinging tightly to him as if my life depended on it. A part of me expected laughing and teasing, but I knew Rocky wouldn't let that happen.

"Get out, *now*," my brother orders through gritted teeth.

"Whatever," Sadie says in her sing-song voice. "C'mon, Masey. Later, losers."

9

Chapter Nine

I'm tired.

I know Rocky is doing his best, but it isn't helping.

It's only been a few days and I'm already tired of the insults.

I'm tired of people pushing disgusting pictures into my locker.

I'm tired of caring.

And now I have another problem, which is crawling up my back.

"What is this?" Marco flicks through the old book, his gaze stony and unreadable. "This isn't about Dragon Mythology."

Wes shuffles in his chair in panic. "It's-"

"Elemental markings? What do they have to do with Dragon Mythology?"

"Elemental markings?" I feel Rocky tense.

"Elemental markings are not just limited to dragons; they can appear on other animals in rare cases. We call this phenomenon-" Wes snatches the book off Marco, who shouts: "Hey!"

"Marco, what were you reading?" Rocky raises an eyebrow.

"He folded the corner of the page in the damned book!" Marco fumes. "What do you want to know about that stuff for?"

Wes doesn't answer, just hugs the book close to his chest.

Without warning, Rocky lifts the back of my shirt, revealing my markings. Marco looks absolutely astonished, while my brother doesn't look fazed at all.

"I thought you might get them," he mumbles.

My brother's standoffishness makes me pull away from him, and his stony expression doesn't change. "Why?"

I move onto the chair beside him as he gets up and takes off his shirt completely before turning around. Pale yellow lightning bolts crawl up his back, some overflowing onto his shoulders. The markings are only just visible on his pale skin; they are nowhere near as noticeable as mine or Wes'.

"I got them when I was your age," he explains, sitting back down on the chair. "The more Cerberus and I learned to control my element, the more markings I got." Cerberus chirps in agreement, nudging his arm playfully. "I thought you might get them because we're siblings. I guess it's hereditary."

Wes flicks through the book to the page Marco read aloud, his gaze flickering up every so often to study Rocky's markings.

"That's weird," Marco scrunches his face up. "So, Haze will have blue markings all up her back by the end of First Year?"

"Have you got a problem with that?" Rocky snaps.

My friend puts his hands up apologetically. "Woah, calm down. I haven't got any problems with it; I couldn't care less."

Rocky's gaze doesn't waver, but his eyes drop when I grab his arm. "Don't fight."

"Uh, you can put your shirt back on now," Wes mutters, his eyes flicking back down to the book awkwardly.

Rocky rolls his eyes but says nothing and does as he says.

"Here!" Wes holds up the book, pointing at a large drawing. "This explains something."

The drawing is of the eight elements, each represented by their markings. The elements are in a circle with a large multi-coloured star in the middle, emanating a white glow.

"What does it mean?" Marco takes the book away from Wes and studies the page.

"There are eight people in total with markings. The ninth is the most powerful, the star: they are the leader. It's how the Original Elementals came to be."

Rocky sighs. "Where did you find this? I spent all year looking for a book that would give me information, and I found nothing."

Wes points to the fourth aisle on the right. "I found it at the back. I went to pick up another book and it fell on my head." He smiles sheepishly.

"So, what does it mean? The Original Elementals are following you lot around?" Marco teases, winking playfully at me.

"Oh, don't say that!" Rocky moans. "I do embarrassing things all the time!"

"Don't worry, we're not being stalked. The Original Elementals were our ancestors! But, I don't know why *we're* getting the markings." Wes scratches the back of his head in thought. "My parents took me swimming; they don't have them."

My brother shrugs. "Mum has never said anything about them either, but we could ask her tomorrow."

My heart stops. Mum's coming tomorrow?

Tomorrow?

What am I supposed to say to her?

Wes shakes his head and flicks through the book once more. "I just don't know what it means…" he mutters to himself.

Marco shrugs. "Don't let it bother you guys; your 'leader' should come soon enough. Hey, maybe you're all aliens? It would explain why you look so weird." He chuckles at his own joke.

"Hilarious." I roll my eyes agitatedly.

86

"At least you're not upset anymore," he points out softly.

It's true: I must have stopped crying ages ago, but not noticed. This is a good distraction from Sadie's harsh words.

"I guess we could look it up." Wes puts the book down and closes it slowly, looking lost.

Rocky sighs deeply. "I've already looked online; there are just pictures of dragon markings."

Normie wails loudly as Aqueous tackles Asteroid, and the two bored dragons get into a play fight. The small kitten jumps into the fray, batting at the duo with his soft paws.

"I think we should sleep on it," Rocky sighs.

"'We'? I'm allowed to join the club?" Marco teases.

"You're my mentor," I point out. "I *have* to confide in you."

Marco fist pumps the air in mock excitement. "It doesn't mean you need to *all* the time."

"Let's meet up here tomorrow, around six o'clock, to do research, okay?" Wes packs the book in his bag, ushering Normie to climb in as well.

"Hazel and I can't. We'll meet you at eight." Rocky wraps his arm around me. "Mum is coming down."

Marco sighs. "See you two at eight, then."

* * *

The day passes far too quickly for my liking. It's soon half five, and Rocky arrived to take me to the hotel Mum is staying at.

I haven't been able to calm my nerves all day.

What if she doesn't like me?

What if I don't like her?

Currently, we're sitting in the hotel's dining room. Dinner is being served so Rocky thought we might as well just eat here. The room is quite small, with dusty red carpets and yellow walls. A few colourful paintings hang from the walls, though some are crooked. Silver trays hold the food at the far end of the room, and many people have crowded around to get their share of the buffet.

My leg won't stop bouncing out of nervousness, so Rocky keeps mistaking me for being cold. Aqueous and Normie are itching to eat, but I've told them both to stay put until Mum arrives. Cerberus is being more patient, sitting obediently at my brother's side with her tongue lolling out. She nuzzles him every so often, expecting a reward for being good.

Without warning, a dark brown dragon rushes towards Cerberus. Rocky's companion jumps up and plays with her new playmate, batting at its tail.

"Mum!" Rocky jumps up and hugs someone behind him.

I take a deep breath and swivel round in my chair.

The first thing that hits me is how beautiful she is. She is tall, skinny, with long jet-black hair tied back in a tight ponytail, not leaving much room for her forehead to move. Her skin is a porcelain white, like Rocky's, matched with a pair of warm brown eyes and soft, delicate features.

"Hey, baby," she coos, ruffling my brother's hair as he pulls away.

Her eyes land on me, and I shuffle nervously in my seat.

Do I hug her too?

Do I sit here?

Do I say nothing?

Mum answers my question for me, by holding her arms out and whispering: "Come here, darling."

Without a second thought, I'm in her arms. It feels warm and familiar being with her again, though I barely remember her as a child.

"I've missed you," she murmurs, so softly I can barely hear her.

"I've missed you more."

She laughs and pulls away, wiping tears off her face, and mine. We both sit down, her dragon settling down next to her.

"This is Warrior." She pats the dragon on the head. "You remember her, don't you?"

Warrior shakes her head, revealing pale blue snowflake markings on her neck and chest. Mum is an ice Elemental, then.

Aqueous jumps on my lap, whining and pointing to the buffet with his tail.

"Who is this?" Mum pats the table, which Aqueous immediately jumps on, expecting food.

"Aqueous. And this-" I reach down and scoop Normie up in my arms "-is Normie."

"Aww." Mum strokes Normie, who confidently struts around the table, soaking up the attention.

Aqueous growls again, pointing towards the buffet once more. "Alright, alright. I give in, come on." My companion grins and flies towards the trays, jumping up and down on a table close by.

"I'll come with you; Cerberus is about to explode." Rocky flicks his hand for Cerberus to follow, and she immediately jumps up and scampers over to the trays, pushing an elderly couple out the way. "Oh fuck!" My brother chases after his companion, apologising profusely to the couple.

"Cerberus is over-excitable," Mum giggles. "She fits Rocky perfectly."

With Rocky gone, I decide it's the perfect opportunity to ask about the markings. The both of us asking about it might make her suspicious.

"Mum, this is a bit of a weird question, but do we have a family history of dragon markings?"

She stiffens before regaining her composure. "What do you mean, dear?"

"It's just that-"

"Look! They've just restocked the spaghetti." She interrupts, though I have the feeling she did it on purpose.

I collect a plate with a few pieces of chicken for Aqueous and Normie to share, before getting a plate of spaghetti for myself. We return to the table with Rocky, who now has Cerberus under control.

Before giving my companions their food I cut up the chicken into smaller pieces, so it's easier for Normie to chew. Aqueous wriggles impatiently, pawing at my knee for the plate. After what he perceives to be a lifetime of waiting, the plate is on the floor and the duo tuck in as if they haven't eaten for a week and a half. Rocky begins wolfing his dinner down, similar to the way Aqueous and Normie are eating.

Mum asks us both loads of questions about school and everyday life. She seemed particularly happy when Rocky mentioned Ciara as his girlfriend. I rolled my eyes at that. She told me about her job as a waitress, and how she earns extra money through cleaning. The question about markings is not brought up again.

"Have you made any new friends since coming here, Hazel?"

"Yeah; Wes is okay."

"Wes is a boy's name," she smiles.

My face heats up at what she's implying. "We're just friends."

"Mm-hm. That's what they all say." She giggles at my horrified expression. "You used to hang around with Marco White a lot as a baby; are you still friends with him?"

"Unfortunately," Rocky sighs.

She raises an eyebrow. "What's wrong with him?"

"He's a pain in the ass."

"He's only a pain in your ass because you *want* him to be a pain, so you'll have an excuse not to like him," I point out, waving my fork in his face.

Rocky just rolls his eyes in reply.

Mum's eyes dart between us, before realization dawns on her face.

"Ah, I see."

"See what?" I question.

"You'll know when you're older," she grins, taking another mouthful of salad.

* * *

After dinner, we headed over to the library, but I was sad to leave my mother. It was nice to catch up, even if only for a few hours.

"There they are!" Marco waves us over by one of the computers.

Wes is too busy scrolling through websites to look up, so he half-heartedly waves with one hand. Two chairs are in between them. I pick the one closer to Wes, so Rocky wouldn't kick off and start an argument.

"Anything?" Propping one elbow on the table, I scan the current website he's on.

"No, nothing," he mumbles. "It's all about dragon markings. But-" He passes me a small pile of paper. "-I found stuff on the Original Elementals, so that could be helpful."

Flicking through the pages, I see that the few diagrams that are on them are like the one in the book.

"I found this website," Marco leans back in his chair. "But it's filtered."

"Filtered?"

"Yeah, the school doesn't want us going on it, basically."

"What's it about?" Wes looks up. "It could be important."

Marco clicks on the website, coming up with a red screen with the word 'FILTERED' in bold white letters. "It's an article called 'Can Elemental markings appear on humans?'"

I bite my fingernail in thought. "Can we bypass the filter?"

Marco shakes his head. "The school has to disable it themselves."

"What about the museum trip?" Wes sits up, rubbing his tired eyes.

"What about it?" I feel a twinge of jealousy about not being able to go on the trip, but I don't let it show. "How can that help?"

"There's bound to be a computer there," he explains. "I could go on it and take photos of the website."

I shrug. The museum could have filters as well, but it's worth a try. "Okay. When is the trip?"

"Next Tuesday," Wes bites his lip. "But if it doesn't work... We're back to square one."

Rocky nudges my shoulder. "How come you didn't tell me about the trip?"

"I'm not allowed to go. No commoners."

"What?" His face scrunches up in confusion.

"That's a load of bull," Marco cracks his knuckles, one by one. "All the commoners could go last year."

I sigh deeply. "I don't really care anyway; it means I can do some research here. I also get a private one-to-one lesson with you, Marco."

My best friend shrugs and smiles. "Fine by me."

10

Chapter Ten

"Have fun, okay? And don't get lost!" I wave to Wes as he leaves with the rest of the Year, all of them piling on to the long silver coaches.

He rolls his eyes cheekily. "Yes, Mum."

With that, he scampers off to join everyone else. He doesn't mix in with the crowd; he kind of hangs around on the outskirts.

I hope all goes well for him. I also hope the museum haven't filtered the website; currently it's our only lead.

Over the past week, we've been trawling through books and websites for information, but there's still nothing. The only book that really helped us was that old one. Wes keeps it safe in his bag until we need it.

Today, I decided to go to the library to catch up on my homework, seeing as I have no lessons because my entire Year has gone on the trip. Marco and I are meeting on the field at three for our lesson. He said he'd focus on teaching me how to control my element more, rather than trying to teach Aqueous.

Speaking of Aqueous, he's sprung up in size recently. He's too big to balance on my shoulder now, but I can just about carry him in my arms. More swirl markings are spreading on his face, and there's even one on each of his front feet now. Normie has also grown, but he's staying in the cabin today to sleep; he was up all night playing with his toys.

I finish off my short story for English, before moving on to collect dragon pictures for my Dragon Mythology class. I need to get pictures of dragons with each element, which shouldn't be too hard. As I type, my companion jumps on my lap, staring at the screen in awe when pictures of different dragons come up. He growls each time I click on a picture and move it into a document to print it off. When I go to collect them, a book catches my eye. It is a shiny gold colour with white writing on the side. I pull it off the shelf to read the title: *Common Dragons – Dangerous Beasts*.

I don't think I'm going to like this.

Despite a sense of foreboding, I flick through the book and land on a random page. A blurry picture of a black blob is in the corner, with the caption: 'third sighting of the black common dragon'. I turn back a page, which reveals two other blurry photos, the first and second sightings. Underneath the first is a warning:

Common dragons are extremely dangerous. That is why they are given to the poor, to eradicate the 'undesirables'. In total, 4,302 people are injured by common dragons each year, while uncommon dragon injuries are at below 3,000.

Do not approach these dragons with food; they will attack with no hesitation, and will kill if they feel threatened.

"What a load of complete and utter bull," I mutter, closing the book and putting it back on the shelf.

Aqueous is too soft to hurt anyone! Plus, what sad person sat and counted every single accident with dragons? There's bound to be accidents. Common dragons tend to be more over-excitable and friendly than other dragons; that's what caused the accidents.

My companion looks at me with his head tilted to one side in confusion.

"You wouldn't hurt anyone on purpose, would you?" I coo, scratching his chin, his weak spot.

He shakes his head vigorously, pawing at my hand. He growls something at me, opening his mouth in his unusual smile.

"Let's not listen to that guy then, shall we?"

He shakes his head, growling again.

I take my homework from the printer and return to my seat, but I'm surprised to see Mr Reedman standing by the counter, eyeing me carefully. Eruption walks up behind him, baring his sharp teeth at Aqueous.

Fuck.

The short man approaches me slowly, dragging each step out for a painfully long time. He eventually reaches me, his eyes narrowed in an angry glare. "Why aren't you on the school trip?" he asks.

"Commoners aren't allowed to go," I reply timidly. "I'm doing homework instead."

"What about your dragon training?"

I swallow back my fear. "Marco's giving me a one to one later."

He stares hard at me for a few seconds, making my heart thump so loud I'm sure he can hear it. "Very well." He looks at the printer. "Which book did you pull out? *Common Dragons – Dangerous Beasts*, I presume?"

"How did you-"

"I wrote that book, and I'll have you know that common dragons *are* horrible creatures. Yours included. But, since the poor reforms, you've been cheated out of an uncommon dragon."

The poor reforms was a law passed by Government to legally discriminate against commoners. It means that we now cannot have uncommon dragons, as they are considered too expensive for us. So common dragons were captured from the wild and given to us.

"Aqueous is perfect for me; I don't want a higher one." My tone is darker than I thought it would be.

He raises an eyebrow in disbelief, before flicking his hand in dismissal. "Think whatever you like, Miss Adams. But beware of your political beliefs; the Cindaraans are getting more and more popular by the day." With that, he turns around and strolls off, Eruption lumbering after him.

***

"That's weird, even for him." Marco scratches the back of his head in thought.

"So, what does it mean? Is he trying to imply that I should become a Cindaraan?"

He shrugs. "I guess. I heard that Krystalan supporters in higher Years are getting beaten up and abused until they give in to the Cindaraans."

"What are you going to do?"

"I'm going to join the Cindaraans, and I suggest you do too." He cuts me off as my mouth opens to protest. "For safety, Haze. I don't agree with their views."

With a loud sigh, I reluctantly nod. I really don't want to join Raymond's group, but I will if it will put Marco's mind at ease. "Okay. Can we do the lesson now?"

A nod accompanied with an eye roll is my answer. "Try not to drench me this time."

"Sorry about that," I apologise sweetly.

"Today, you're going to learn to conjure water without using natural water."

"Huh?"

He rolls his eyes again. "You're going to make water out of thin air."

"That's a thing?"

"Yeah." He clicks his fingers and a short burst of flame burns in the air for a second, before vanishing.

Cool! I can throw water at people when they annoy me now!

"How do I do it?" I bounce excitedly.

"Just think about water rising from your hand. It'll get easier the more you practise."

Water rising from my hand?

I think hard about a small ball of crystal-clear water rising from my empty hand, but when I open my eyes, I only see a tiny drop.

"It's a start," I shrug.

At this moment, Aqueous shrieks and zooms towards me as Drea chases him, shooting a bright purple beam from her mouth.

"Drea, stop!" Marco commands, instantly freezing the terrifying creature in her tracks.

She shoots Aqueous a venomous glare before laying down in the grass, looking extremely sulky and not in the mood for talking. My companion clings to my legs, not keen on approaching the white dragon again.

Marco looks at me expectantly, so I try again. This time, there's a small puddle in my palms, which slips between my fingers and onto the grassy ground.

"Better," Marco comments. "Not perfect, but better."

After a few more tries, I manage to get the water in the air for a split second, before it splashes onto my shoes. I try one more time, and I'm astonished to see a perfect sphere of water float above my hand for a second, before dissolving into thin air.

"Well done!" Marco claps sarcastically. "Took you a while."

I roll my eyes. "Thanks. Is the lesson over?"

"Thankfully, yes," he sighs and sits on the ground, staring at the cloudy sky. "When is the sun gonna come out?"

I settle down next to him, sitting cross-legged so Aqueous can sit in my lap. "It's supposed to rain tomorrow."

"Fantastic, but at least you'll be dry."

"I guess."

He pushes my shoulder teasingly. "You're not upset about the trip, are you?"

I shrug and lean against him, resting my head on his shoulder. "No. I'm just upset about being discriminated against."

He snorts. "Don't be. I know you haven't had a great start over the past month, but I'm glad you're here. Rocky is too, so please try to ignore what people are saying."

"I know. But it's not just the insults, Marco. People are posting things in my locker. I'm scared to open it sometimes."

"What kind of things?"

"People calling me names and guys posting pictures of their you-know-what."

He scrunches his face up in disgust. "Do you have a spare locker key?"

"Yeah, why?"

"I'll clean out your locker every morning. You shouldn't be seeing that stuff."

"Thanks. I'll make it up to you, promise."

* * *

Wes paces up and down the room, his face contorted in anger. "And then, the stupid guy threw me off the computer! I was *so* close!"

"It's okay, Wes. We'll pick up another lead." I try to reassure him, grabbing his arm as he storms past to pull him onto the bed.

He kicks the floor childishly, his eyes burning with fury. "This is so important! We have nothing to go on now!"

"Look," I say. He raises an eyebrow suspiciously when I squeeze his hand. "There will be more opportunities, better ones."

He goes silent, which I'm partially thankful for. Yes, he's stressed and worried, but I'm worried too. If anyone finds out about this, we could be in real danger. The school won't hesitate to contact the government; I realize that.

Asteroid noses Wes affectionately, patting his face with her foot. The brown-haired boy lifts her on his lap with obvious difficulty.

Plus, it won't just be us who are affected. The connection would have to be broken between Aqueous and I, and that can only be done with one of us dying. I don't want my companion to die because of some stupid markings on my back; I'd rather take the blow.

What's worrying me most is that the markings are spreading, like Rocky said they would. The more I learn, the more they spread.

"If another trip comes up, will you go on it?" My friend asks suddenly, his eyes pleading.

"I don't know," I admit. "If I'm allowed to go, and it's not expensive… "

He sits there in silence once more, stroking Asteroid's head, careful not to let his fingers catch on her stubby horns.

Do I really want to go on a trip, though? Even if I had permission and the money, I don't think I could bring myself to. The people outside are obviously discriminatory, and I don't want to get caught up in all that crap.

Still, it would be nice to go on just one trip, to see if I'm missing out.

* * *

We were all surprised to get a letter the next day. The envelopes were bright white, with our names handwritten on them. When I open mine, my nostrils are assaulted by the smell of ash and dry leaves. Two necklaces lay inside, which I tipped out. One had a gold chain with an orange flame-shaped pendant. The other had a silver chain with a green leaf-shaped pendant. Intrigued by these items, I read the letter quietly to myself.

Dear Miss Adams,

Due to a communication error, the school has been asked to send pupils this letter as an apology. It is required for all students to pick their political sympathies immediately.

If you are still unsure, we have provided a short biography of each party and what they wish to accomplish. Please take time to read it, and choose wisely: there are no second chances.

<u>*The Cindaraans*</u>

This group was recently founded by Sabrina, Kyle, Cameron and Sophie Williams. The Williams family are extremely wealthy, and their businesses prosperous. They have never tried to hide their hatred for the Krystalans and always voiced their opinions on Krystalan decisions.

They believe that all dragons should be put to work, as humans are. They believe dragons are lazy and take life for granted. They want dragons to do hard labour, such as building, mining and stopping crime. Dragons will work until they die, or are too injured to continue.

The flame is their symbol; this recognizes that determination and hard work are key to training a dragon to live in our society.

<u>*The Krystalans*</u>

They are the 'softer' party. They were formed one hundred years ago by Robert Brown. His goal was to run the country in a fair way, and to treat everyone equally.

He wanted children to learn to be responsible, respectable people from a young age, so he set up the towns we know today. There are now thousands of Primary and Secondary Towns across the country, and we must thank him for that. It was also his idea to give children dragons at the age of fifteen, so they would be more responsive and focused while in education.

The leaf is their symbol, as it symbolizes growth in society.

By the end of the week, you will be expected to pick which party you want to join. There will be two stalls set up in school in the main hall. Wear your party's necklace and register at the correct stall.

After joining the party, there will be regular meetings and events for you to attend, so be sure not to miss out.

If there are any problems, talk to your base tutor.

We hope to hear from you at the end of the week.

Choose wisely.

11

Chapter Eleven

Three months have passed since I received the letter, and life hasn't been any easier. The teasing has died down, but people are looking to find something else to bully me about. I can't wait for that day.

Rocky and Marco have joined the Cindaraans, along with quite a few others. Since then, a political war has sprung up between the Cindaraans and the Krystalans, which led to one dragon getting killed. The owner was immediately thrown out of school for allowing his companion to be killed, although I think his Krystalan sympathies were the real reason. Many Krystalans are now facing abuse; physical, emotional and even sexual in one case. After hearing about this, many students in our Year joined the Cindaraans for protection. I wear the Cindaraan necklace, but Marco and I don't agree with their views.

Wes convinced me to join; Raymond is his mentor. Despite him sharing a surname with his father, I didn't make the connection until he mentioned it. Among the Cindaraans he goes by Ray, probably to try and make himself more likeable and approachable. I still don't like him, although he was very pleased when I joined the Cindaraans. I guess he wants everyone to see how 'pathetic' I am.

My markings have spread along my back. I have to wear my hair down now, as they have also crept up my neck. Rocky was as confused as I was; his markings go no higher than his shoulders.

Aqueous is too big to carry now; he has to walk beside me or fly above my head. His horns are becoming a problem; they're starting to curl, so his head keeps getting stuck in railings or ladders. Normie is also growing, but he isn't talking to anyone right now. He had to be neutered a few days ago and hasn't got over it yet. He's been sleeping a lot, and his taste in food is starting to get expensive, as Wes keeps fussing over him like a baby. The silly thing doesn't need five different flavours of treats; they probably all taste the same anyway.

At the moment, Mr Knight is giving us a tutorial on how to create a bubble of air so we can breathe underwater. Marco hasn't been excited; he keeps fidgeting and pulling at his swimming trunks uncomfortably.

"My penis is too big!" he complains jokingly. "It won't fit in properly!"

After ten minutes of that I just ignored him, I don't want to listen to his perverted jokes. Plus, I have other problems.

I have to wear a swimming costume.

It's not just that I'm insecure about my body, it's that someone might spot my markings. Then what the hell am I supposed to do?

"Before you dive underwater, think of a large bubble around your head. Don't forget about your mentor though, they need a bubble too!" Mr Knight pops the clear bubble around his head with his finger, then folds his arms. "Any questions?" No-one responds, so he claps his hands together. "Great! Off you go!"

"Alright, Haze. Let's get in the river already, I want to get these stupid things off as soon as possible." The girls in the group turn to stare as Marco takes his shirt off and leaves it crumpled on the ground.

My face burns as people start glancing at me from the river. While they were getting in, I'm still fully clothed.

"Haze? Come on," Marco whines.

"I can't," I mutter. "They'll see the markings!"

"What? Your tattoos? It's no longer a tramp stamp, you should be fine."

To get on my nerves, Marco's recently decided to call my markings tattoos, and is constantly asking when I'll get a sleeve.

"Marco!"

"Okay, okay. Just keep your back to me, and you'll be fine."

After a few more seconds' hesitation, I take off my white top and denim shorts before wading into the river. Aqueous paddles next to me, swimming confidently as if he had been born in the water.

"There, now, was that bad?" My friend grabs my arm and clings to me like a limpet; it's obvious he's not confident in the water.

"Will *you* be okay?" I swim further into the river, making him tense and grip me harder for support. "You don't look like a confident swimmer."

"When you're fire and dark, swimming isn't really a top priority," Marco complains, brushing my fringe out of my face. "Let's try to get this done as quickly as possible, and don't get me killed."

"Would I?"

"Yes! You'd leave me to be eaten alive by seaweed!"

"It's a plant, dumbass."

"Whatever! Just don't let go!"

The other students start diving down in the water to practise their air bubbles, ignoring our squabbling. I breathe a sigh of relief, knowing that no-one has noticed my markings so far.

"Hide my back."

Marco mutters something inaudible under his breath, wrapping his arms around my waist for support. "Don't go down too far. Not until you can do the bubble thing."

"I know," I sigh.

Aqueous dives under the water, only to re-emerge with a small, clear bubble around his head. Show-off.

"Ready?"

Marco squeezes his eyes shut and buries his face in my hair. "No."

"Too bad."

I take one last breath before submerging myself in the water. I concentrate hard on creating a bubble around my head, but I feel no change. After a few seconds, I rise back to the surface, Marco coughing and spluttering behind me.

"Fuck! That was horrid! Why are you water? Couldn't you have just been wind and make my life ten times easier?" he whines, rubbing his eyes half-heartedly.

"You wanted to be my mentor…"

"I didn't think this through at all," he says. "Are we done? I need to adjust my trunks." He wriggles, yanking at his costume once more.

"Why have you got it if it's so uncomfortable?"

"I dunno, I think someone's put something down there."

"Why, and who, would do that?"

"Fuck me!" He waves a needle-thin piece of plastic in my face. "That's what's been bothering me."

"Gross!" I whack his arm away in embarrassment. "Didn't you check to see all the labels were off?"

"Guess not. Let's go again. I feel better now." He pulls at the blue strap of my bikini top. "Nice costume, by the way. You look good in a bikini."

I roll my eyes in agitation and try to hide my reddening cheeks. "I didn't want to be bullied for not wearing one."

He shrugs. "I wouldn't have minded; you could have come in the buff."

"That's not what I meant and you know it," I mutter through gritted teeth.

"I know, but-"

I dive underwater again to take him off guard. This time I relax a bit, letting my mind wander instead of thinking so hard and straining myself.

"You did that on purpose!" Marco coughs, spitting water on my neck.

My friend's voice makes me realize that I'd managed to create the bubble successfully. "I did it!" A clear bubble is wrapped around our heads, allowing us to breathe with no worries.

"Yeah, great." My friend relaxes his grip around my waist slightly. "That doesn't mean I forgive you."

His fringe is now draped over his eyes, and I highly doubt he can see anything.

"You need a haircut."

"Gee, thanks."

"I'm not a fan of the shaggy look."

He sighs irritably. "Whatever."

Once we reach the surface, Mr Knight inspects my bubble, and deems it worthy enough for us to leave. "Well done, Hazel. You can go."

To our dismay, someone had thrown our clothes in the river, so we have to walk home in our towels. Marco didn't seem to care that much, but he complained when I wrapped a towel over my shoulders.

"You're a quick learner," Marco comments.

"Thanks. I guess I have to thank you for that."

He grins and jabs me in the stomach. "Thanks. Just try not to drown people, okay?"

* * *

"Another meeting?" Rocky sighs. "I hate them!" My brother crosses his arms at the table, not touching his breakfast.

This morning we were informed about a Cindaraan meeting that will be held tonight. No-one knows what it's about, or how interesting it will be.

Knowing Ray, it will probably be extremely dull.

"We joined," Marco points out, his mouth full of pancake.

Drea growls, nudging Marco's shoulder, as if to say: *why did we do that again?*

Marco pats his companion on the head, but her stony expression doesn't change. I think that when she's alone with Marco she secretly softens up; not that she would let us know that.

I take another bite of toast before they could ask for my opinion. The Cindaraans are hiding something from us, but I'm too frightened to probe any further. Who knows what I'll find if I start sniffing around?

My brother rolls his eyes. "For the wrong reasons. I don't want to watch people getting beaten to a pulp for joining the Krystalans."

"I'm glad you saw sense," I squeeze my brother's hand. "I don't want you to be one of those kids."

He huffs. "I still think I should have joined them." He strokes my hand softly. "At least you're safe though. That's all I care about."

Marco makes sick noises, sticking his finger in front of his mouth for emphasis. This is not appreciated by Rocky, who pushes him so hard he falls off the chair and into a messy heap. I snatch my hand away and cross my arms, glaring at my brother.

"What?"

I don't answer.

"I'm not apologising."

Narrowing my eyes, I can see him cracking under the silence.

"Fine. I'm sorry."

Marco climbs back into his seat, a sour look on his face. Drea growls at Rocky, lashing her clubbed tail and baring her teeth, daring him to do it again.

Rocky raises an eyebrow before changing the topic. "Did Wes find anything about the markings in the book?"

A few days ago, Wes found a book in the library about dragon markings. We both read it carefully, but we hit another dead end. Everyone has started to lose hope; I'd be lying if I said I wasn't.

"No, nothing. Again."

He frowns. "This isn't going well. With all the censorship in place, we can't find anything."

"There's that book shop we haven't tried," Marco sighs, pushing his empty plate into the middle of the table.

"They won't let us in; that's why we haven't tried it," Rocky replies through gritted teeth.

Marco shrugs and his face contorts into an angry expression. I don't understand why they can't get on. They don't have to be best mates, just civil.

Aqueous jumps on my lap frantically, growling and tugging my arm. "What's wrong?" As soon as I stand up, he speeds off down the road, kicking up a cloud of dust and dirt behind him. "Aqueous!"

Rocky tries to grab my arm to stop me chasing after him, but I'm already halfway down the road. My companion is jumping in front of a large crowd that has gathered in the town square. Agonised screams are coming out of the middle, making the crowd whoop and cheer hysterically. Aqueous whimpers and hides behind my legs, shaking violently.

Getting grabbed from behind makes me jump, and Rocky angrily mutters in my ear: "Don't ever do that again!"

"Aqueous ran off, I wasn't just going to let him go by himself!" I rip my arm out of his grip.

"Shut up!" Someone hisses in front of us.

Confused, I stand up on my tiptoes to get a better look. The screaming starts again, this time more anguished.

The orange pendant around his neck gives Ray away as he balls his hands into fists. Maya is on the ground in front of him, her face battered and bleeding. A rock levitates from the ground beside him, which then promptly strikes Maya in the face, producing a sickening crack. More people cheer as the rock collides with her face again, but I'm unable to continue looking.

Why is he doing this?

"Mase!" Rocky grits his teeth.

"What?"

"They're beating Mason up."

"And Maya."

"What's going on?" Marco's voice makes me jump as he comes up behind me.

"I don't know. Ray is beating people up." Rocky replies, his teeth still gritted.

"Marco, Mason is one of them." I mutter, grabbing his hand for comfort.

This shocks my friend into silence, who slouches slightly. I stand on my tiptoes again, trying to get a better look. Screams divert my attention to Mason, who is now getting electrocuted by one of Ray's cronies. His body convulses and his eyes bulge as the hot electricity flows through his body before abruptly stopping as Ray turns to address the crowd.

"This-" Ray pauses to face the large crowd "-is what happens if you disobey us! You have pledged your loyalty. Do *not* go back on it!" He looks back at Maya and spits on her, a dark smirk on his face. "You are one of the lucky ones."

Ray and his cronies sneer as the crowd parts for them, letting the intimidating group go past. He catches my gaze as he walks by, the smile turning into a scowl. Once he breaks contact, I feel like I can breathe again.

For whatever reason, he does not seem to like me.

The crowd starts to disperse, but some people come forward to kick dirt in the faces of the people left on the ground. Mason writhes around in the ground half conscious, his eyes fluttering and bloodshot.

"Shit!" Rocky runs up to him and crouches in the dirt, holding his friend's head in his hands.

"I'll... I'll call my mum." Marco murmurs before taking off down the road.

Despite every bone in my body telling me not to, I approach Maya as she lays unmoving on the ground. Her eyes briefly open to look up at me before slowly closing as she loses consciousness. Members of the ground boo, as I wipe blood from her face with my jacket sleeve, but I ignore them. If I face them, it'll only give them a reason to hurl abuse at me.

"What do we do?" Rocky shakes in the spot, still clutching Mason as if his friend would just drift away.

"Marco is calling his parents, they'll come get Mason. He'll be fine, I promise."

My brother nods, but doesn't seem to listen to what I'm saying. His eyes are glazed over and empty. Mason means as much to him as Marco does to me.

Marco runs back over, kneeling in the dirt between the two of us. "They've sent out for a medical helicopter, he's being airlifted out of here."

"Good, once they get here we take Maya to the hospital here."

12

Chapter Twelve

"Hold her for a second, I'll run the bath." With shaky hands, I set the bath up for Maya, while Rocky and Marco stand awkwardly at the door.

I couldn't just leave her. As soon as I saw her lying there, it didn't matter how much she'd ignored me or refused to hang out with me; she didn't deserve that.

"How will this help?" Marco asks.

"It'll get the blood off. I don't know what else to do."

"I can't believe the hospital refused to treat her," Rocky mutters. "Just because Ray told them not to; how petty."

As soon as the helicopter picked Mason up we took Maya to the hospital. Ray had beaten us there and was threatening the staff to not treat any of his victims. Long story short, we left with a few medical supplies thanks to a sympathetic nurse. We had little idea what to do with them, but I knew washing the blood off was a priority. It would allow us to see the wounds and reduce the chance of infection.

The hot water starts to run, and I see Maya stirring in Rocky's arms. Her eyes flutter open, then just as quickly close and her breathing slows once more.

Marco shuffles his feet uncomfortably. "Can I help at all?"

I turn the tap off as the bath fills up to a reasonable level. "Marco, put her in the bath please?"

Hesitantly, Rocky hands Maya's limp body carefully over to Marco, trying not to hurt her. Marco heads towards the bath and freezes. "With her clothes on?"

"Yeah. I'll take them off when you two are outside."

Maya is placed carefully in the bath. Upon impact with the warm water her eyes fly open. "Wha..."

"You can leave now."

Rocky opens his mouth as if to protest, but quickly thinks better and shuts it before leaving. Marco stays behind for a second and strokes my arm softly before leaving. Maya looks at me, her eyes wide with a mixture of fear and confusion.

"Shh. It's okay," I whisper as her eyes dart around the room.

"Haze..."

"You're fine." I wipe some of the blood off her face with a sponge before beginning to take her clothes off.

She puts up no resistance, just looks at me with tear-filled eyes. "I hurt..." she mutters.

"I know."

She winces as I pull her shirt over her head. "What are you...?"

"Unless you want soaking wet clothes, I think it's best I take them off." I reply, throwing her wet shirt in the sink.

She sniffles. "But I embarrassed myself..."

"I'm sure you didn't *ask* to get beaten up." Her bra is also thrown in the sink.

Sniffling, she unzips her jeans slowly and tries to pull them down, but can't push them father than her knees. "No. I pissed myself..."

I didn't want to bring up the fact that I saw the wet patch between her legs before she came in. "It's okay, it wasn't your fault." I pull her jeans down the rest of the way for her.

She grabs my arm and pushes her cheek against my hand. "Why are you doing this for me?"

"I couldn't leave you there." I put a towel over her body to make her feel more at ease, while also throwing her jeans and underwear in the sink.

"Why?"

"Because… Well, we were friends once. It wouldn't feel right to leave you there to suffer."

"What about Mason?"

I shuffle uncomfortably. "Marco called his parents to take him to a hospital outside of Aria. I can't remember the name."

"They won't let him go, surely…?" She protests, pulling the towel further up her chest.

"I don't think Mason's parents were in the mood to argue."

She sighs and sinks lower into the bath, so her mouth is just above the water. The water has taken on a pink tint, so it might be time for her to get out.

"Are you okay to stand?" I pull the plug out and she sits up fearfully.

"I think so…"

With a lot of effort, she manages to stand and step out of the bath, clinging to me shakily. I swap her soaking wet towel for a dry one, and let her sit on the toilet seat while I usher the boys in. They both step in hesitantly, their concerned gazes locked on the injured girl. She looks a little better not covered in blood, but now the bruising is revealed, huge purple splotches covering her face. The dark-haired girl looks up as they walk in, and clings to the towel wrapped around her, tugging at the bottom in embarrassment.

"Are you okay?" Rocky asks softly.

"Is Mason okay?" Maya ignores Rocky, her attention fixed on Marco. My friend nods slowly. "He will be. He's got the best doctors in the country looking after him now."

Maya sighs in relief. "Thank fuck."

Rocky scrunches his nose at her use of the language, making me roll my eyes. I'm not a baby anymore. I know what the words mean.

"What happened?" I throw the wet towel in the sink with the rest of her clothes. She doesn't seem interested in putting them back on.

Her lip quivers. "We were spying on the Cindaraans for the Krystalans. But we were reckless. I didn't realize it was so serious around here; I just thought it would be a bit of fun. A fight between Mason and Ray lead to Rayna getting interrogated, because she was close to Mason. She let everything spill, and Ray wanted to punish all of us. Now Rayna's dead and the rest of us are injured. The Instructors did nothing, the assholes; Ray has connections everywhere. This whole Cindaraan thing is a lot worse than you think it is. I regret spying in the first damn place."

Marco stays silent, but Rocky says, "You must have known spying wouldn't end well."

An elbow in the stomach from me makes him smile sheepishly.

Maya shrugs. "I don't need to justify my actions to you."

"Woah, no need to get nasty," Marco snaps, crossing his arms over his chest. "We had no obligation to help you."

Maya considers this and sighs. "Sorry."

"Where can she stay?" Rocky bites his lip thoughtfully. "We can't take her back to the cabin yet, she'll get beaten up again."

"We could book a hotel room for her for the night." Marco waves his mobile phone in the air. "I could ring up now."

Before Maya can protest, I nod at him enthusiastically. "Yeah, do it."

Marco looks between us before walking outside to make the call. Maya glares at me, but says nothing.

"You need to rest." I cross my arms as she snorts irritably. "Going to your cabin would be suicide. You're not stupid; you know what will happen."

She rolls her eyes. "Whatever. I just want to see Mason."

"Well, you can't. He's off-site." As I squeeze the water out of her clothes in the sink, I can feel her angry gaze burning into my back.

My brother takes a threatening step towards the injured girl. "If you're going to be stroppy, we could just take you back to the Square."

She calls his bluff. "Fine. Go on."

Thankfully Marco re-enters the room, preventing an argument from breaking out. "I've booked a room for three nights for you."

Maya keeps a careful eye on Rocky when speaking. "Thanks. I appreciate it." Her tone is slow and agitated, but Marco makes no comment.

"Great. You can have a few minutes to rest and then we'll take you over."

Maya rolls her eyes as I talk, which is just rude.

What the hell happened to her? A minute ago, she was vulnerable and in tears, and now she's rude and uninterested. If that's the way she's going to be, we'll take her to the hotel and leave her to it. Seeing as she can't appreciate what anyone is doing for her, why should we help her further?

"I am *not* going anywhere without any clothes." Maya pushes my brother away roughly as he tries to help her stand.

She's deliberately being difficult.

I've had enough. "Fine. Wait here."

I'm thankful that I'm able to leave the bathroom for a bit, to give myself a chance to cool down. Sifting through my drawer, I look for anything that could fit the injured girl. She'll have to make do with whatever I find.

"Hazel!"

The door swings open, slamming against the wall and leaving a large grey mark. Wes runs up to me, his eyes wide with excitement.

"I've got a lead!" He presents me with a small black leather book with the title: *Markings*.

I take the book from him and flick through the pages, surprised by sketches and photographs of lions and leopards with elemental markings. "Where did you...?"

"Ray found out about my markings," he confesses. "He convinced his Dad to buy the book for him. Apparently, that bookshop has an entire *shelf* on elemental markings on anything!"

"Which shop?"

"'Advanced Readers'. The one that students are barred from entering."

"Of course."

He scuffs his foot on the floor repeatedly. "But..."

"But what?"

"I told Ray that you and Rocky also have the markings. He wants to see you two after the meeting tonight."

Fuck me.

I don't want to go anywhere near him after what he did today! Plus, I hate the Cindaraan HQ. It's gloomy and I feel as if my every move is being watched. One step out of line, and they'll know.

"Look, Wes I-"

"I know you hate it! But Ray can get us information! We can't turn this down, we can't afford to." He looks up at me with big, sad eyes. "It won't be for long, Hazel. Please?"

I *really* want to say no.

"Ugh, fine."

Fuck!

His gaze brightens again and he takes the book from me. "Yes! I'll go tell him. I'll say that you don't feel well so he won't keep you for too long!" Before I can say anything, my friend has rushed back outside, slamming the door against the wall again.

There's too much going on.

I can't keep up.

Remembering the clothes for Maya, I pick out an old pink top and black shorts. Both are tatty, but they'll have to do. A soft paw strokes my leg, and I look down just as Normie decides to climb up my body, leaving me no choice but to hold him like a baby. Aqueous chirps from my bed, repeatedly pointing at the beige cat with his claw. The cat doesn't reply, just closes his eyes and purrs in my arms.

Apparently, I'm forgiven for having him neutered.

With Normie in my arms, I return to the bathroom, and realize how cramped my stall is with four people in it. Everyone inside is shooting filthy glares at each other, but I don't ask about it.

"Here," I throw the clothes to Maya. "Put them on."

She scrunches her face up. "Don't you have anything better?"

"Fine." I snatch the clothes away from the ungrateful girl. "You can wander around naked. Rocky, pick her up."

"N-No! I'll wear them!"

"Make up your bloody mind!" The clothes smack her in the face as I throw them at her again, this time with more force.

She looks taken aback by my sour attitude, but I'm not going to apologise. Why should I? She's the one being an ungrateful brat.

"Hazel, come outside," Marco whispers and leads me outside, shutting the stall door behind him.

He looks at me expectantly, his body language relaxed. He wants me to talk to him, but I don't feel like talking.

"I'm not apologising." I grit my teeth.

He chuckles and tucks my hair behind my ears. "You sound just like Rocky, you know that?"

I don't reply, just cross my arms like a sulking toddler.

"Tell me what you're thinking."

With a sigh, I voice my concerns. "Ray wants to see Rocky and me

117

tonight. Wes told him about our markings."

My friend raises an eyebrow. "Wes told him?"

"Ray found out about his somehow, so Wes spilled the beans when Ray got him a book about elemental markings from the non-student bookshop."

"Oh? Is it helpful?"

"I haven't looked through it yet." Normie stretches in my arms, purring once more as he settles down.

My friend is silent for a few seconds before sighing. "Please don't worry about it."

"I don't need to relax, okay?"

At this point, Maya and Rocky emerge from the stall, Maya now wearing the clothes I offered her. My brother looks angry; he's had enough of Maya as well.

"Let's go."

13

Chapter Thirteen

Escorting Maya to the hotel is a nightmare. Many Cindaraans we pass call us traitors and throw rocks at us, but our companions fight them all off. No-one dares to touch Marco with Drea flying above their heads, her stony gaze locked on the crowd, waiting. Cerberus and Aqueous shoot electricity and water at the crowd's feet, making them back off. For some reason Normie decided to come; he's currently sitting on Cerberus' back, ears swivelling and nose twitching at all of the noise and new scents. He probably thinks we're going to go to a place full of food, and doesn't want to miss out.

He's going to be disappointed when we arrive.

"Magma!" Maya suddenly shouts, waving her arms excitedly.

Her companion limps towards us, one of his feet drawn up next to his chest. He looks pretty badly beaten up, and one of his horns has been snapped off at the base, leaving a short stump. He noses Maya affectionately but pulls away upon noticing her injuries. He whimpers softly, his emerald-green eyes wide with concern.

At least her companion is okay. I heard that having your connection broken is like dying; part of you can never be replaced.

"Let's keep going, the longer we hang around the higher the risk that

Ray will come along." Marco nudges Rocky forward who shoots him a venomous glare but listens to his advice anyway.

The yellow walls of the hotel soon come into view. I feel a pang of sadness that this is where I'd seen Mum for the first time. She hadn't been able to come to see us since; she's been too busy with work. Rocky and I still get our allowance each week, which isn't much compared to others, but it's enough to buy meals when we want to go out.

Rocky stops at the door and hauls Maya onto Magma's back. "This is as far as we go."

"Okay," is all she says.

Magma turns and limps through the entrance. Maya doesn't even look back at us.

No 'thank you'? Really?

"Where to?" Marco breaks the silence, making me inwardly relieved.

Rocky shrugs. "I dunno." He tears his gaze away from Maya. "What time is it?"

My friend checks his watch, and his eyes widen. "Haze, we need to go back and get our costumes, we've got ten minutes!"

"So? Mr Knight won't mind," I shrug.

"Mr Reedman is taking the lesson today!"

Before Rocky can question us, we're tearing down the road.

Cerberus follows us, her mouth wide open in the wind. She probably thinks we're playing some kind of fun game, and she doesn't want to be left out. Drea flies overhead, Aqueous clinging to her tail for dear life.

"Take Cerberus! I'll meet you on the field!" Marco and Drea break off, running in the opposite direction.

What the hell am I supposed to do with Cerberus?

My cabin finally comes into view, so I throw the door open. Grabbing my costume from my drawer, I rush into the stall to throw it on. Aqueous clings to my back the entire time, which doesn't help.

When I'm done, Cerberus is waiting outside for me. Upon noticing me, she stops chasing her tail and lowers herself to the floor. Aqueous chirps and climbs on her back, taking a seat next to a frazzled Normie. The brown dragon curls her tail towards her back, motioning for me to climb on.

"Really? Are you sure?"

The dragon growls her approval. Carefully, I climb onto her back. Her scales are rough and slightly warm, but they don't scratch my skin. As soon as I'm comfortable, she rushes forward in a sprint. Taken by surprise, I lean forward and wrap my arms around her neck, squeezing my eyes shut. A furry ball presses against my stomach, meowing and wailing loudly.

Why does Mr Reedman want to take the lesson anyway? He has Monday to Thursday lessons, and he just makes us have one to ones with our mentors anyway! He wanders around to make sure we're working, but he's never taught us once.

Cerberus dodges people who are blissfully unaware of her in the street. The field isn't too far away from my cabin, so I don't have to endure this for long. The brown dragon screeches to a halt, kicking up dirt and grass into my face. She stops a few metres from the large crowd that has gathered on the field. She allows me to get off before trotting over to Rocky, who looks amused at her performance. Normie still clings to my shirt, his ears flat on his head and his eyes wide with terror.

"Hey, you almost killed me!"

Marco jogs up to me, Drea trotting at a steady pace beside him.

"Huh?"

"Cerberus almost ran me over!" he wheezes, stopping to get his breath back.

"Well, you're fine now."

He pries Normie off me and strokes his head. "Aww, he's spooked."

"Well, you were. Why wouldn't he be?" I tease, jabbing his shoulder.

"Everyone sit down! The lesson is starting!" Mr Reedman booms, his face bright red with anger. A tiny vein throbs on his head, which students have nicknamed the 'volcano'; it appears when he's furious.

Immediately everyone drops to the floor. All conversations end and all dragons sit patiently with their partners.

"Today you will be working with your element to attack each other. It is time your mentors taught you and your dragons some offensive and defensive moves." Many people exchange worried glances. "All water Elementals will be in the river and all earth Elementals will be in the ditch so they can get used to their environments." He shakes his hand dismissively. "Off you go."

Marco grabs my arm and pulls me close as people push and shove to get to their places. Normie clings to my friend's waist, making him wince and mutter under his breath. When the coast is clear, we make our way over to the river, where the others have already waded in. My heart thumps at the thought of attacking my best friend, or him attacking me, for that matter. He hasn't let go of my arm yet, and I can tell he's uneasy. We undress and wade into the river in silence, with me keeping my back from everyone. Aqueous wades in next to me, while Drea settles on the riverbank with Normie sat between her front legs.

"What are we going to do?" I ask, breaking the awkward silence.

He's silent for a few seconds before sighing. "Let's get into the shallows."

I follow him silently until we are able to stand up, our waists above the water.

"Are we doing offensive or defensive?"

He dodges my question. "I don't know why you're learning this stuff this year. I only started a few months ago." He looks up at me again, his eyes burning with fury. "We'll do defensive. I'm not attacking you."

"Okay. Whatever you think is best."

Inside, I'm panicking. I've never seen him so upset over a lesson. These moves must be bad, otherwise he wouldn't want me learning them.

"You need to create a wall of water in front of you," he explains. "If you struggle creating it from thin air, use the river water. Just push your arms up, hands balled into fists."

I do as he says, but for the first few times I'm just picking up a small amount of water from the river. However, Marco points out that each time I try it grows bigger, which makes me feel a little better. Finally, after a good fifteen minutes of trying, I'm able to throw up a wall of water in front of me that's big enough to cover my body, head to toe.

"Good." Marco's mood hasn't improved. "Now you need to try curling the water around your body like a ball."

He pushes me towards the ground, arms and legs tucked close to my body. With my head bowed, he tells me to think about a thick layer of water covering my body. I find this easier to do, and have water surrounding me, front and back, as a defensive shell. With no warning, I'm hit by a ball of fire. It explodes against my defence, flinging me into the river. I'm shell-shocked for a few seconds before remembering to form an air bubble around my head.

I'm too scared to return to the surface.

I can see silhouettes swimming above me. A few people dive down with their air bubbles before returning to the surface again.

They're looking for me.

My body hits the bottom of the river but I don't care; I'm too scared to move. Despite the scratchy sand rubbing against my skin I make no move to swim upwards.

Aqueous comes into view and paws at my side. He opens and closes his mouth in his air bubble, but I can't hear his quiet yaps. He grabs my hand with his claws and tries to pull me to the surface, but I'm not sure if I want to. I could get attacked again.

But Marco will be worried.

And Rocky.

At that point, I decide to swim up to the surface. My brother will be worried sick once he finds out; I don't want to keep him waiting if he already knows. Upon emerging from the dark water a familiar face throws himself at me, clinging to my waist as if I was going to sink.

"Are you okay?" Marco whispers in my ear while hugging me tightly in his arms.

"I'm fine. I just got scared."

"I know. I was scared too."

"How despicable."

I look up fearfully at Mr Reedman, who is standing on the riverbank, smirking. It was him. It must have been. Marco wouldn't do that to me, and it came from the opposite direction anyway.

"That behaviour would have got you killed," he glares at me coldly, his face expressionless. "You need to react faster. Come on, attack me now."

"Leave her alone!" Marco pulls away from me and puts his middle finger up at Mr Reedman. "She hasn't learned any offensive moves. She's staying on the defensive side."

The strict teacher shakes his head. "She needs to learn offensive moves! Otherwise you'll get her killed!"

"Why do we need to learn this?" I demand. "I don't understand!"

"You could get attacked at any moment!" Mr Reedman starts pacing up and down. "Everyone needs to learn to fight because *I* said so!"

Marco opens his mouth to argue more but Mr Reedman storms off. He pauses for a second to kick Drea in the leg, making her hiss and jump up. Eruption lands behind her and grabs her tail, making the white dragon roar in fury and attack him.

124

"Drea, no!" Marco clambers onto the riverbank and tries to get between the two fighting dragons, only to be held back by other students standing nearby.

My friend's companion bites Eruption's wing, shaking her head violently. The black and red dragon howls in pain and hooks Drea's leg with his claws and trips her up. The white dragon isn't prepared to back down, however, and swipes at him, leaving long claw marks on his front leg. She then jumps up and spreads her wings to propel herself into the air, only for him to bite her wing and yank her back down to the dirt. While she's down, she lets go of Eruption in the confusing fray, allowing him to pin her head down with his foot. She can't move or her head will be crushed by the larger dragon. He bares his sharp teeth, gloating over his victory.

However, he isn't done yet.

His teeth plunge into her neck, making her squirm and scream in pain and fury. Blood flows down her face, her mouth open in a horrified scream.

"No! Stop!" Marco's screams can barely be heard over his companions'.

Mr Reedman looks on smugly, not intending to help.

Then Aqueous flies towards Eruption, breathing ice-cold water at him. The large dragon looks up only to jump back as cold water blasts his face, rendering him unable to see. This gives other dragons the courage to help. Soon Eruption is surrounded by dragons, big and small. They look ready to pounce on the large beast, their claws digging into the dirt and their wings spreading out to propel themselves forward in a coordinated attack.

"Enough!" Mr Reedman finally intervenes, waving Eruption over to him.

The large dragon roars at his enemies, before he lumbers over to his companion with one eye closed, the one that Aqueous hit. His mouth is covered in Drea's blood, staining his teeth crimson red. The two of them walk away, not even bothering to apologise or explain themselves.

I look back at Drea. Marco is leaning over her, his head on hers. I hesitate about approaching; he might not want me to interrupt. Quickly I wrap my towel around myself to hide my markings.

I can't just leave him alone.

As I get closer I can see tears rolling down his face. He hardly ever cries; he's really worried about her. If I were in his position, I'd be crying bucketfuls like he is.

The second I crouch next to him, he buries his face in my hair with his arms wrapped around my waist. Drea's chest rises and falls slowly.

She's still alive.

"There!"

Three people in white uniforms crouch next to Drea, holding shiny silver boxes. One briefly looks over the wound.

"She's alive, but we need to fix her up immediately."

The people push Marco and me back, which he surprisingly doesn't react to. He stares blankly at Drea, fear written all over his face.

I've never seen him like this.

I hope to never again.

"She'll be fine," I whisper. "She's strong; she won't let go so easily."

Marco nods slowly, but his worried gaze doesn't move from Drea's body. Sweat covers his face and I can feel him shaking violently.

It kills me to see him like this.

No-one wants to see their best friend cry.

The vets rush around, carrying various tools and bandages to save Drea. Most of the crowd have dispersed to give the vets room to work or feel too awkward to stick around. Marco stays rooted to the spot with his arm practically glued to my waist, but I make no attempt to move it. We must have stood there for an hour before the vets stopped and approached us. I can't read their expressions, so I have no idea what they're thinking.

"She'll be fine. We'll transfer her to the emergency ward to keep an eye on her until she's well enough to leave," one says, a tall man with fuzzy brown hair.

Marco nods wordlessly, his gaze unmoving. The three vets nod and start calling their dragons over. Between them, the three dragons carry a white stretcher in their mouths, placing it on the ground next to Drea before slowly picking her up by the feet. The white dragon roars in pain as she's lowered onto the stretcher, lying limply on the white material.

"Do you want me to come with you?" I murmur, squeezing his hand softly.

He shakes his head slowly. "No."

"Okay."

Gently I step out of his grip, letting his arms drop to his side. For a few seconds, I stand there watching him, before Aqueous starts yanking at my towel. Reluctantly I leave him alone. As I trudge across the field, I feel bad for leaving him. What if he changes his mind? What if Drea's condition worsens in the night, and he has no-one to support him?

What if she never recovers?

14

Chapter Fourteen

Ray shouts for silence above the chatter, his gaze cold and stony. When we arrived we realized he isn't in a good mood, but no-one has dared to ask him why. Yes, he's friendly to people he likes, but get on his wrong side and you'll wish you never had. .

"Tonight, we are meeting because of an incident that has occurred among our members," he booms, pacing up and down the aisle, meeting the gaze of anyone who makes eye contact. "As you may have heard, there have been Krystalan spies in our group."

Boos and hisses erupt from the crowd, but I'm reluctant to join in. I'm just hoping he doesn't harm anyone else.

He puts his hands up for silence. "These spies have been dealt with. However, we are sure that there are still spies lurking in our ranks." He pauses to sweep his gaze around the room slowly, studying everyone's faces. "We have no choice but to investigate *everyone*. We cannot allow the Krystalans to know about Cindaraan plans. Investigations will begin tomorrow. Do not fret about them; we will just ask a few questions."

Questions? Maya said Rayna was interrogated. If that happens, I'll panic and won't be able to talk, guilty or not.

Aqueous wriggles under my chair, struggling to fit his growing form under the seat. He's one of the smallest dragons I've seen, but he's still too big to fit in the places he used to. He's as big as a medium-sized dog now, so I can't carry him around like I used to. His horns how stand out straight before curving in the middle back to his forehead.

"Meeting dismissed." Ray waves his hand for everyone to go, and relaxes as the crowd starts to leave.

I choose to stay in my seat as people push and shove to leave. Large and small dragons try to squeeze through the exit all at once. The impatient people aren't helping either. I'm glad I'm not part of that crowd tonight. Returning my gaze to the front, I see Rocky sitting near the podium. Cerberus is standing in the aisle growling at him, pawing at the air.

"Ah, you stayed!"

My heart thumps wildly as Ray steps off the stage at the front. A pale blue and white dragon with dazzling icy-blue eyes steps off with him. It has twirling horns that curve back towards its forehead. Emerald-green markings in the shape of vines cover its back, cheeks and chest. Aqueous emerges from the chair upon seeing it, his head cocked to the side in awe.

"Come with me; we will chat in private." He waves me over, smiling warmly.

He leads Rocky and me into a room behind the black curtains on the stage. It's a large grey room with a long wooden table in the middle surrounded by at least twenty plastic chairs. Ray motions for us to sit down, before taking a seat opposite us. His dragon sits behind him, its tail curved around its feet.

"This is Winter," he explains. "She is quite friendly, so do not fear her."

Cerberus paws Rocky again, chirping and yanking at his shirt sleeve.

"It won't be long, Cerberus," he murmurs, patting her neck softly.

"Is she okay?" Ray tilts his head to one side quizzically.

"Yeah, she's just hungry."

The blond boy chuckles before continuing. "And you, Hazel? Where is your dragon?"

Aqueous hops onto the chair next to me, peering at Ray suspiciously. The blond boy doesn't react, just stares at my companion in awe.

"This is Aqueous. He's a little impatient." I shrug sheepishly.

"A black common dragon," he mutters. "I never thought I would see one of these." He taps the table for my companion to hop up, and Aqueous obeys. He relaxes when Ray strokes his back softly.

"Where's Marco?" Rocky nudges my shoulder.

"I think he's still with Drea. He didn't feel like coming tonight."

Ray sighs. "I heard what happened with Eruption. It was best for him not to come." He clears his throat and allows Aqueous to sit back down again. "Anyway, I just want to talk to you about your 'markings', as Wes calls them."

"I presumed Hazel would get them because I did," my brother shrugs. "But hers have spread in a different way to mine."

The blond boy nods slowly. "Can I see them?"

"Uh, yeah, sure."

My brother stands up, takes his shirt off and turns around. Ray shoots to his feet and walks around to study them carefully. "Interesting. They reflect your element?"

"Yeah. We don't know what caused them, though."

Ray bites his lip in thought. "And they appeared when?"

"After I discovered my element, when Cerberus got her first mark."

"And they have spread ever since?"

"Yeah. They stopped spreading when I started Year Two."

"Yes, I see," Ray mumbles. "You can sit down now."

The two boys return to their seats, and Rocky puts his shirt back on. Ray is quiet for a few seconds, still biting his lip. "Hazel, can I see yours?"

His eyes watch me carefully as I pull my shirt up to my chest. I can't see his expression, but the fact that he is staring at me makes me horrendously uncomfortable.

"Okay, this is what we will do." He leans forward in his seat, resting his hands on the table. I take this as a sign to pull my shirt down and sink into my seat. "You two and Wes keep researching this. I will get him to report to me each week with your findings. Any books or articles you may need, come and find me and I will get them for you. But, do not tell anyone else about this, okay? Keep it secret for now. I will bar you two from the interrogations. I want you focused on these markings, understood?"

"Marco knows as well," I murmur, uncomfortable under his gaze. "He's been helping too."

He nods slowly. "Okay, be sure to inform him about what I have told you tonight. He will also be excused from interrogation." I nod reluctantly and he continues. "Be careful. If anyone else finds out about this, it could be disastrous."

"We will be." Rocky promises.

"One last thing before you go." My heart thumps as his expression darkens and the atmosphere thickens. "If I ever find out that you two have helped a Krystalan spy again, I will have no choice but to put you in your place."

"I couldn't leave her." I blurt out.

His eyes narrow and he sighs irritably. "You are too soft. You need to toughen up if you want to be a Cindaraan."

"She's young," Rocky snaps. "Give her time."

"This meeting is over. You can go."

I grab Rocky's arm and drag him out of there before he can start an argument.

15

Chapter Fifteen

A month passes with little excitement. Today is Rocky's birthday, however, December twenty-first. He's asked me not to get him a present for Christmas, as my gift can be for both occasions. Seeing as Christmas is coming up I've been busy buying presents for everyone. I got my gifts quite early, while all the good sales were on.

My companion has been learning fast. He has perfected his defensive moves while I'm still struggling with some of them. I'm proud of the little guy; he doesn't care when Mr Knight gives him no attention because he's only a common dragon. However, I can see that he's dying to join in on the higher classes. The higher dragons are learning how to shoot through the air like a dart, and how to perfect their Elemental breathing. He tries to join in, but Mr Knight's companion, Shark, always shoos him away. Instead, Cerberus is teaching him these moves, which is making him much happier. Since Drea is recovering quickly from her injuries, she sits on the sidelines and offers chirps of encouragement every now and again, but at least she feels well enough to go out and about. Mr Reedman and Eruption were never punished for what they did as they hold quite high positions in the school. Even though they attacked a child and nearly killed a dragon there were no repercussions.

"Okay, your homework is for your dragon to perform a little display on how the mythological dragons behaved," my Dragon Mythology teacher, Miss Dean, says. "Class dismissed."

Everyone practically throws their stuff in their bags, ready to go home for two weeks off school and dragon training. I welcome the break; we've been working hard for the past couple of months. The only time we get off is at Christmas and the end of the academic year in summer. Both breaks last for two weeks.

Aqueous sticks to my side as we pass through the crowded hallway. He looks up at me often, his gaze excited and quizzical at the same time. Royal blue swirl markings now snake up his legs completely, and most of his face is covered. He's been developing markings less often now, which indicates that he doesn't have much left to learn in mastering his element.

I approach my locker with caution. Even though the notes stopped coming through months ago, I'm still anxious to open my locker sometimes. Hesitantly, I swing the door open. A small yellow note floats to the floor.

Not again, please.

Aqueous sniffs the note curiously and looks up at me, his gaze concerned at my stiff body language. Slowly I bend down and pick up the note, wracking my brain as to why someone wrote it. It smells flowery, as if someone sprayed perfume on it before posting it.

Hazel,

Meet me at the square at eight o'clock tonight. Come alone; tell no-one.

What the hell?

Is this some kind of joke? Am I going to get pranked?

I look around but see no-one who might have posted the note into my locker.

Should I go? What if it's a trap?

* * *

"Happy birthday!" I squeal, presenting my gift to my brother.

"Aww, thanks!" He takes the box of colourful paints from me, studying them closely. "Are these the limited offer ones?"

"Yeah, I was lucky I got there early; the queue was massive."

"Thank you." He pulls me into a quick hug, not letting go of the paints.

"Don't forget to blow out your candles!" Ciara coos, wriggling onto his lap.

Unfortunately, Rocky wanted Ciara to be invited to his birthday dinner. She's been insulting me behind his back all night and even openly flirted with Marco at one point. Rocky didn't notice, but Marco ignored her.. But I can't cause an argument on his birthday. Plus, I don't want to give him an ultimatum. He'd be upset if he has to pick between his sister and his girlfriend.

A gust of wind blows out the seventeen candles on the chocolate cake. Cerberus sits behind Rocky with her tail curved innocently around her paws. She's been dying to blow out the candles since she first heard there was going to be a cake. Her little escapade earns a few chuckles from around the room, except from Marco, who just rolls his eyes irritably. Rocky said I could bring a friend to keep me company at dinner, so naturally I chose Marco. Who else would I bring?

"Well, that works, I guess," Rocky chuckles.

Ciara looks far from impressed, but says nothing. "Okay, who wants a piece?"

Cerberus' pleading barks are ignored by the rude girl, so she cuts herself a small slice and a larger one for Rocky. Afterwards, she places a small plate of food on the floor for her companion, Angel. After taking a bite, he stands up and stretches, showing off his snowy white scales. He then curls his tail around his feet and continues his meal, growling when Aqueous gets too close.

"Can I go yet?" Marco mutters, slumping in his chair.

"No. We're staying a little longer," I hiss back.

"Rocky keeps glaring at me though."

"It's his birthday. He can beat you up if he wants."

My friend mulls this over. "He doesn't know that, does he?"

"Keep complaining and he will."

He mutters something under his breath and crosses his arms sulkily. One of Rocky's friends – I think his name is Kyle – glares at Marco and taps the table impatiently.

"Dude, why are you even here? Rocky doesn't like you, and you don't like him. It makes no sense to come to his birthday." Kyle brushes back his shaggy dark brown hair, so his fringe doesn't fall over his eyes. He's been doing that a lot, I've noticed.

"Haze wanted me here," Marco snaps sulkily.

Kyle looks between the two of us irritably, his eyes narrowing. The room is dead silent. Everyone is staring between Marco and Kyle with a mixture of concern and excitement. Some want them to fight; some want them to shut up and not talk to each other for the rest of the night.

I'm in the latter category.

"C! Can I have some cake, please?" Naomi cuts through the tense atmosphere.

"But you've done so well on your diet!" Ciara reluctantly cuts a small slice for her friend.

Naomi rolls her eyes. "It's my treat day, silly!"

With one last second of hesitation, Ciara hands the plate over. Concern is written all over her face, which is a rare look for her.

Chatter rises once more, and everyone relaxes. Although I'm enjoying myself I'm still thinking about the note. I've been counting down the minutes until I have to leave ever since I arrived.

My gaze turns to the clock on the wall. Ten minutes left.

My friend fidgets in his seat and sighs quietly. Maybe it was a bad idea to bring him. I didn't think Rocky's friends would be so hostile. Drea is obviously uncomfortable being surrounded by dragons that are not happy with her there. She sits close behind Marco, resting her chin on his shoulder. It's adorable how close they are.

"So, you and Hazel are full siblings?" Another of Rocky's friends, Luke, starts a new conversation.

"Yeah, why?" A defensive edge creeps into my brother's tone.

Luke shrugs. "You two don't look alike."

Kyle rolls his eyes. "Not all siblings are twins, fuckface."

"Language," Rocky warns, glancing at me.

This makes the two boys snicker.

Marco tugs my arm roughly, sending a sharp pain up my shoulder. "Can we go now?"

I know Rocky will be disappointed, but there is no point in us staying if Marco's stroppy and I have to go to the Square. I'll make it up to him some other time.

"Yes."

Before I can say anything else, Marco is out of his seat and out the door. This raises a few eyebrows around the table, but people quickly return to eating as Drea lumbers out after him.

"Are you leaving? You've barely touched your dinner." Rocky's face falls sadly.

"Yeah, I don't feel well," I lie.

I hate lying to him, but it's the only way he'll consider letting me go.

"Do you want me to walk you home?"

"No, no. You stay here and have fun. I'll catch up with Marco and walk most of the way with him. I'll see you tomorrow."

Before he can argue, I hurry away. Aqueous is hot on my heels, glancing back every few steps to growl at Angel, who pays no attention to my companion's empty threats.

The cool evening breeze buffets my face as I close the door behind me. It feels nice to cool down after staying in that stuffy restaurant. Down the road, I can see Drea and Marco walking back to their cabin. At least I don't have to explain where I'm going.

Aqueous looks frazzled as I walk in the opposite direction to my friend. He looks between the two of us before trotting after me, glancing backwards every now and again. He yanks at my socks every so often and tries to pull me in the opposite direction. He throws me accusing glares, as if to say: *home is the other way, stupid! You're going somewhere we're not supposed to! The others will be angry!*

It's scary wandering around at night. The streets are empty, the shops are closed, and the only light source comes from the dim grey street lamps that are dotted around the roads. The only sounds come from owls, hooting continuously.

As I turn a corner, a sharp feeling of foreboding makes my stomach roll. I'm starting to doubt whether I should be doing this.

Maybe I should have told Marco where I'm going.

Maybe I shouldn't have come at all.

I should have thrown the note away and forgotten about it.

As I turn another corner, the Square comes into view. To my surprise, candles dot the floor, each a different colour. They are arranged in a tight circle, with the largest candle in the middle. The middle candle is snowy white, and the flame is a little more orange than the others.

"You came."

The voice behind me makes me jump. Aqueous clings to my leg for a second before composing himself and growling in a way that he views as threatening, but really comes off as a squeak.

Someone steps in front of me, a smirk on her face. "I'm Braith." She has a thick Welsh accent, but she speaks slowly and clearly so I can understand her.

Braith has dark skin and short black hair, a lot shorter than Rocky and Marco's. It's spiky with bright blue highlights scattered around her head. What strikes me most are her big, brown doe eyes, which are warm like my Mum's but hard to read.

"You're a lot prettier up close." She looks me up and down, biting her lip thoughtfully.

Shifting uncomfortably, I mumble: "Why am I here?"

She sighs wistfully. "Let's go to the circle."

Braith skips into the middle, checking each candle as she laps the length of the circle. A black and white dragon lands next to her, its bright orange eyes locked on Aqueous and me. Pale blue snowflake markings cover its face, tail and feet. Its horns are similar to a ram's, curved in the middle back to its ears.

"This is Damayanti." Braith wraps her arms around her companion's neck; she looks slightly bigger than Drea.

"Damayanti?"

"After the Hindu myth. Because she's absolutely beautiful." She scratches Damayanti's chin, cooing over her.

I don't know much about Hinduism, but it's a pretty name. Most of the dragons have unique names, so most don't surprise me. Damayanti is an unusual name, though, one of the only ones that have really stuck out from the rest.

"What are ya waiting for? Come 'ere!" She waves me over impatiently.

I'm starting to feel *really* uncomfortable. Something about this seems a little…off. I could be ten seconds away from getting kidnapped for all I know.

I don't know this girl.

I don't know what she wants.

I don't know what all these candles are for.

Why did I do this?

With a little prompting from Aqueous, I carefully step into the circle, trying to avoid knocking the candles over. Now that I'm closer, I can see the candles are all the same size, apart from the one in the middle, which is considerably taller. Braith sits down in front of the large candle, beckoning me to sit on the other side. Aqueous and I swap quizzical glances before settling down.

"So, what's his name?" She points to my companion.

"Aqueous."

"That's weird."

"Excuse me?"

Ignoring my hostility, she stares into the flame. "You have markings, no?"

How does she know?

My heart thumps so loudly I swear she can hear it. She looks up at me, waiting expectantly for my answer.

"What do you m-mean?" I stutter, cursing myself for fumbling my words out of nervousness.

"You know." She reaches over to move my hair out of the way, looking at the intricate details on the back of my neck. "They're pretty."

With a harsh swipe, I whack her hand away. "How do you know?"

She looks hurt at my reaction, sighing: "I've been watching you."

How long has this been going on? What has she seen?

"*What?*" I back off a little bit, making hurt flash across her face.

"Fuck, that came out creepier than I thought it would," she mumbles, her eyes darting around the circle. "I mean; I saw them. When you were practising your defensive moves. Ya know, with that guy. Marcus?"

"*Marco.*"

She waves her hand dismissively. "Whatever. I saw them, and I was intrigued. I thought I was the only one."

I'd thought about others having markings, wondering if Rocky, Wes and I were the only ones. I didn't expect to find out like this, however. But, if she thought she was the only one, that means she doesn't know anyone else with them.

"You have them?"

"Mm-hm. Wanna see?"

Before I can reply, she's stripping off in front of me. She removes her black dress, and she's completely naked. I see pale blue snowflakes on her shoulders.

"Like whatcha see, huh?" she taunts, jiggling her breasts.

Embarrassment reddens my face. "Put your clothes back on."

She looks like she's about to argue, but then her face falls. "What a buzzkill."

"Is this some kind of joke?"

Slowly she pulls her dress over her head. "Nope. That was a test."

For fuck's sake. What the hell is going on?

"A test for what, exactly?"

"To see if you would stay and listen to what I have to say." She must have noticed my annoyance because she speaks more softly. "We can help each other, Hazel. You know stuff I don't; I know stuff you don't."

I raise my eyebrow suspiciously. "Oh yeah? Like what?"

"There are nine people with markings. So far, I only know of you and me. But, don't ya see? The ninth is missing."

She's speaking in riddles. If her aim is to piss me off, it's working. "No, I don't."

"Each candle has its own colour," she points out, looking around the circle. "Except this one." She gestures towards the candle in front of us, which is a snowy white. "Stellar is missing."

I stiffen as I realize she's right. One candle is red, one blue, one yellow, but the middle one has no colour at all. "Who's Stellar?"

With a smile, she whispers: "Our saviour." She leans close to me, making me lean back out of her reach. "Stellar isn't here right now, but two are."

"Four are," I blurt out.

"Huh? Four?" Her eyes widen in excitement. "You know more of us?"

I'm not sure if I believe what this crazy girl is saying, but it could be the most important lead we have. "Rocky, my brother. My friend Wes also has them."

The mysterious girl claps her hands loudly. "Yes! This is going to be *so* much easier now!" She takes a deep breath before continuing. "Each person has their own markings. The markings represent our element – in your case, water. Once we're all together, we can do something! Although I haven't been able to figure that part out yet..."

She's talkative. I'm surprised she has enough time to take a breath between each sentence.

"Okay...? What are the candles for?"

She looks around wistfully. "Just a little creative idea of mine, to demonstrate the hierarchy of the markings. But mostly to make it a bit more romantic, I guess." Wriggling her eyebrows, she reaches forward to touch my face before I whack her hand away roughly.

This could be a joke. I could be falling for a huge prank right now. Someone could have taken pictures of all of this, and I could be bullied again tomorrow.

"What's wrong?" The excitement slips from her face, replaced with concern.

"Is this a joke? Am I going to get the shit beaten out of me for this tomorrow?" Tears are forming in my eyes, so I bow my head.

A few seconds of silence drag out between us. After what seems like years, she picks up one of the candles, blows it out and passes it to me. It's pale blue, like the reflection ice gets when it freezes over a large body of water.

"It's my candle," she mutters. "It represents ice. You keep hold of it, to show ya my sincerity."

I don't know how a candle is supposed to convince me, but it feels *strange*. As I roll it in my hands, I see the word 'Frost' on either side of it. For the representation of ice, I guess.

"Take care of it," she whispers, before standing up. "You can go now. I'll find ya tomorrow."

I stare at the strange girl for a few seconds, before rising to my feet and leaving. I feel bad leaving her, knowing that tomorrow she'll have to wander around trying to find me.

"I'll be in the library at twelve," I call behind me.

"Great! See you there, hot stuff!"

16

Chapter Sixteen

It's close to Christmas so the library is empty. My friends are the only people in here, and we're waiting for Braith. I haven't yet told them what happened last night; Marco and Rocky are in a strop and Wes has been reading all morning.

I've been on the computer for a while, trawling through websites only to find that over half of them are filtered. It's frustrating to know that what you're looking for is right in front of you, but you're unable to see it.

"Hey, gorgeous!"

For fuck's sake.

Before I can turn around to greet Braith, she's on my lap, looking at the computer screen curiously. "No luck, huh?"

"Nope, none."

She shrugs. "It's fine. Have ya got my candle?"

"Not on me, no."

"Ah, I see. Go to bed with it, huh? Have a little fun?"

My face reddens at what she's implying. "No," I hiss through gritted teeth.

Braith snickers and slips onto the chair next to mine. "Where's

Rocky?"

Why does she want to know that? For the candle thing?

"He's with Marco, sulking."

"Why?" She eyes the two boys up and shakes her head.

"I dunno. Neither have spoken to me all morning."

She tuts and rolls her eyes. "Boys."

Wes chooses this point to join us, finally tearing himself away from his book. "Hey, Hazel. Who's your friend?"

Braith beats me to it. "I'm Braith. I've got those markings too."

Wes pauses for a second to mull over her words before his eye widen. "You found another person? That's great! It's more common than we thought!"

"Yeah," Braith's mouth curls in one corner. "I think I know why they appeared too. I could only show Hazy here a bit last night," she elbows my side sharply, making me wince.

"Wow! What do your markings look like?"

Braith smiles at me and wriggles her eyebrows flirtatiously. She stands up and goes to pull off her shirt until I yank her back down to her seat.

"That will not be necessary," I mutter.

"No, no! I don't think you got a good enough look-"

"What's going on?" Marco seems to have recovered from his sulking session, and leans on my chair to join the conversation.

"Braith has the markings too!" Wes explains excitedly. "She was showing Hazel last night!"

Marco's eyes widen in realization. "Oh! Rocky saw it wrong..."

What's happened now?

"Saw *what* wrong?" I demand, glaring at him as he avoids my gaze.

"He thinks you and Braith are dating."

"*What?*" Braith and I scream in unison, though hers is a lot more excited than my more agitated tone.

"Let's do it, Hazy!" she screams, wrapping her arms around me and nuzzling my neck.

I push her off and ignore her look of mock hurt. "Is that why he's been ignoring me all morning?"

He fidgets uncomfortably and casts a stony look at my brother. "I guess so."

Rubbing my temples, I can feel the stress building up inside of me. If he's that worried, he can just *talk* to me. He's behaving like a bratty child.

"Go correct him, please," I sigh, rubbing my eyes tiredly.

Marco nods and, thankfully, doesn't argue. Wes looks confused, but knows not to start asking questions. Braith pouts and crosses her arms.

"What, am I not good enough for you?" she whines mockingly.

"I'm not discussing this."

She grabs my hand. "So, there's a chance?"

I yank my hand away and roll my eyes. "No."

"You'll change your mind. You can't resist my charms forever." She winks and wriggles her eyebrows.

I ignore her as Rocky comes over, looking apologetic, his hands stuffed into his pockets and a sheepish grin on his face. He rubs his arm and mumbles: "Sorry."

"We'll talk about it later." My tone is harsher than I wanted it to be, but I don't take it back.

He nods mutely, refusing to meet my gaze.

Why does he need to create such a fuss? I'll get a partner someday; I'm not planning on staying single forever!

The trouble is, he will always see me as a vulnerable child that needs protecting.

I've grown up now.

I still need him, but not nearly as much as I used to.

I'm *not* a child anymore.

"Alright, can we talk about the markings now?" Wes whines impatiently.

Braith nods enthusiastically. "I found information from my sister. She's twenty-four and left camp years ago, so she could sneak stuff in. That's how I found out about the myth."

Wes hangs off her every word, while Marco rolls his eyes in disbelief. "The myth?" he snorts disbelievingly. "Myth about what exactly?"

She waves her hand for quiet, shooting Marco a stony glare. "The Original Elementals passed their powers on to present-day humans. They evolved in a way that other people didn't, and they were able to survive the Primordial Dragon attacks with the help of their leader, Stellar." She pauses to wink knowingly at me. "The Original Elementals have been reborn through us. That can only mean that the Primordial Dragons are coming back."

I learnt about them in Dragon Mythology. The Primordial Dragons were the first dragons to evolve. They were huge, with long claws and teeth the size of an average person. Destroying villages and eating cattle were their only goals in life, but they died out due to natural selection. They were too big, they ate too much, and there wasn't enough food for all of them. They eventually killed each other or starved to death. But they died out thousands of years ago. How can they be coming back?

"That sounds like a load of complete and utter bull." Everyone turns to Marco as he speaks. "They don't exist anymore."

Braith taps her nose knowingly. "They're being created. Scientists are close to giving the extinct creatures life."

Whose idea was that exactly? These creatures are unbelievably dangerous, and they want to bring them back to life! Some things should just *stay* dead.

"How do you know all this?" Wes breathes, in awe of her story.

"My sister is a scientist working on it."

Rocky has stayed unusually quiet throughout this conversation, and he still looks as if he won't question anything. I'm pretty sure he's waiting for my reaction, so as not to agitate me any more than he has done already.

"Okay, so let's say that your story *is* true," Marco squeezes onto my seat, so I'm partly dangling off it. "Where's your proof?"

The girl considers this for a second, before snatching my keyboard and typing into the search bar. She types: *Primordial Dragons resurrection,* but of course the results are filtered. She clicks the filter log-in and starts putting in the details of Mrs Alhmer, one of the maths teachers. Once finished, the website page loads fully, allowing us to see its contents.

"You bypassed the filter!" Wes scrolls up and down the web page, fascinated by the new information.

"It's pretty easy actually, Mrs Alhmer always shows her password as visible when she types it in, loads of people from her classes use her log-in." Braith grins and grabs my arm. "Am I in the group now?"

Rocky's expression darkens and he opens his mouth to say something before Wes exclaims: "Definitely! This is all new stuff!"

The new member punches the air excitedly. "Great, because it was a bit of a sausage fest before."

I rub my eyes tiredly, ignoring her comment. "Okay. Let's print this off before someone sees us."

17

Chapter Seventeen

Life has become much easier since Braith joined the group. She can access areas we can't and gathers information from her sister, who visits regularly. Wes has informed Ray about Braith's markings, and he was more than pleased to discover how much she knew about them. However, Ray hasn't been informed about the Primordial Dragon, as she didn't feel comfortable discussing it with him.

"Hazel, you've barely touched your food." Rocky nudges my shoulder, pushing my plate closer to me.

"Huh? I was daydreaming."

Chewing a mouthful of turkey, he smiles, happy to see me eating. Christmas came around quickly, and the school are hiring out the hotel dining room for a Christmas dinner. The tables and chairs have been replaced by long rows of benches and large wooden tables. Red and green decorations are strung up from the ceiling, and a small tree covered in baubles stands in the corner by the door, with empty presents scattered beneath it. Some parents even came along, but not mine. I haven't heard from Mum in months. Neither has Rocky. We're both starting to get worried.

Marco's mood has improved greatly over the past few days, especially after hearing that Drea is doing better than expected and can return to dragon training again. Mason was allowed back into town last week, as he had been given the all-clear by the hospital.

"Guys!" Braith skips over to our table, carrying a tray full of potatoes and vegetables.

The crazy girl squeezes onto the bench in between Marco and me. She wraps her arm around my waist and wriggles her eyebrows.

"Braith, you have friends now?"

A tall woman with thick-rimmed brown glasses approaches us, smiling sarcastically. She's almost identical to Braith, apart from the fact that her hair is in a long ponytail down to her waist and she has a faded scar on one cheek.

"Olwen, sit down!" Braith cries. "Guys, this is my sister. The scientist."

Everyone on the table either waves or mumbles hello in between bites. Olwen sits at the end of the table and keeps an eye on her sister while she's eating.

"These are the people with the markings I told ya about," Braith shoves some salad in her mouth and rests her head on my shoulder, stroking my hair lovingly. "My future wife is right here. Expect a wedding invitation any day now!"

Rocky rolls his eyes and mutters: "Not on my watch."

I try to push her away, but she clings to me like glue. I swear she only does it because she knows it annoys me. Yesterday when she saw me in the street she screamed and jumped onto my back, begging for a piggyback ride.

Her sister chuckles. "You say that about every girl you see."

Braith pouts. "But this one's for keeps."

"Do you have markings?" Wes enquires, having forgotten about his food since Olwen arrived.

"No, I don't." Olwen points at her sister with her fork. "I only found out when Braith came to me panicking about them. I did some research and sent her some books to calm her down."

"I wasn't *that* scared," Braith mumbles in between chewing.

Her sister shoots her a disbelieving glare before continuing. "They have a deep significance, but I have no idea what that could be yet. I don't even know what the link is to Primordial Dragons."

"No-one does," Braith sighs.

"*Someone* will," her sister retorts. "We are so close to creating the Primordial Dragon, we've used preserved DNA to create an egg. Its survived all odds so far; with it will come answers."

An egg?

I don't doubt the scientist's plans, but is this the right thing to do? Bringing back dead species, especially dragons of such horrible reputation, sounds like a terrible idea. I mean, what if it escapes?

What if it goes on a rampage?

What if it comes for us?

* * *

I don't know where I am.

Everything is dark, and my whole body aches like hell. The only thing I can see is an inch of light right in front of my eyes. A blast of wind hits my face, blocking out the light for a second. It stings my eyes horribly, so I squeeze them shut, gasping at the sharp, icy cold air. When I'm able to open my eyes again, the light is gone.

I'm so cold.

My arms and legs are trapped. They feel imprisoned in ice. The only sound is my jagged breathing, and the screams of the muffled wind. The air is so thin I feel as if I'm choking. All I taste is my own sweat, with a coppery taste.

Blood.

When did I start bleeding? Why am I bleeding?

The worst part is: I'm all alone.

No-one is around. If they are, I haven't seen them.

What's going on?

Two seconds ago, I was in my bed, and now I have no idea where I am. Is this a really vivid dream?

"Marine! Marine! Are you there?"

Who the hell is that?

"I'm here! Help me!"

I didn't say that, yet my mouth moved. I'm unable to speak. It's my voice, but not in my control.

"Where'd it come from?"

"There! Dig there!"

Rummaging noises come from above and I feel the weight around me loosen a little. Whoever is up there is working hard to get me out. After a few minutes a hole appears in front of my face, and two blurred faces look back at me.

"She's alive!"

"What are you waiting for? Haul her out!"

As my body rises, a stinging cold freezes my body. They lower me to the ground, shivering violently. The ground is cold and crunchy; snow.

I'm buried under snow.

"Oh, Mari," *One person strokes my cheek with thick, furry gloves, leaving a second of warmth on my freezing skin.* "You're okay. I was so worried."

"What happened?" *Not my words again.*

"Avalanche. You got caught right in the middle of it."

"What about the others?" *My teeth chatter uncontrollably, making it hard to speak properly.*

The two blurred people look at each other before sighing. "William is dead. We found him higher up the mountain. I'm so sorry."

Who?

I have no idea what's going on, but warm tears roll down my face. I start sobbing uncontrollably. Someone lifts me up to hug me closer.

Who is William?

Why am I so upset about him?

"Draca attacked us again. William tried to fight back, but he didn't stand a chance."

"What's the point?" I sniffle. "Why should I go on now?"

"Shh, don't say that. He'd want you to continue, and survive, for him. Please don't give up. We're so close now, Mari."

"Lightning, we've gotta go." The other person speaks for the first time.

A loud roar sounds in the distance, and everyone freezes and jumps to their feet. I'm lifted onto the back of the first person, who passes something to the other.

"Let's go; Draca is coming!" The first person starts clambering up the mountain, kicking up layers of snow behind them.

As I'm jiggling around on this person's back I try to figure out who these people are. They sound familiar, but my vision isn't clearing up. Everything is still blurry, and it doesn't help that everything around us is white and grey.

"Run! We have to hide!"

Another roar, this one closer and angrier. A loud beating sound fills my ears, and a strong wind suddenly picks up, flinging snow and jagged rocks in all directions.

Before I can contemplate what's happening, everything goes pitch black.

* * *

My eyes fly open from the dream. I sit up in my bed, throwing the duvet off and letting it fall onto the floor with a soft thump.

What just happened?

What was that about?

Where was I? I was nowhere near home, that's for sure. The people there, they seemed so familiar. Yet... They were too different.

It rings a bell, but I don't know where from. It must have been when we were learning about aquariums in school. Despite my half-assed explanation, I know that I'm just making excuses. My heart tells me it's much bigger than a stupid lesson on aquariums.

Marine.

Why is that name in my head? What significance does it have to my life?

My heart won't stop thumping wildly, and I scrunch my face up in disgust at how sweaty I am. I must have been more scared than I thought. I want to go back to sleep, but I don't want that nightmare again. I still feel as if I'm trapped underneath the snow; my chest feels tight and restricted. My head feels as if I've just slammed it into a wall.

With a loud sigh, I swing my legs off the bed and step down the ladder. The wood is cool underneath my warm feet and the air is crisp and fresh. Someone opened the window in the night. The snores of the other kids fill my ears, along with the constant fidgeting of someone up the front. I feel a twinge of jealousy at the thought of them sleeping soundly with nice dreams, but I bury that feeling and rub my eyes tiredly. Careful not to wake anyone, I tiptoe to the bathroom and squeeze into my stall.

I couldn't open the door too far because Normie and Aqueous are fast asleep against it. Aqueous is now too big to sleep in my bed, and he won't sleep in the stables. Instead, he sleeps in my stall with Normie, before he gets too big and *has* to stay in the stables. The cream cat stirs as I step in front of the mirror, cracks an eye open lazily to look at me, then falls back to sleep.

Marine.

My head is really hurting now. Allowing the sink to fill up, I splash my face repeatedly with cold water in an effort to calm my nerves.

The dream is over, but I still feel as if I'm trapped in that avalanche.

What was I doing in an avalanche?

Something about a Draca?

Marine, look up.

Shock freezes my body. My hands grip tightly on the sink, my knuckles white.

I didn't think that.

Look up.

This sounds like a bad horror film. When some idiot wanders around clueless and gets jump-scared by the monster.

Look. Up. Now.

Gathering all my courage, I move my head slowly up towards the mirror. At the last second I squeeze my eyes shut.

I'm such a wimp. Why can't I be braver? Why can't Rocky be here?

With a deep breath, I count to three and open my eyes.

Nothing.

I stare hard into the empty mirror, tilting my head this way and that to try to make my reflection appear. "Oh fuck, I'm a vampire."

Well, I think it's time for bed. Definitely time for bed.

I never want to look at a mirror ever again.

I think I've just scared myself into sleeping.

Wiping my face with shivering hands, I turn towards the door when my hand collides with something. *Someone*, rather.

It's me.

Same dirty blonde hair, same hazel eyes, same pale face, same everything. Even the scar is the same, but the usually pink line looks red and angrier than normal. Is that what mine looks like right now? The only thing that is different is her age; she looks a lot older than I am, without the acne and greasy hair.

Her eyes are wide open, and dark blue swirly markings curl on her neck, creeping up to her face. They look like worms writhing around in the dirt. She reaches out to me, her mouth wide open but no sound coming out.

I'm dead.

I'm actually dead.

I want to scream, but my throat closes. I'm defenceless against her.

My companion opens his eyes and looks up at me groggily. His eyes widen at the scene, his gaze flickering between us, unsure what to do.

"End it." The girl, the other me, finally speaks. Her voice is dry and raspy, like she hasn't so much as *seen* water for months.

Aqueous stands up, growling and baring his teeth at her. She ignores him, her gaze unmoving from me.

"End it," she repeats.

"End what?" I'm thankful that my voice finally works again, even if it does come out as a whisper. I ask.

"End it. Please."

"I don't know what you mean."

"Save us." Her body starts to dissolve from the feet up, making her look more distressed.

"Wait, I don't know what you mean!" I plead, watching her disappear before my eyes.

"Marine, please. End it."

When she utters the final word, she's gone. Where she once stood lies a silver bracelet.

I sink to the floor, cradling my legs in terror. Aqueous nuzzles my face, looking distressed.

What should I do?

What did she mean?

Why did she look so terrified?

18

Chapter Eighteen

"Are you sure you weren't dreaming?" Rocky presses, squeezing my hand softly.

"Yes, I'm sure. I've got the bracelet." I point underneath the sink.

The bracelet is shiny silver, surrounded by charms in various shades of blue in the shape of rain drops. Every time I touch it, it glows and shakes.

I stayed in a foetal position all night, only moving when I heard people mulling about in the bathroom. I'd kicked the bracelet under the sink in case the girl reappeared. I told Wes to get Rocky after quickly telling him what happened. He'd sped off, returning with my brother minutes later.

My brother hooks the bracelet with his finger, inspecting it thoroughly. "She just…left it?"

"When she disappeared, yes. But, I feel like I've *seen* it before even though I haven't. It's so familiar, yet not familiar at all."

He rolls the strange bracelet around in his palm. "Do you want to wear it? To keep it safe?"

Ever since she left I've felt the urge to wear it. My wrist has been itching uncontrollably all morning; it feels as if ants are crawling under my skin. It has some effect on me, and I don't like it.

"Haze?" he presses.

"I don't know." My wrist burns as he brings it closer to me. "I feel like I *need* to, you know?"

"Put it on then. It's not as if it will bite or anything."

"You don't know that. It could be carnivorous."

He rolls his eyes and pushes the bracelet into my hand. "If it starts eating you, I'm here to snap it in half."

"You're not even strong enough to lift Aqueous." I nudge his arm playfully, watching him pout in mock hurt.

"Fine, I'll let you get eaten then."

I snatch the bracelet from him and slip it slowly onto my hand. As soon as it touches my wrist, the charms glow and it clamps onto my skin.

I try to pull the bracelet off to no avail. "Rocky!"

My brother tries to wriggle the glowing thing off my wrist, yanking and pulling in all directions. It may as well be cement; it melds with the flesh on my arm. The bracelet returns to its normal state, and in all of Rocky's panicked pulling, two charms fall off. Time seems to slow for me as the two charms clang as they hit the floor. They glow brightly and clatter on the floor, spiralling in different directions.

Normie starts batting at one as it falls into his paws, fascinated by the tiny blue charm. Aqueous chases the other, picking it up in his mouth and placing it at my feet.

"It's stuck!" My brother cries.

"I knew this would happen!"

I don't understand; does this mean the girl will come back?

"It's okay; we'll sort this out." I don't believe what he's saying, and I know from his distress that he's just trying to reassure himself.

"Are you two okay? All we can hear is your squawking." Marco pops his head around the door, amused.

"It's stuck!" I wave my arm around wildly, trying to yank the thing off my wrist.

Wes also comes in, with one eyebrow raised. Braith squeezes through the small crowd, wincing at my predicament.

"Why did you bring *everyone*?" I glare at Wes, who holds his hands up innocently.

"They followed us when I got Rocky." He smiles sheepishly.

Braith presses against my side, staring at the bracelet enviously. "It's so pretty! Can I have it?"

"It's stuck!" I cry. "This isn't the time for trading!"

She pouts and crosses her arms sulkily. "Fine, be like that."

"Okay, how about we all pull on three, okay?" Rocky grabs one part of the bracelet, with the others grabbing different parts. "One... Two... Three!"

Everyone prepares to pull, but the bracelet just goes limp on my wrist, allowing them to slip it off easily. They all go flying in different directions, crashing into the walls and the floor because of the unnecessary force they used.

"It's off!" Marco twirls it on his finger triumphantly.

"Thank fuck!" I hold my hand out to Braith, who gladly takes it, but doesn't let go when she's up.

The two charms that fell off dissolve into the floor, before magically reforming on the bracelet itself. This is just getting weirder and weirder by the minute.

"Let's take this-" Rocky snatches the bracelet from Marco "-and put it in a safe place."

"Agreed," Wes nods enthusiastically. "I'll hide it in my suitcase."

The bracelet is gladly passed over, but Wes gives the mysterious thing a wide berth, holding it in front of him as if it's a bottle of poison. There's more room as he leaves, which makes me feel less claustrophobic.

"Now what?" Marco bites his lip and sighs.

"Let's get the full story from Hazy." Braith squeezes my hand gently, smiling slightly in reassurance. "I couldn't understand a word Wes was saying."

* * *

Braith hands me a glass of water, bouncing excitedly next to me on Wes' messy bed. "First time we've shared a bed, Hazy." She pouts her lips like a fish.

With an eye roll, I reply with: "And the last."

Her lip quivers in mock sadness.

Rocky scuffs his feet on the floor impatiently, annoyed that Braith is so close to me. "Well, what happened in your dream, then?"

I tell my friends everything. I pause each time the few people left in the cabin stir, and keep my voice hushed in case someone is awake and overhears. I tell them everything from the dream, to the blurred faces and the girl; the older me. Wes interrupts a few times, but after annoyed hisses from Marco and Braith he stays quiet for the majority of the story. Braith is bouncing excitedly at the end of the story, seemingly armed with explanations.

"Go ahead." I motion for Braith to talk, making her grin proudly.

"Marine is the name of the original water Elemental," she explains. "She must have visited you, but appeared as you because no-one knows what she actually looks like! The Primordial Dragon must be close to being created!"

"So, our situation is getting worse?"

"Must be. I've got a book on the lives of the Original Elementals. It describes the aftermath of the death of the last Primordial Dragon in it; that may help us!"

Before I can open my mouth, she's off. The crazy girl runs outside.

159

Peering out the window I spot Damayanti sprinting down the street. Braith is sat on her back with her arms up in the air. Wes isn't sure what to say after Braith's surprising exit, but Marco sits in her spot and lets me rest my head on his shoulder.

Rocky crosses his arms and clears his throat. "So, you saw one of the Original Elementals?"

"She told me to 'end it' and 'save us'. I don't know what she meant."

My brother nods slowly, his lips pursed. "It's not good, whatever it is."

Loud scratching at the window catches everyone's attention. Cerberus is trying to stick her head through the bars on the window, growling and pawing at the air.

"Can we go outside?" My brother moves towards the window, reaching out to touch his companion's nose. "She's getting anxious."

Asteroid happily takes the lead in showing us where the door is. The weather outside isn't too nice: grey sky and bitterly cold wind. I'm happy I remembered to grab my thick blue coat before going outside. It's *freezing*. It's uncomfortably similar to my dream, which worries me. My companion jumps around wildly as it starts to drizzle, darkening the mood even more. Despite my element, Rocky puts my coat hood over my head, stroking my hair behind my ear softly.

"The weather is crap." Marco crosses his arms and closes his eyes as another blast of sharp wind buffets our faces; and I only just realize that we're all in our pyjamas outside.

Aqueous and Asteroid wrestle playfully, rolling around on the damp earth. Cerberus jumps out of the way as they roll towards her, nosing the two of them away from Drea as they get too close. The two finally break apart as they fall into a slight dip in the ground. Asteroid darts upwards, hovering in the air as Aqueous writhes in the hole, before rolling onto his stomach and huffing at his friend. The orange-footed dragon grabs her friend's tail in her teeth and yanks him onto his feet.

The two playmates then return to wrestling, until Cerberus separates them with her foot. She finds it hard to stop Asteroid, considering the young dragon is now almost half her size.

"Is she coming back?" Wes shivers violently, his hands shoved under his armpits.

Rocky shrugs, watching the two dragons play. "Who knows?"

Just as Asteroid and Aqueous manage to pin Cerberus playfully to the ground, Damayanti stops a few metres away from us, Braith squirming wildly on her back. She waves a book around with a picture of a dark blue water swirl surrounded by bright blue dots on the front of it. She slips off her companion and throws the book towards me. I have to dart forward and stumble to catch it.

"It's about Marine!" She takes the book from me, pointing excitedly at the cover. I'm not entirely sure why she even threw it to me if she was just going to take it back. "It could give us answers!"

"Okay? Which page?"

She flicks through the book before stopping near the end, landing on the first page of the last chapter. *"The fourth encounter with Draca left Marine trapped in an avalanche. She was rescued by Lightning and Frost mere minutes later, only to be told of the news that would break her heart, the news that she never fully got over. Her lover, William, was killed by Draca during the avalanche. The large beast had picked him up, flown high in the air, and dropped him on a ledge of sharp rocks. It was believed that this was her motivation for killing Draca in the end. She believed she was sacrificing herself to kill the beast and to see her lover again."*

"That's my dream! I was in an avalanche, and someone told me about William!" I exclaim excitedly.

Rocky raises his eyebrow quizzically. "That's a tragic love story, but what has it got to do with Haze, exactly?"

Braith glares at him and puts her hand up for quiet. *"She failed. She did indeed kill Draca with her plan to lure it into a narrow cave and collapse it, but she survived. The others pulled her out of the rubble and she went on to live until she was ninety years old. Her legacy left a daughter, Mary, who was born a few months after the death of Draca. Mary went on to have between five to seven children, who have created the family tree that leads to their current descendants."*

"Jeez, Mary was busy," Marco mutters, squeezing his eyes shut as the wind buffets his face once more.

After a few seconds, Rocky speaks again. "So...? What does it mean?"

"Marine had a daughter, Mary, who must be related to you! We're all connected to the Original Elementals; they're our ancestors."

My brother scrunches his nose up in confusion. "But Haze and I are completely different elements, yet we share the same ancestor...?"

Braith is silent for a second, before flicking to the front of the book, staring at some sort of family tree. "Marine and Lightning were siblings. It would make sense that you're siblings as well."

My brother nods slowly. "So, how useful is the book, exactly?"

"Very." She hugs the book close to her chest lovingly. "I've read it many times, along with the books about the others." She strokes the spine of the book, her gaze locked on the ground. "Frost is my favourite. She's my ancestor."

"Who's mine?" Wes steps forward, still shivering from the cold. "You haven't mentioned wind."

"Squall."

Marco snorts and bites his lip to stop himself from laughing. He isn't even *trying* not to hurt Wes' feelings. It's just a name; I've heard weirder from the dragons.

"So, what does it mean?" Rocky's gaze is locked on the cover of the book. "It's a nice story, but why did you bring it?"

"I know these things off by heart," she explains. "I could re-read them, and give us core information. Like, for example, Marine and Squall shared a pet cat, Tobias. Sound familiar?"

Normie?

Next I'll be haunted by a cat ghost. Sounds fun.

"Are you telling me that even the *cat* is involved in all of this?" My brother rubs his face, pinching the bridge of his nose agitatedly.

"Yep. He was a partner to both of them. However, our lives aren't following theirs exactly, thank goodness. Marine and Frost met through Lightning, who was Frost's boyfriend." She sticks her fingers down her throat. "I am *definitely* not doing that."

Rocky rolls his eyes and mumbles something under his breath.

This is getting weirder and weirder.

For one, I'm being haunted by one of the Original Elementals, who left me with a bracelet that does nothing but try to cut my hand off.

Two, a Primordial Dragon is about to be re-born. Enough said.

Three, now I've got to worry about the damn cat. Normie's involved in this, but what part does he play? Purr the dragon to death? Complain and complain about a lack of food, causing the dragon's eardrums to explode?

This is not getting any easier.

"So... What's the plan?" I ask, seeing as everyone else is dead quiet.

Braith doesn't meet my gaze, her shoulders slumping. "I... I'm not sure," she confesses. "What more can we do? There's still five people to discover, and we have no clue who they are. As for the Primordial Dragon... What can we do? The oldest person here is seventeen, and the Original Elementals didn't face Draca until they were in their late twenties."

"'Draca'?" Marco raises an eyebrow quizzically.

"That's what they called the Primordial Dragon they killed. It was the last one alive that they knew of at the time."

"Basically, we have no plan." Rocky scuffs the floor irritably, anger written all over his face. "We can't just sit around for ten years."

She shrugs. "Continue with our lives, I guess. There's nothing more we can do until Stellar arrives."

Wes finally speaks up, jarred from his train of thought. "There's someone out there with every single element?"

"Yeah, we have to wait for them. According to Stellar's book, they were one or two years younger than the others. We can't do anything but wait. Because of that, we don't know how to defeat the Primordial Dragon. Our lives won't follow theirs. Who knows what will happen this time?"

"Maybe the people and animals involved are the same, but not the chain of events," Wes suggests. "If we were 're-born' then why wouldn't Normie be if he was a part of Marine and Squall's lives?"

19

Chapter Nineteen

"A dead end?" Ray slams his hands on the table, his eyes blazing with fury. "You have *not* hit a dead end! I can supply you with more books, anything you need!"

I sink in my chair; his fury is making me increasingly fearful. He could strike any one of us whenever he wants with no warning, now that we have no new information for him.

"We can only wait," Wes mutters, the only person here who isn't afraid of Ray's temper.

"Not good enough!" Ray storms around the table to us, eyeing us with hatred and disappointment.

Braith fidgets in her seat, anxiously glancing at Damayanti, who is ready to spring to her partner's aid if needed. "We've explored all the options. What would you suggest we do?"

The blond boy's furious glare lands on Braith, but she doesn't meet it. He leans in close to her face, making her whimper and bow her head. "I cannot understand a word you are saying. *Speak properly.*"

Damayanti growls as Braith doesn't move. The usually loud girl swallows meekly before talking again, this time a lot more slowly. "What would you suggest we do?"

"I suggest you look *harder*," he hisses before returning to his pacing.

Braith sighs with relief as he moves away from her, and Damayanti relaxes slightly into a sitting position. I grab Wes' hand, squeezing it tightly for comfort. He squeezes back, but he is much calmer than I am, his breathing level and his gaze stony.

He's scaring us all to death.

Everyone is silent for a minute or so, casting distressed glances to each other. Rocky is watching Ray's every move, carefully studying his behaviour. He's worried Ray will lash out, and he wants to be ready in case the angry boy makes him his target. He deliberately separated us, moving Rocky to the end and putting me between Wes and Braith.

"Everyone leave!" he orders. He turns to face us, his gaze locked on mine and Wes' hands. "Except Hazel."

What?

Why me?

For a few seconds, everyone remains seated. That is, until Ray slams his hand on the table, making Braith jump up and scamper out, casting pitiful glances towards me. Wes and Marco are up next, brushing my arm as they leave and the latter muttering apologies as he goes. Rocky stays stubbornly in his seat with his arms crossed sternly, his mind set on staying with me. He is not going to leave willingly. Ray rolls his eyes and opens the door, waving someone over. Three of his friends enter, listening carefully as he whispers in their ears. The three boys nod and grab Rocky, yanking him out of his seat.

"Get off me!" My brother kicks out, managing only to knock one or two chairs over.

"You can't stay!" one boy grunts, struggling to get a hold as Rocky struggles wildly.

One stumbles backwards as my brother kicks him in the stomach. He sinks to the floor and breathes heavily, his arms cradling his winded stomach.

I can only watch timidly from my seat as Rocky is dragged out of the room, kicking and screaming wildly. Cerberus follows him out, lunging forward to try to bite the three boys. As the winded boy leaves, Ray slams the door behind him and turns his angry gaze to me.

Aqueous growls as Ray steps towards me. My partner emerges from under the table and bares his teeth, water streaming from his mouth. He's getting ready to attack if necessary.

"He-" Ray points to my companion "-will leave."

"I'd rather have him-"

I'm cut off as Ray's companion, Winter, grabs Aqueous' tail. My companion screeches in fury and turns to attack her, only to freeze in his tracks as his entire body becomes encased in hard brown dirt. As the dirt covers his face, I shoot to my feet, only to be immobilized by rocks crawling up my legs.

"No harm will come to him." Ray opens the door again and waves Winter out, who can now easily drag my companion without any interference.

I should have done something.

I'm water *for fuck's sake! I could have helped him, or at least tried!*

Aqueous trails dirt behind him as he's dragged out, but the dirt around his mouth is starting to fall off in wet clumps. At least he can breathe now.

"Now." This time Ray closes the door gently; his anger has cooled considerably. "You obviously have close ties with everyone in the group."

I shrug shakily. "I guess."

"So, if I teach you a lesson, the outcome will affect the entire group, yes?"

What does he mean?

Am I going to get beaten up like Maya?

"I don't want any trouble." I try to move back, only to remember my predicament when the sharp rocks scratch my skin.

"Then you should have looked harder."

The rocks around my feet crumble, allowing me to step back as he swings. Before I can react, he lashes out again, this time colliding with my left cheek. Pain shoots across my face, and one eye closes from the stinging. He lets me sink to the floor and hide under the table, cradling my throbbing face.

"Be glad I was not harsher with you."

"Rocky will kill you." I wince as he crouches down to peer under the table.

"No. Because you are going to keep quiet."

As if.

"Fuck off."

He narrows his eyes. "Tell them you tripped over or hurt yourself."

My brain is screaming at me to stop arguing, but I can't. How can he expect me to stand there and lie to their faces?

"How will you teach the group a lesson if I keep quiet?"

"You have a lot of leverage with the group. You can spur them on when they stop working."

"It's human to get tired," I retort.

He reaches under the narrow table and grabs my hair, yanking me out from underneath. He then grabs something from the table. Taking my chance to attack, I punch him in the stomach. He wheezes heavily, but his grip doesn't loosen.

"Do as I say," he hisses between breaths.

I have no fight left. I just want to go home, but I can't agree. He's taking this too far. If I try to fight back again he'll overpower me, or call for back-up.

I have no choice.

"Fine. I... I... I'll tell them I tripped."

"Good." He drops me, but keeps a tight grip on my hair. "Just for good measure..."

I cry out as he releases me, but as I look up at him, there is a large clump of blonde hair in his hand.

He cut my hair off.

It now falls unevenly above my jawline, cut into a slanted bob. Some bits stick out at weird angles, making me look like I've just dived into a hedge head-first.

"What was-" I quickly shut my mouth, not wanting to argue further.

The intimidating boy rises to his feet, a dark smirk on his handsome face. "Leave. Before I change my mind."

Don't let him think you're a weak pushover. Teach him a lesson.

Despite my mind saying otherwise, I raise my hand and shoot a stream of water at him, content in seeing him stagger back and struggle for air. Not slowing the stream, I back out of the door, ignoring his wheezing as he struggles for air. When I'm at a safe enough distance, I sprint away, dodging his cronies as they go inside to check on him.

Once I'm out of the building, I don't dare to look back.

* * *

"Damayanti!" Braith rushes towards her companion, who sinks to the ground so her partner can easily reach me. "Oh, Hazy..."

After running down the street for a while, I bumped into Damayanti. Braith must have sent her to look for me.

I hold my friend's hand for support as she helps me step down from her companion. She throws her arms around me, muttering under her breath.

"What happened?"

Braith is ripped away from me and is quickly replaced by my brother. He squeezes me so tightly that I feel like I'm going to explode. He releases me when he notices my hair.

"What happened?" he repeats, more softly this time.

"I... I fell..." I lie, unable to meet his gaze.

"And your hair?" Marco twirls a strand in his finger, eyeing the lopsided cut.

"I fell."

"You fell over, punched yourself in the face and then chopped all your hair off?" Rocky strokes my cheek, making me wince and wriggle out of his grip.

"Um... Yes."

Braith elbows Rocky out the way, looking crestfallen. "He chopped all your hair off!"

"Good eye," Marco says sarcastically, tucking a few strands covering my face behind my ears.

"It'll grow back," she tries to reassure me. "It'll just look a bit weird for a while."

"I don't care about my hair."

"You will tomorrow when one side of your face is black and blue with a haircut that looks like you've had a narrow escape from man-eating scissors."

My brother steps in front of me again, studying my face closely. "He did this to you?"

I bow my head in shame. "Yes."

"I'll kill him."

"No! He'll just hurt you too!"

"I'd like to see him try."

"That's what he wants, Rocky! Just pretend you don't know, okay?"

"What? No!"

"Please!"

Marco grabs my hand and squeezes it tightly. "Rocky, if you go back there, he won't just hurt *you*. He'll just come back to use Hazel as a human punch bag."

Realization dawns on my brother's face, before being replaced by frustration. "So we're just supposed to ignore it? Carry on like normal?"

"Yes," Wes has been quiet throughout the argument. He didn't come over to check if I was alright. "We do as Ray says, and we don't anger him again."

We're all silent for a few moments, before Braith nods and mutters: "Okay."

Marco takes his chance to hug me while Rocky is lost in thought. He whispers in my ear: "I'm sorry I left."

"I'm glad you did," I mutter, gritting my teeth as my face throbs painfully when I knock it against his shoulder. "I don't want you to get hurt."

"I'd rather me than you."

"Well, I'm glad I was the one who was hit, then."

He rolls his eyes. "Whatever. It won't be happening again."

"Hopefully."

20

Chapter Twenty

Wes hasn't spoken to me all morning.

Ever since he found out Ray punched me he hasn't so much as looked at me. He's completely blanked me. I try to talk to him, but he won't answer. Instead he'll look around the room and shrug.

It's like I'm a ghost to him.

Asteroid is still talking though; she's been following Aqueous and Normie around all morning. They huddle in a little group, murmuring amongst themselves only to stop when someone passes by. Every time I approach they move away as if I can understand what they're saying.

A few people have asked about my injuries and hairstyle, and now they have the idea that either Rocky or Marco beat me up. Despite denying the rumours, they've continued to spread.

"Hey, Hazy!" Braith shoots up the ladder and sprawls out on my bed, holding a brown package in her hands.

"Hey."

She frowns and strokes my cheek lovingly. "Poor Hazy… Does it hurt?"

"A lot." I don't tell her how hard it was to sleep; every time I moved my face stung horribly.

Puckering her lips, she coos: "I could kiss it better!"

Gently I push her away as she leans forward. "That won't be necessary."

"Okay. On the lips, then."

"*No.*"

With a loud sigh, she taps her lips. "One day."

"Are you a postwoman now?" I point to the package.

"Sure. If that's what you're into." She licks her lips and winks cheekily.

"Where did you learn all this stuff?"

"Internet." She shoves the package into my arms. "Open it."

As I unwrap the brown paper she bounces excitedly, grinning. Underneath the messily wrapped paper is a large black scrapbook. I open it up and find it's filled with photographs of Aqueous and Normie from when they were smaller, along with scattered pictures of my friends.

"Have you been going through my-"

"*Happy birthday!*" she screeches, planting a large kiss on my cheek.

Out of surprise I jump back and hit my head on the ceiling, much to the amusement of the people about to leave the cabin. Braith stares at me innocently, the book now sat in her lap.

"My birthday is next month."

Her smile disappears and she looks mortified. "What? No, it's not!"

"I know when my own birthday is!" I snap, scrunching my face up when she still looks confused. "Braith, it's the third of January today. My *birthday* is February the seventh. What made you think it was today?"

"But... Marco lied to me!" She's silent for a few seconds before her usual smile appears. "I knew this. It was planned."

I roll my eyes and cross my arms. "Whatever you say..."

"I purposely did it early. Until you get the rest of your presents, mine is the best."

"Nice save," I reply sarcastically.

Pressing herself against my side, she balances the book on both of our laps. "I got all these pictures of you with Rocky and Marco and Aqueous–"

"So, you *have* been looking through my stuff? What else have you stolen?"

"Nothing!" Her eyes dart around in mock suspicion. "I haven't been in your clothes drawer…"

"Stop looking through my stuff!"

"I wanted to borrow that cute frilly top!" She pouts and crosses her arms childishly.

I turn another page, filled with more photographs surrounded by colourful hand-drawn borders. One or two are from when I was little, posing with Marco next to piles of his toys that we hardly ever played with.

"Aww! Look at baby you! You were so cute!" She points to a picture of me when I was about a year old, my mother holding me, grinning. "You were chubby too, jeez."

"All babies are chubby!" I protest.

"I bet I wasn't. Came out thin as a twig."

With an eye roll I turn the page over, scanning through the pictures of Aqueous a few days after he'd hatched, losing nearly all his wrestling matches with Asteroid. A picture of my brother and me catches my eye.

Something isn't right about it.

Braith raises an eyebrow as I peer at the picture, staring hard at the background. "What are you doing? You're going to wreck your eyesight."

"There's something wrong with the picture."

"Did I damage it?" She peers at the picture, smoothing down the edges.

"No, no." I point behind myself, at the figure. "Who is that?"

She takes the book from me, her eyes wide. "I didn't notice that before."

"Who is it, though?"

"It looks like… You?"

We swap a worried glance. Please, not again. I can't handle another visit from her and her man-eating bracelet.

"Is she in the other pictures…?" I turn back to the beginning, scanning for any sign of her.

"Oh my… She's in that one! And this one!" She points from picture to picture, each time pointing out the girl. She's in every single one, even in my baby ones. In the one with my Mum she's poking out from behind a tree.

Braith rocks me back and forth as I sob, murmuring in my ear.

After a minute, she speaks up: "We need to know for sure." Reaching into her pocket, she pulls out a small silver phone. "Let's take a picture."

"I don't want to…"

"We have to. Just to know if… If she really is doing it."

With a bit more prompting, we lean in close to each other and she holds out the phone in front of us. With a quiet click, the picture is taken. For a few seconds we both hesitate, afraid to flip over the phone and see the photo.

"On three?" Braith holds my hand shakily. "One, two, three."

When she flips the phone over we both scream and throw it off the bed. This time the girl isn't behind me, she is *me*. She'd also brought a friend. Her friend looked exactly like Braith, except older and with snowflake-shaped pale blue markings all over her face. They were pulling the exact pose we were, including Braith's wink and big smile. They really are taking on our appearances to substitute their own.

We cuddle each other tightly, lying on the bed shaking and crying. I can't move; I'm paralysed with fear. Braith's eyes are tightly closed, tears running down her cheeks and onto the pillow.

What is happening?

Why is it happening?

Something glints by our feet. Using my foot, I push it upwards. It's a small, flat pale blue ring in the shape of a snowball.

Like the bracelet.

With great care, I kick it back down to the foot of the bed, but it has caught Braith's eye. Sitting up, she picks the ring up, rolling it in her palm and staring at it curiously.

"I think it's like the bracelet," I mutter.

"I want to put it on..." Braith breathes. "It must be from the other me."

"We got lucky last time. Don't put it on unless you want to lose a finger."

"I need those." She leans over the bed railing, placing it on the drawers. She then falls back to lie beside me, her eyes brighter and less watery. "Are you okay?"

"Yeah. You?"

"I didn't know we were starring in a horror movie," she jokes.

"Hope not. I'd probably die first."

With an eye roll, she waves her finger at me. "Not on Rocky's watch."

"Oh no. He'd kill the monster."

Sighing, she touches my cheek delicately. "Plus, the girl who fucks everyone always dies first." Laughing nervously at her own joke before going silent, she asks: "What do they want?"

"I dunno. It's obviously important."

She sighs and rubs her eyes. "I'm tired. I couldn't sleep."

"Me neither. My face hurt too much."

"Are you sure you don't want a kiss? I've been told mine have magical healing properties." Wriggling her eyebrows, she puckers her lips and leans towards me once more, determined to get a kiss this time.

Gently I push her away. "Who said that, exactly?"

She shrugs. "People."

As I wriggle into a more comfortable position, pain shoots through my cheek. "Whatever. Can you create an ice pack for me?"

With her hand just above my face she creates a thin layer of ice over her palm. I sigh in relief as the ice cools my cheek. At least the pain will numb for a bit.

"Better?"

"Yeah, thanks."

Braith giggles as I yawn loudly. "You can sleep now if you want. I'll keep ya safe."

"I'm not sure about that." I close my eyes and snuggle into my pillow. "You screamed louder than I did."

"I was *surprised!*"

"So was I."

Before we can argue further, I'm fast asleep.

* * *

"Don't wake them up…"

"Shut up! She's my sister, I can wake her up if I want to!"

I'm roused from my sleep as something jabs at my face, and I shoot up at the thought of that girl being back.

"Afternoon, hun." Rocky strokes my hair softly, smiling gently.

"Afternoon?"

"You've been crashed out a while. Luckily we've got you up before dragon training," Marco chuckles.

Braith fidgets next to me, her mouth wide open and her side of the pillow covered in drool. One arm is locked stubbornly around my waist while the other is in the perfect position to cup my breast as I was sleeping. With a red face, I pry her arm off me and slap her back. Her eyes fly open with a start and she looks up at me fearfully for a second before her eyes adjust as she recognizes me.

"You two looked so peaceful locked in each other's arms." My best friend leans on the ladder, a cheeky grin on his face. "I wish I'd taken a picture."

"*No!*" Braith and I scream in unison.

He raises an eyebrow at our reaction. "Alright, alright. No pictures."

Braith crawls to the edge of the bed, peering at the phone lying on the floor. "It's still there."

"It's not alive, Braith," I retort.

Rocky picks up the phone and offers it to Braith, who jumps back with a petrified squeak. The two boys swap worried glances and Rocky turns the phone on.

"Did your phone turn into a robot or something?" my brother asks.

"No. You watch too much sci-fi." I jump back as he tries to hand the phone to me.

"Get down from there! You're not planning on hiding in your bed all day, are you?"

Braith yanks the duvet out from underneath me and pulls it over our heads. "It's safe up here! Away from stupid pictures!"

"Pictures…?"

After a few seconds, there is a loud yelp and the clatter of the phone being thrown at the floor again. The duvet is yanked off our heads, Marco having pushed it further down the bed.

"Get down!" He grabs my arm and pulls me down the ladder angrily.

Braith remains on my bed, peering fearfully at everyone below.

"Why the hell was the phone flashing 'end it' over and over?" Rocky demands, his anger directed solely at Braith.

"What do you mean? Look at the picture!"

The two begin to squabble, throwing insults at each other. Marco

178

hasn't let go of my arm; his grip tightens.

"What are you two doing here anyway?" I butt into their petty argument, crossing my arms irritably.

"Rocky had some sort of dream," Marco rolls his eyes. "He thinks it's like yours."

Has the girl visited him too? Or another one of the Original Elementals?

My brother sighs irritably. "It wasn't a dream. I was visited by Lightning. He left me something."

Digging around in his pocket, he produces a golden bangle with lightning bolts carved all around it. The bolts glow as my brother touches the bangle, but it returns to normal when he drops it onto the chest of drawers.

"Oh!" Braith points to the ring. "I think Frost left me this!"

"Why are they giving you gifts?" Marco asks.

"Not gifts, mementos."

Everyone whirls around as Ray and Wes enter the cabin, both looking stern. Marco steps in front of me as Ray approaches, making the blond boy's eyes burn with fury.

"The Original Elementals are leaving behind parts of their past," Ray explains, offering a brown leather necklace with a dark grey pendant to Wes. "Wes figured it out when he saw Squall. He noticed that he was wearing the same necklace."

"How long have you had that?" I ask, staring at the strange necklace.

My friend shuffles his feet uncomfortably. "A while. I'm sorry I didn't tell you. I just wanted to be sure."

"So, when I said that we've hit a dead end, with no more information we could find, you actually *knew* something?" Braith grabs my hand; I didn't notice she'd climbed down.

He doesn't meet her gaze. "I'm sorry."

Aqueous noses my leg, carrying the bracelet in his mouth. When I hold my hand out, he drops it, licking my fingers comfortingly.

Do I have to put the stupid thing back on?

Really?

The last time it clamped to my wrist. I don't want that to happen again. What if it doesn't come off this time?

"You need to put them on," Ray orders.

Crap.

Wes pulls the necklace over his head. The pendant glows brightly, but settles after a few moments. The leather looks as if it's attached to his skin, but Wes doesn't seem to pay any attention to it.

"Are you joking? The damn things are carnivorous!" Braith looks at her ring suspiciously.

"But you want to put them on, no?"

Wes really has told him everything. I feel as if I'm being forced to do whatever he wants, simply because he wants me to do it. Whenever we fail him, he throws a fit like a toddler.

He's just a spoilt brat.

He thinks he's better than us because he went to some private town.

"Just put them on; it doesn't hurt," Wes reassures us, fiddling with the pendant.

What happened to Wes?

Wes puts this guy on a pedestal; he'd better not abuse his trust.

"I'll put mine on first." Rocky slides the bangle onto his wrist, jumping as it glows and clamps on with no intention of letting go. "I don't want you two suffering any negative-"

"No harm will come to them," Ray interrupts, balling his hands into fists.

Braith squeezes my hand tightly, her eyes wide with fear and confusion. We both want to speak out, but know that the possible consequences won't be worth it.

"Well?" The blond boy crosses his arms expectantly.

Why did Wes have to tell Ray? I feel imprisoned by this guy. We're being pushed too hard, and for what reason? Why does Ray care so much? To make himself look better? So he can stamp his name on this discovery?

As he steps forward, I slide the bracelet on my wrist. I don't wince when it clamps onto my skin. The blue charms glow for a second, before returning to normal.

I don't think it's going to come off any time soon.

Braith slides the ring onto her right ring finger, the only one it fit on. Ray smiles at our work, letting his arms drop by his sides.

"Well done." He claps softly. "Find out what significance these mementos have. I want to hear your report in two weeks' time."

Before Rocky can even open his mouth to argue, Ray is out of the door, letting it slam behind him. Braith starts to pull at the ring on her finger, but it doesn't budge.

"Now what?" Wes asks, but he can't meet anyone's eyes.

"*You* can explain what you found out," Rocky says. "After all, it must be important enough to allow one of your friends to get beaten up over it."

Wes looks at me, but I don't meet his gaze. He didn't tell me anything. Why did he keep it from us? I thought we were friends, but I guess friendship means nothing compared to praise from Ray.

"Squall visited me last week. I didn't want to tell you guys because I wanted to find out on my own. It was only when Braith mentioned Marine that I realized I'd had a similar dream to Hazel. The necklace that Squall was wearing was the same as the one I have now. But I don't know why we have them. It's just that... I wanted to do something on my own."

"To make yourself look better for Ray," my brother counters. "I hope it was worth it."

"No!"

"Yes!" Braith snaps, making the boy wince at her angry tone. "You don't care what happens to us, as long as you're in Ray's good books!"

"Shut up!" His eyes tear up and the necklace starts to glow dazzlingly bright.

Asteroid looks up at her partner before lunging forward and snapping at Braith's legs. As she jumps back in horror, she pulls me back with her and we land in a messy heap by the bed, inches away from hitting our heads on the chest of drawers. My companion roars in fury and fires water at his friend, making her jump back in shock. Asteroid looks hurt for a second before spreading her large wings and flapping them, creating a gust of wind that blows everyone back. Braith and I are pushed under Wes' bed, squeezed against the wall hard I swear one of us will come out of this looking like a pancake. Aqueous is also pressed flat against the wall, imprisoned by the strong wind.

"Stop!" Rocky screeches, covering his face with one hand and clinging to a door frame with the other.

Asteroid ignores him, sending items flying around the room in a frenzy. A picture frame hits Aqueous in the face, making him hiss and breathe a stream of water at the angry dragon. Because of the harsh wind, however, it's blown back and drenches Marco, who grunts when the ice-cold water hits him.

"Asteroid, enough!"

At the command of her companion, Asteroid eases the wind, dropping Aqueous on the floor with a loud thud. Before I can ask if he's alright, he's climbed to his feet and hisses at her, his jet-black wings spread in an attack stance and his mouth wide open.

"Aqueous, don't!" The second I touch my companion's tail, he relaxes, dropping his threatening stance.

Nosing me softly, he grabs my shirt collar as I climb out from underneath the bed, pulling me up into a sitting position. Braith follows suit, squeaking as Aqueous sits her up too.

"Let's go." Rocky yanks me to my feet and pushes past Wes and Asteroid, shooting them both warning glares.

Cerberus, Drea and Damayanti are crowded around the door as we leave, each peering inside to try to get a better look at the havoc inside. The three dragons swap worried glances as Aqueous follows me sulkily out, his tail dragging in the dirt.

Marco shivers violently as a cold wind starts to blow. "C-c-can w-we go inside s-somewhere?" His teeth chatter uncontrollably, and his arms are locked around his body for warmth.

My brother says nothing, just rolls his eyes and walks down the street, dragging me along with him. Small sparks of electricity fly around his feet as he walks, but he doesn't pay any attention to them, engrossed in his anger. Drea noses Marco's hands, breathing small puffs of fire into them in an effort to keep him warm.

This is a disaster.

What on earth compelled Asteroid to do that? Wes wasn't in danger; he was just upset. It doesn't help that he didn't even attempt to stop her, even though she could have hurt someone. Aqueous was just standing up for Braith, but still Wes kept quiet and watched as Asteroid nearly squashed us all to death.

Did that stupid dream really mean that much to him?

If it did, I hope it was worth hurting his friends over.

Asshole.

21

Chapter Twenty-One

"Happy actual birthday!" Braith screeches, balancing on the ladder precariously.

"Braith, it's six in the morning…" I mumble, draping the duvet over my head.

Groans and irritable sighing tell me that Braith has woken the entire cabin. But at least she got my birthday right this time.

"I know… But Damayanti and I wanted to be the first ones to congratulate you!" She pulls the duvet off me and dangles it over the foot of the bed. "So, happy birthday!"

"Thanks. Leave me to sleep, please."

With a sigh, she says: "Okay… I'll go see Aqueous then… Seeing as I'm not wanted here!"

"Bye, unwanted person."

With a gasp of mock hurt, she goes into the stables to see my companion. Aqueous moved in there after he couldn't fit through the cabin door a few weeks ago. At first, he was really reluctant, but I spent ages making him a nice sleeping area, which I think he appreciated. A soft blue blanket, one of my pillows, and a stuffed toy lion to keep him company. Normie moved in with him, swapping between Aqueous' and Asteroid's bed every few nights.

Wes and I made up in the end. He was apologetic about what happened, and Asteroid apologised profusely to Aqueous, though it took him longer to forgive than I did.

I must have fallen into a light sleep because when I open my eyes people are starting to get up to go to school. With a long stretch, I get down and grab my clothes for today and go to my stall. What I was not expecting was Braith to be already in there with a surprise cupcake for me.

"You scared me half to death!"

She ducks playfully as I go to slap her.

"Sorry!" she says in a sing-song voice. "Blow out your candle!"

On the cupcake is a large candle in the shape of the number sixteen. It looks far too big for the small cupcake, so I quickly blow it out before it can topple over.

"Okay, you can get changed now." She places the cupcake by the sink, biting her lip excitedly.

"Braith…"

"We're both girls, I have what you have."

I can't be bothered to argue with her, so I just turn around and carry on like normal. Once finished, she looks absolutely delighted.

"Here, breakfast." Grabbing the cupcake from the sink, she shoves it into my hands and looks at me expectantly.

Again, I didn't want to argue, but I will admit that the cupcake was really tasty. It was a tangy lemon flavour with a vanilla frosting – my favourite because of the way it makes my lips curl. She probably spent ages picking out the right one for me. Once we're outside, Aqueous runs up to meet me, greeting me with a headbutt to the back.

"Hey, I'm pleased to see you too." When I pat him on the head he calms down a little, though he still stays overly happy.

"Hey, wait for me!" Wes sprints up to us, panting heavily with the

---

effort.

"Have you never heard of a gym?" Braith teases, elbowing him in the stomach.

With a harsh swipe, he whacks her in the arm, making her lip quiver in hurt. "Hazel, I got you this."

From his bag, he produces a large package wrapped neatly in red paper with a small golden bow tied around it.

"Oh, Wes you didn't have to..." I weigh the package in my hands; it's quite heavy.

"I wanted to."

"Open it! I'm excited!" Braith bounces on the spot, shaking my arm vigorously.

Underneath the wrapping paper is a bright blue book. The cover has a silver border and the title in big silver letters reads: *The Key to a Dragon's Heart – Book One.*

"It's a timeline of all the dragon species, from Primordial to Avian, and everything in between, of course. I thought you'd like it, because you're really interested in that stuff." He shrugs sheepishly.

"Aww, thanks, Wes."

He stiffens as I hug him, but relaxes once I pull away. Do I smell or something?

"Mine's still the best!" Braith sticks her tongue out at the uncomfortable boy and crosses her arms defiantly.

"Oh? You mean the one with the pictures?" Wes snaps.

We're both taken aback by his sour change of attitude, which renders Braith silent.

"Let's go to school, okay?" I'm the first to recover from his grouchy reply.

"Gladly. Oh, there's a Cindaraan meeting tonight. Don't be late." He grits his teeth and walks ahead of us. Asteroid lands on the floor to walk with him.

What is going on with him? He's getting grumpier and grumpier by the day. What happened to that sweet quiet boy that I first met?

It's a phase. He'll get over it.

I hope he's just going through a rough patch at the moment, so that he'll recover from it soon. Maybe he's tired, or upset about something.

If he was upset, he hasn't told me anything.

Maybe he just wants some time alone. After all, the only people he really talks to are Braith and me; Marco and Rocky still aren't fond of him after what happened last month.

It's probably a guy thing.

* * *

"Fellow Cindaraans! We have just been given news of new funding opportunities, which will be spent on furbishing our headquarters." Cheers and whoops erupt from the crowd as Ray finishes his sentence.

This place does need brightening up.

Everyone is sat on plastic chairs, and the only other piece of furniture in the gloomy hall is Ray's podium, which he puts his notes on for when he loses track of his words.

The blond boy raises his hand for silence. "The last announcement I want to make is an unusual one. I have decided to host a dragon fighting match on the field tomorrow at six." Winter bangs her foot on the floor for silence as quizzical chatter starts to rise. "All Cindaraans will attend, and we will see who the strongest dragons are. Depending on what place they fall in, they will get a job. Those who finish in the top places will be guards and patrollers. Those who finish in the final places will be cleaners and helpers. Any dragons that fall in between will be working on building a bigger Cindaraan headquarters. This building is being expanded."

Fuck. No.

187

I will not have my companion work some stupid job. He will most likely get ridiculous working hours. Plus, he's my friend. How am I supposed to be okay with him being pitted against other dragons? He could get seriously hurt, especially as the dragons have to drive each other into collapsing!

"All dragons will have an equal playing field. No favouritism. Even my companion, Winter, will be involved."

This calms the crowd down a bit, but not much. How can he allow this to happen? Some dragons are stronger than others, and these stupid fights are sure to turn violent quickly. Aqueous isn't competitive, it's not in his nature, and he's quite small compared to the other dragons in the room.

"Will they get paid for working?" a guy at the back shouts.

Ray's eyes narrow slightly. "We'll see. If they work hard enough, they may be fed and paid for their work."

"How many hours will they work?" another person shouts.

"We have yet to decide. No more questions! The meeting is dismissed!"

Instead of dragons pushing and shoving to get out the door, they run up to their partners, worry and guilt filling their eyes. Aqueous lands beside me as I step out into the aisle with his eyes full of foreboding and fear.

How can I let him do this?

If he gets hurt, it will be my fault.

My gaze lands on Rocky and Cerberus, who are both sat down and looking up at Ray with hatred burning in their eyes. Who willingly wants to do this? We all know if we fail to show up or not let our companions fight, then we'll have to face Ray's wrath.

He'll probably beat up any 'traitors' as he did with Maya.

"Haze, don't stand around; let's go." Marco yanks my arm and nudges Aqueous forward with his foot.

We pass through the doors with little effort, as most have people stayed behind to talk to their companions or try to question Ray further. Damayanti spots us, and waves us over to Braith, who is sat on a step with her face in her knees.

"Braith?"

Her head shoots up as I sit next to her. Her eyes are puffy with tears and her shirt is damp from where they have fallen.

Laughing, she wipes a tear from her cheek. "Oh, hey. I didn't want you to see me like this, Hazy."

"Everyone's upset." I let her rest her head on my shoulder for comfort.

"I know." Snuggling into my shoulder, she sighs contently as I rest my head on top of hers.

Marco sits down next to me, unsure of what to say. I'm glad he's here, even if it is just for wordless comfort. He must be worried sick about Drea. She's only just fully recovered from her neck injury; one bad hit could leave her bedridden once more.

Aqueous sits in front of me, his gaze suddenly steely and determined. *No, you can't do this. I'll suffer any consequence I have to.*

His gaze doesn't waver, and he lashes his tail angrily. Obviously, he wants my blessing to do it, and he won't accept anything but.

"No. You're not."

Curling his lip, he nods vigorously, as if to say: *tough, I am!*

Before I can reply, Marco puts his hand on my shoulder. "He wants to do it. All the dragons will be forced to do it either way, so you may as well back him up."

Aqueous chirps in agreement, his turquoise eyes now shining happily without fear.

I should have more faith in him.

He might be okay in all of this.

He might get through it.

If the worst comes to the worst, I can tell him to fake exhaustion to stop a bad fight from escalating too far.

He could do this.

With a deep breath, I say: "Fine."

Pressing his snout against my forehead, he allows me to hug him tightly. Usually he doesn't let me in public; I think the other dragons tease him about it.

"I think in dragon training tomorrow we'll focus on fighting moves for him." Marco strokes my companion's cheek roughly.

"What about our dragon training?" Braith cuts in. "Drea and Damayanti could practise together."

Both of my friends nod in agreement, and both dragons seem happy with the arrangement as well. Aqueous vocalises his approval by chirping loudly and beating his large wings.

I hope we can do this.

No, we *need* to do this.

* * *

"No, Aqueous. Try not to use the river water. In the fight, you're going to need to conjure it up on your own," Marco instructs, nudging my companion away from the river.

So far, he's been doing well. I've asked Marco to focus on defensive moves, seeing as Aqueous will be too small against most dragons. I want him to use his agility to his advantage.

My companion stomps his feet deep into the ground again, spreads his wings and closes his eyes. As he catches the wind he jumps back, spraying water on the sandbag target in front of him.

My friend rolls his eyes as I clap hysterically, but Aqueous prances around, happy with his achievement.

"Remember, only use that if your opponent is down for a long time," my friend repeats. "It takes too long to charge; you'll be knocked down straight away otherwise. Try using that other move on Drea, but be careful."

Drea steps in front of the sandbag and stands perfectly still with her legs spread far apart. My companion breathes a stream of water at her knees, knocking her off her feet and into a soaking wet white heap.

"Okay. Let's discuss strategies." He waves both dragons over and we all sit in a tight circle.

"Strategies?" I don't object as Aqueous lies down behind me and rests his head on my shoulder, almost as if it were a pillow.

"Yes. You know, like, um… Aqueous is against a dragon with the element electricity. That dragon is going to use the water to electrocute Aqueous while he's firing it."

"I see. So, in a battle like that, he shouldn't use his element?"

"Yes." Both Drea and Marco nod in unison, making me smirk. They're so cute together.

"So… What should he do?"

"Just stick to the defensive moves and the flight. He'll be a harder target to hit, and the dragon doesn't get the advantage of using the water. This goes for the element ice as well. It will have no effect whatsoever; the dragon will just freeze it."

"What dragons would he be most effective against if he uses water?"

Marco and Drea glance at each other for a moment, before my friend hesitantly says: "Fire, obviously. But possibly earth as well. Any dirt or small rocks could be softened if he sprays water hard enough."

My mind flicks back to when Winter encased him in hard dirt, and how as he was leaving clumps of wet mud were falling from his snout and chest.

"You two are so lucky to have two elements. You don't have any weaknesses."

My friend ponders this. "I don't think we'd do too well against light.

The whole area would be lit up and fire wouldn't be very effective – those dragons are used to high temperatures. That's the only one we've got to worry about."

"How long now?"

My friend rolls his eyes and checks his watch. "Four hours. Stop fretting."

"I know, but…"

"Look. We'll all be fine. Braith and I are practising in our dragon training lesson in an hour. We even invited Rocky. You could always practise with Wes for a bit." As my gaze locks on the floor, he tilts my chin up with his finger. "We all know the back-up plan; just feign exhaustion. We've got you to thank for coming up with that. Once it's done, it's done. We can all go home and have a nice rest. We've wasted our entire Saturday going through moves. Let's take a break, okay?"

"Okay."

Aqueous whines as I move forward to hug my friend. He huffs and rests his head on his feet and curls his tail around his nose. Even though he's trying to sleep he keeps one eye open and permanently locked on me.

* * *

Aqueous and I had to leave after Year Twos started arriving for their lesson. The Cindaraans among them looked scared stiff, and their dragons weren't faring much better. Rocky caught me as I was leaving, however, to give me my birthday present. He'd sent it into a shop to get it framed and preserved neatly and it had only just been finished. It turned out to be a beautiful painting of Aqueous a few days after he'd hatched. He's sat on the floor with his wings outstretched and his eyes wide and playful.

I love it.

It was a pain to carry home, though. The brown frame isn't light, and I was careful not to let it scuff on the floor or bang into anything on its journey.

Thankfully I bumped into Wes on the way home, and asked him how he would feel about Aqueous and Asteroid training together. He politely declined, which surprised me. But, we both decided to go out for something small to eat, as the others wouldn't be done until five.

"Have you and Asteroid been training with Ray today?" I ask, taking a bite of my muffin.

"Yeah. It was great to train with Winter; it showed us Asteroid would be good at fighting against earth." Asteroid looks up from her plate to nod, but quickly returns to her food as Aqueous eyes it up.

"Cool. We think Aqueous will be good against fire and earth." My companion paws at my leg and taps his empty plate with his tail. "It's meant to be small – we're eating dinner with the others later." He doesn't look impressed, but stops bugging me anyway.

"How do you feel about doing this?" He looks up from his brownie to watch me carefully.

Why is he acting so strangely?

"I dunno. I don't want to let Aqueous get hurt, you know? I just don't think it's fair that he has to fight to do some stupid job."

My friend nods slowly. "I understand. But, it'll be worth it in the end. The dragons will be building more of the Cindaraan headquarters! We'll be able to have multiple rooms! You know, offices, halls, dining rooms-"

"Dining rooms?"

"Yeah. Ray wants to separate us from the Krystalans as much as possible."

Wow.

One surprise after another.

This is all about getting one up on the Krystalans. I heard they got funding for a fancy new TV room. Now they just go over whenever they want to watch films or sports.

I'd prefer a TV room to a fucking dining room.

"Okay…"

"Yep. Cool, huh?"

With a shrug, I say: "I guess…"

"You guess?"

"Yeah. I'll have to see it to like it."

He rolls his eyes but doesn't probe me further. I feel as if I'm being interrogated. Maybe Ray asked him to question my loyalty.

"Anyway, I have to go. I need to print my maths homework off." He shoves the rest of the brownie in his mouth and Asteroid rises to her feet.

"Oh, yeah. I did that yesterday. The table isn't hard to find; there's loads of them."

"Uh, thanks."

Before he can leave I grab his arm, making him jump slightly. "Good luck, Asteroid."

His companion nods and nudges Aqueous playfully, most likely offering words of encouragement to her best friend.

"You'll do great out there." He pats my companion's head and then smiles at me before rushing out the door.

We're growing distant.

I do hope Asteroid does well. Wes looks up to Ray immensely; I'd hate for him to be disappointed if the large dragon doesn't do as well as they'd hoped.

22

Chapter Twenty-Two

It's time.

A circle has been marked out in white tape on the grassy ground of the arena. The crowd has been told to stay on the outskirts of the field, as the circle takes up all the space but the corners. We've been told that there are four rounds to the competition, and the overall winner will be given a thousand pounds and their own office as a reward for their partner winning.

A dark blue collar has been put around Aqueous' neck to symbolize the water element. I have to wear a matching scarf to show the same. There is no order to who goes when; names are randomly generated for each fight. If a dragon wins their fight in round one, they proceed to the next round, and so on.

The first fight was Asteroid against a dragon with electricity. Both dragons had bitten and swiped at each other until Asteroid flew up high and blew the other dragon to the ground, rendering it unconscious. It was a quick fight, over in less than a minute.

Each time they generated names in the judge's box I've held my breath, hoping that Aqueous would never be called.

"Cerberus against Aqueous!" Ray's voice echoes through the

speakers.

No.

No.

My companion looks to me for guidance, but what can I say? He basically has to fight against his sister.

"Do your best," I tell him. He presses his face against mine. "Don't worry about letting me down. I'll be proud of you whatever happens."

With a flash terror in his eyes, he flies off to take his place on the field. Cerberus faces him, her teeth bared and tail lashing. She's not afraid to hurt him, but I don't know if he's okay with hurting her.

I can't see my brother in the crowd. Is he hiding from me? Is he upset?

"Hazy!"

I'm thankful to see one familiar face push through the sea of people. Braith grabs my hand and kisses it softly.

"Have you seen...?"

"Yeah. He told Cerberus not to bother with who he is, just to fight to the best of her ability."

Fuck. Fuck, fuck, *fuck*.

What have I led Aqueous into?

"I should have stayed home," I whimper.

"No. Everyone *had* to do it. Ray would have just come for you anyway."

We turn to the battle as the horn to begin blasts. Cerberus opens her mouth immediately and shoots electricity at my companion, but all she hits is empty air. Aqueous circles her in the sky, eyeing her for weak spots or injuries. Another bolt of electricity is fired; it misses his head by inches. With an angry roar, he swoops down and drags his claws along her back, making her scream in fury. He's not fast enough to get away, however, as she grabs his tail tip. He convulses violently as electricity streams through his body and crashes to the ground, leaving a trail of upturned earth behind him. She jumps on him and clamps her jaws around his leg, shaking her head in a bid to get him to give up. He screams and whacks her in the face when he unfolds his wings. This makes her angrier, however. She digs her claws into his hide and drags them down his body. With a terrified screech, my companion kicks her off, but she gets up just as quickly as she goes down. Just as Cerberus opens her mouth to fire more electricity, my partner scoops dirt in his claws and throws it at her face. Blinded, she desperately paws at her face to recover her sight.

I know what he's going to do before he does it: the move he learned from Marco.

He fires water at her legs, making her crumple into a heap. Then, he quickly rises to his feet and stomps them in the ground. With his wings spread and his eyes closed, he leaps backwards into the air, throwing ice-cold water at the defenceless dragon. After a few seconds she gets up, the water having washed the dirt out of her eyes. Out of rage she launches into the air to attack my partner, only for him to move out of the way and slam his tail on her head. Dazed, she falls to the ground and lands on her back, her foot twitching slightly.

It seems like a lifetime before Ray starts counting. Cerberus makes no move to get up; she just lies on the ground with her feet in the air.

"...Ten! Aqueous wins!"

Finally, Cerberus clambers to her paws, leaning on Aqueous for support as they limp towards the crowd. As soon as they reach the outskirts I throw my arms around my companion's neck and he lifts a foot up to my back to hug me closer.

"Cerberus, are you alright?" Rocky runs up to Cerberus, holding her face up to his.

She blinks painfully and lies down, allowing him to see the three bloody lines on her back. He's silent for a second, before turning his angry gaze to my partner.

"Before you even *start*," I step in front of Aqueous, hands balled into fists. "Look at his leg *and* his back!"

My brother considers this and turns back to Cerberus, though his angry gaze doesn't waver.

"That was *so* cool!" Braith breathes. "You two were awesome! Throughout the entire fight, I thought you were equally matched!"

Cerberus chirps and stands up, allowing Braith to pat her on the head, though she winces when the girl gets too close to her eyes.

"Both of them need to be fixed up," Rocky says, pointing to the team of vets running towards us with white bags. "Let them do what they need to."

We all step back as the two dragons are treated. They're able to pay close attention to Cerberus' wounds, but seeing as Aqueous will be going into another round they can only dress his wounds and make sure they are heavily wrapped up so as not to be damaged further.

Rocky and Cerberus leave after she's treated. He doesn't look at me. It's not my fault she lost. I thought they both fought well. Braith is still scared about Damayanti going for her fight. Every time they call names she grabs my hand and refuses to let go. Several battles are fought before it's finally her turn.

"Damayanti against Hula!"

The colour drains out of my friend's face as she turns to her partner. "Be careful. Don't do anything stupid, please."

The black and white dragon licks her cheek before flying into the arena. Her opponent has pale pink markings on its face that look like a sunset with a mix of green, white and red scales. Its tail is long and slim, but doesn't have any spikes on it, so Damayanti doesn't need to worry about grabbing her tail. The two dragons crouch defensively until the horn is blown to begin. Having the advantage of size, Damayanti rushes forward and knocks her opponent off their feet. Hula, however, quickly illuminates her entire body in a blinding bright light, making the black and white dragon stagger backwards with her eyes squeezed shut.

"No..." Braith squeezes my hand so hard I swear she'll break it.

Come on, Damayanti. You can do it!

As the dragon is blinded, Hula sees her chance to land a few hits. Shooting up into the air, she comes spiralling downwards and slams onto Damayanti's back, making her screech in pain. Before the dragon can do it again, a layer of ice grows on her wings and she falls to the earth, landing heavily and lopsidedly on her feet. Her opponent is up at this point, and is beating her wings quickly to blow the other dragon back with ice-cold air. Hula freezes in the harsh cold, a thin layer of frost spreading on her face and chest. The tri-colour dragon then collapses on the floor, motionless. Ray begins the count, but at three seconds Hula is up again, pouncing on Damayanti and pinning her down. The smaller dragon then bites and scratches her face and chest, with the bigger dragon powerless to kick it off at the angle the other dragon is sitting.

"Stop!" Braith's eyes are tightly shut. "Give in. Don't get hurt."

Hula then jumps off and crouches with her teeth bared, daring Damayanti to get up. Ray counts to ten, and Hula wins. Braith rushes to meet her companion as she exits the arena with her head bowed in shame.

"You're okay!" Her partner buries her face in her neck. "You're okay..."

Aqueous says something to Damayanti, but the older dragon looks away, her orange eyes glazed over.

This is really taking its toll on everyone.

It's been over an hour, and we're finally on the last fight of round one. Then we have three more rounds to get through.

"Finally, Drea against Poppy!"

Braith grabs my hand once more as Drea flies into the ring, looking determined to win. Her opponent is a small red dragon with red fireball markings on his wings. He looks terrified, almost as if his feet were trapped in stone. The horn is blown to start, and Drea wastes no time sprinting at the scared dragon. To everyone's surprise, Poppy falls to the ground and lies perfectly still. For a few seconds nothing happens, but then Ray starts counting. Throughout this the poor dragon doesn't move, its gaze locked on a confused Drea.

"Ten! Drea wins!"

As if nothing had happened, Poppy sprints through the crowd, running down the street as if a pack of dogs is chasing him. His embarrassed partner chases after him, calling and waving his arms crazily to try to get him to stop.

"What the hell? Did that dragon faint or something?" Braith watches the two of them run, an amused expression on her face.

"I have no idea. At least Drea is okay; her wound didn't re-open."

"Of course it bloody didn't! She just stood there for ten seconds!"

"Are you going home? Now that you're done here?"

"What? And leave you here by yourself?" Her arm snakes around my waist. "It'll get cold out, and you *need* a heat source."

"I'll just get Marco to light a fire," I tease.

"Not when you've got a better, more *passionate* option right here you won't!"

"Round two is starting. All participants who lost in round one are welcome to leave." Ray's voice booms out of the speakers, making us both jump.

A few people leave, their dragons limping or flying beside them. Some of these fights were quite brutal; they should be happy they don't have to fight further.

Neither of us really pays attention for the first few fights; we just listen out for dragons we recognize. Aqueous takes this time to snooze lightly. Unbeknownst to him, Damayanti has pressed up against him, her tail curved around his nose. After the second fight, Braith bought some hot food for us both. We shared a packet of chips, which kept us warm for a while when the cool night air rolled in. I presume Rocky went home, but I haven't seen Marco or Wes. They're probably further up the field somewhere.

"Drea against Wren!"

"Finally! Hopefully Drea actually gets to fight this time!" Braith stops picking at the grass, her eyes now glued to the impending fight.

When Drea enters the arena, I finally spot Marco on the other side, bolt upright and chewing his nails worriedly.

She'll be fine.

At least, that's what I keep telling myself. Her neck is an obvious weak spot, which gives her opponent an easy advantage over her.

Wren is red and white, with dark blue water swirls covering his face and back. His wings are stretched out in an obvious taunt, but Drea doesn't seem to notice. The horn blows, and time seems to slow as the white dragon steps back into a shadow and dissolves into the darkness.

Wren swings his head round in confusion, trying to pinpoint where his opponent will re-appear. A loud screech fills the air and Drea slams into Wren from behind, tackling him to the ground. Grabbing one of his wings, the white dragon twists her head to the side, making her enemy scream. A stream of water knocks Drea back, but she gets up and shoots into the air. The red and white dragon follows her, despite the damage to his wing. His sharp, straight horns puncture Drea's leg and the white dragon drops. Both dragons fall to the ground, but at the last second Drea opens her wings and darts back into the air. Wren isn't so lucky, and slams face first into the dirt.

Drea seizes her chance to strike and pins the other dragon's head down while her back claws dig into his hide. They both stay still as Ray starts counting, and Drea sprints away towards her partner as she's announced as the winner.

"Cool." Braith's mouth opens in a wide yawn.

"You're tired already? It's not even eight." I jab her in the side as she starts to drift off.

"Huh? Oh... I know. I couldn't sleep last night; my mind wouldn't slow down. All I could think of was your boobs."

"Braith!" Instinctively I cover my chest, even though I'm fully clothed. "You've never even-"

"Yes, I have. I peeked into your stall one time when you left it unlocked, and there was yesterday morning too."

This time I don't give her the chance to move out of the way, I just punch her fiercely on the arm.

"Ow! Hazy, why? You're so abusive!" She sniffles as her lip quivers.

"Aqueous against Bumble!"

My partner shoots to his feet at the sound of his name, making Damayanti huff in annoyance. I don't get the chance to say anything this time; he just quickly licks my cheek and flies into the ring. His opponent is also water, so he'll have to rely on his wits. Bumble is a yellow dragon with a black vertical stripe running down his back. He looks surprisingly calm – unlike my companion, who looks nervous.

Be careful.

The horn blows, and Aqueous charges at Bumble, but the yellow dragon sidesteps out of the way and lets him shoot past. With narrowed eyes, my companion charges again, this time managing to hook his leg with his claws. He doesn't cry out; instead he launches into the air and kicks my companion off. Aqueous quickly recovers, however, and head butts Bumble's stomach, making the yellow dragon grunt in pain. Before my companion can get another attack in, Bumble opens his mouth and a cascade of water pours onto my partner's head. The black dragon is forced back onto the ground, drenched to the bone.

The yellow dragon sees an opportunity to strike and grabs one of Aqueous' horns and starts yanking. My partner cries out in pain and can do nothing but keep up with his opponent as he proudly trots backwards around the ring, dragging my companion with him.

I'm relieved as Ray starts the count, but at six seconds Bumble drops my companion. Instead of waiting for the end of the count, he continuously scratches his back, ignoring his screams of pain.

"Ten! Bumble wins!"

Bumble finally stops attacking my partner and trots off, but not before kicking dirt into Aqueous' face. Braith pulls me back as I try to run out onto the field, screaming for Aqueous. At the sound of my cries, he clambers to his feet and sprints over to us, a trickle of blood running down his face.

"I'm so sorry!" I throw my arms around his neck as he approaches. "I shouldn't have let you do it..."

With an eye roll he shakes his head sharply and nuzzles my cheek, lifting his foot up to my back again in a hug.

"See? Even *he* thinks you should stop blaming yourself!" Braith pats my back softly. "It's all over now. Neither of our companions has to fight anymore. Let's go home, yeah?"

"What about Marco and Wes?"

"Wes was being a grumpy little shit yesterday and Marco can man up for once. It won't kill them if we leave."

With a little more encouragement, we push through the crowd after Aqueous has been treated. Damayanti hasn't left his side; she even offered to let him lean up against her. Braith took a picture of that little scene, and exclaims how adorable they look.

"Um, excuse me?"

We swing around at the sound of a new voice. A handsome brown-haired boy stands behind us sheepishly.

"Is something wrong?" Braith scans the ground, lifting one foot up to check underneath it. "Did we drop something?"

"Uh, no. My name is Tyson, and this is my partner, Pine." A small light brown dragon steps out from behind him, with dazzling green eyes and a short spiked tail. He has indigo markings on his chest and feet, so Tyson must be a dark Elemental. "You're Scar... Sorry, Hazel, right?"

"Uh, yeah."

My heart quickens as he smiles at me, and my face heats up. What am I doing? I've never acted like this before!

He is cute, though.

"I saw your dragon fighting, and it's just... I've never seen a black common dragon before. I've seen you around school a few times, but I've never seen him up close."

Aqueous immediately nudges Damayanti away to stand up on his own. He puffs his chest out and eyes Pine carefully.

"Oh. Um..."

Say something!

Anything!

Really, nothing?

"Pine's a common dragon too, so I recognized his lack of 'desirable' features, you know? I just wanted to see if he was real, or a trick of the light."

I don't have to say anything, as Aqueous steps forward and allows Tyson to stroke his nose softly, making both him and Pine relax [and drop their tense statures].

"It was a surprise when I got him." Inwardly I breathe a sigh of relief as I finally say something. "I wasn't expecting it at all."

"Yeah, I can guess. Do you want to meet up for dinner tomorrow, Hazel?"

His request is quite sudden, and his gaze drops to the ground as I meet it. He looks embarrassed.

For a second my mind flickers to Marco, and what he'd think. But why do I care about what he might say?

"Sure. Where?" My fringe falls over my scar. It's not the most attractive thing in the world.

"Um... We can meet up in the park and decide from there, if you want."

"Yeah, that sounds cool."

Is this a date? Or am I just being *optimistic*?

"Cool. I'll see you at six, then. Bye." He hurries off, his companion trotting behind him looking amused by his behaviour.

It must be a date!

My first date! What am I supposed to do?

As the two of them leave Braith taps her foot on the ground angrily. I'm surprised she stayed quiet throughout.

"Oh! I see how it is! I give and I *give* but I don't get a date! Not even one!" She fumes, turning her back on me.

Pinching the bridge of my nose, I reply: "Well you don't need a date."

"Oh? And why is that?"

"You've already seen me naked; you skipped a few stages."

This gets her thinking. After a moment, she perks up and waves her middle finger behind his back. "In your face, Tyrone!"

"*Tyson.* Braith, I'll need your help with this."

We begin walking again, and Aqueous returns to leaning on Damayanti for support, much to her delight.

"What? With your outfit and stuff? Go dressed as a tramp; guys dig homeless chicks."

I slap her arm. "Be serious!"

"Okay, okay. But he must have had his eye on ya for a while; he came up with the date thing pretty quick. He didn't even hesitate; he must have been rehearsing it. It was pretty awkward too; you'll have to work on that."

My heart still hasn't stopped beating, and my stomach feels as if it's filled with butterflies. I have a *date* tomorrow. An actual date!

"I dunno."

Catching wind of my quietness, she pats me on the back. "Congrats on your first date! I can't wait to tell the others-"

"No! Braith, if Rocky finds out he'll lock me in my cabin for my entire life. Let's just... Keep it to ourselves for a while, okay?"

As much as I hate lying to my brother, I know that I have to. If he finds out he'll probably kill Tyson and lock me away from people for the rest of my life. He'd *freak* if he found out that I'm going out on a date with a boy alone.

As much as I love my brother, he can go overboard with being protective.

"What about Marco? Are you going to tell him? He is your second best friend after all."

"No, I'll tell him... Wait. Second best friend?"

She points to herself. "I'm numero uno, obviously."

"I don't think that was ever established."

"Say I'm number one or I'm telling Rocky."

"You're number one."

Her arm snakes around my waist lovingly. "Good. I get loads of perks for being number one, okay? I get full wardrobe access and bathroom access. Even if you're in it."

With an eye roll, I refuse her terms and we spend the rest of the walk home laughing. As long as Braith behaves, getting ready will run smoothly.

23

Chapter Twenty-Three

The day goes painfully slowly. Every few minutes I check my watch and worry about not having enough time to get ready. Marco picked up on my behaviour in dragon training, and kept asking if I felt ill. Despite saying otherwise, he's suspicious.

At five o'clock on the dot, Braith bursts into the cabin to help me get ready. She's already picked out my outfit, a simple black dress with a sparkly belt, thanks to her new 'perks' of being my 'number one'. She scolded me for wanting to put make-up on, but gave in and helped me put a tiny bit on, us both wanting me to remain as natural as possible. A dark blue scarf with frayed ends hides my markings, as my hair is still too short to cover them completely. She found it funny that the colour matched my element.

"You look beautiful! Let *me* take you out on this date, dump that Tyler guy."

"*Tyson*," I correct him. "And, no. I've already agreed to go."

"Fine." She passes me a small black bag. "I've already put your money in it. You are *not* walking around with that awful brown thing. It's beyond dead, throw it out already."

The bag slips through my fingers, making me roll my eyes as I pick it up. "If you say so…"

Finally, she lets me exit the bathroom to go out into the cabin. Some eyebrows are raised as to why I'm dressed up, but no-one asks any questions.

That is, until Wes spots me.

"Hey, what are you all dressed up for?" He closes his book to look me up and down.

"Uh…"

"Shh! Wes, Hazy's got a date! Don't tell anyone!" She presses her fingers against his lip but jumps away when he tries to hit her.

"A date? You're too young for dating," he says.

"No, Wes. I'll be fine, okay?" I try to walk past him, but he stands up and blocks my way.

He crosses his arms stubbornly as I sigh. "Does Rocky know about this?"

"Yes."

Immediately he sees through my lie, his mouth forming a disbelieving scowl. "No, he doesn't. He'd never let you."

"Please don't-"

"I *have* to tell him."

"Why? Why do you? Stop being such a tattle, Wes! Grow a pair!" Braith balls her hands into fists and pushes past him, knocking him to the floor and dragging me with her.

Aqueous and Damayanti are waiting for us outside. Damayanti is trying to get my companion's attention, but he's too focused on his bandages to notice. I feel bad for her sometimes; Braith says she always had a crush on Aqueous but now she thinks that he's more interested in Winter, so she's trying to up her game.

"Do you want us to walk ya over?" My friend grabs my hands and squeezes them tightly.

"No, we'll be fine. I'll tell you all about it tomorrow, I promise."

"Okay... Now is your last chance to swap him for me..."

I giggle and hug her quickly. "I'll stick to the original plan, thanks."

* * *

Once at the park I decide to sit on a bench near the entrance in the shade. I'm glad Braith mentioned the scarf; it is cold today. Aqueous sits bolt upright beside me, his worried eyes locked on the entrance.

With each second my stomach fills with more and more butterflies. I swear it's going to explode.

Calm down, it's just a date.

"Hey."

Tyson sits down on the bench next to me, his hands stuffed into his jeans pockets and a large smile on his face. Pine goes to say hello to Aqueous, and the two dragons seem comfortable enough to sit together.

"Hey." I smile shyly back, already feeling my face warm up.

"You look nice."

"Thanks. Are you cold?"

He smirks and looks down at his hands. "You aren't?"

I feel like my face is on fire, so no.

"Not really."

"I've found a nice place for dinner. Are you ready to go?"

"Yeah."

It feels incredibly awkward to walk beside him and make small talk, especially since I know nothing about him except his name.

"So, what are your family like?" I ask.

"My Mum died a few years ago. I don't remember much about her. But my Dad is a miner; he's quite cool."

"Any siblings?"

"Nope. I'm an only child. What about you?"

"My Dad left soon after I was born, and my Mum is a waitress. She tries her best, but she struggles. I have a brother, though: Rocky. We're really close."

"It must be nice to have a family member here," he mutters.

"Yeah, I love being able to see him every day."

We soon make our way to the restaurant, a quiet little burger place. It's nice to get into the warm, but I feel sorry for Aqueous and Pine, who have to stay outside in a paddock while we eat. I know they don't really feel the cold because of their thick scales, but I still feel bad.

As the evening goes on we begin to feel more comfortable with each other, laughing and chatting about our lives. We don't leave until half eight; they were late bringing our food. I don't really care; it's nice to be able to talk to Tyson for a bit longer.

He's nice enough to walk me home, despite the freezing cold wind that blows in our faces. I'm both relieved and sad that the date is over, but I don't let either show.

"Thanks, I had fun."

He chuckles and looks down at his feet. "Me too."

"I'll, uh, see you tomorrow, maybe?"

"Yeah, I'd like that."

For a second we just stand there staring at each other, but then he steps towards me and leans forward.

Kiss back, idiot!

My heart is beating faster than ever before, and my lips feel red hot despite having been exposed to the cold air. When we pull away, I can't stop smiling like a crazy person.

"Goodnight," he whispers.

"Night."

As he and Pine leave, I squeal as silently as I can before stepping into the cabin. As I thought, loads of people are awake playing games or chatting. My gaze falls on Wes, who is sat cross-legged on his bed looking sour.

Here goes nothing.

"Hey, Wes," I say carefully as I approach him.

"Hey."

"I'm sorry about-"

He cuts me off by putting his hand in the air. "It's not your fault. I'm angry with Braith; she pushed me over and everyone laughed at me."

"They'll get over it."

"I know. I'm sorry about the way I acted. I didn't actually tell Rocky."

I throw my bag on the bed and sit next to him. "Are you okay? You've been grumpy lately. I ask you an innocent question and you practically bite my head off."

Unable to meet my gaze, he stares at the floor, kicking his feet slowly. "I'm sorry. I'm just struggling, you know? School, research, dragon training, dragon fighting... And we've got an exam at the end of the year! I just..."

Gently I rub his back, surprised to see a tear forming in his eyes. "We've all offered to help with the research, Wes. You don't have to do it all on your own. I know you want to make Ray proud of you, but I'm sure he is anyway for how much work you've put in."

My friend nods slowly and wipes his nose on his sleeve. "Thanks."

"No problem. Who won the dragon fight thing anyway?"

"Asteroid came in fourth." He smiles slightly. "Bumble came out on top; his partner is a friend of Ray's."

I shiver at the thought of that yellow dragon dragging Aqueous around the ring; the determination in his eyes was terrifying. "So, what happens next?"

"No idea. Ray's currently sorting each dragon into an allotted job. All dragons who lost in round one will be cleaning and serving, that's all I know."

My mind flicks to Cerberus and Damayanti, I hope they'll be okay with not having a higher job. Marco told me today that Drea came in third, so she'll most likely get one of the highest jobs. I have no idea what Aqueous will get though; it could be anything.

"Why are you smiling so much?" Wes raises an eyebrow playfully.

"We kissed," I mutter, my smile growing wider.

"Oh, how did your date go by the way?"

"It went really well. I hope we can do it again."

"That's good. How are you going to break the news to Rocky?"

"I have no idea. It won't be pretty, that's for sure."

He shrugs. "If you're happy, he shouldn't have a problem with it."

"He'll have a problem with it, regardless of how happy I am. If Tyson wants to, we'll go out on a few more dates, then I'll break the news to Rocky."

"Does Marco know?"

I shake my head slowly. "I'll tell him tomorrow. I wanted to wait until after the date, so then he wouldn't randomly show up half way through."

My friend's mouth widens in a large yawn. "I'm tired."

"Go to sleep then. And *actually* sleep for once. No reading, and no fretting. Give yourself a break, Wes, we all know you deserve it."

Mouthing 'okay' he gets up and starts getting ready for bed. I should probably do the same, but I'm still buzzing after the date.

I hope Tyson kisses me again.

Despite trying my best to stop, I'm still smiling. It felt nice, and his lips were so soft...

Go to bed. I'm seeing him tomorrow.

24

Chapter Twenty-Four

Tyson and I have been seeing each other for three weeks now, and it's going well. He admitted that he's liked me for a while, ever since he saw me hanging out with Wes and Marco in the library. However, he was always too shy to approach me, so decided to take a chance at the dragon fight. I really like him; he's kind and has been nice to my friends. I've met one or two of his and they seem alright; a little immature, but alright.

Unfortunately, it means I have to tell Rocky.

I've asked to meet up with him after today's Cindaraan meeting, Ray has finally allocated each dragon a job and has decided on working hours and pay.

"What do you think Aqueous will be doing?" Marco asks, glancing back at my partner, who is happily trotting ahead of Drea.

"I dunno. Hopefully nothing too taxing."

"What about lover boy, huh? What's his companion doing?"

After the second date, I told Marco what I was doing, and he was supportive. He isn't a huge fan of Tyson though. He doesn't like the fact that he's a year older than I am; he says it will cause 'problems'.

I blush and whack him on the arm, flicking my hair over my face in embarrassment. "We're finding out tonight, remember?"

My friend rolls his eyes and brushes my hair away with a finger. "I know *that*, smartass. But his dragon lasted until the third round, didn't he?"

"Yeah."

The hall is quite full as we walk inside. There's no seats left, so we just lean against the wall next to our companions. Ray is already at the front, sorting out his notes. I scan the aisles for Tyson, but I can't see him or Pine. I spot Braith and Rocky near the front, however, seemingly in the middle of some jokey argument.

"Speak of the devil." Marco nods towards the door.

"Tyson!" I wave him over, making my friend roll his eyes irritably.

Pine mixes with Aqueous and Drea, chirping to them both excitedly. The three dragons are soon engrossed in conversation, listening to each other intently.

We kiss each other gently, making Marco sigh loudly. Tyson wraps one arm around my waist and leans against the wall as Ray calls for silence.

"After much deliberation, we have decided what job will be allocated to each dragon." He steps off the stage to walk down the aisles, eyeing everyone in their seats. "All dragons who lost in round one will be cleaners and light builders. They will work from nine in the morning until seven in the evening each day until the building work is done." Winter roars loudly as kids shout abuse. "They will earn four pounds per hour of work. Those who lost in round two will be heavy builders. They will work from eight until six, earning five pounds an hour."

"This isn't fair! You can't expect them to work for that long!" someone at the back shouts.

Aqueous is going to be doing hard work; he'll be exhausted by the time he gets home. These hours are ridiculous. If it were for something important I'd understand, but for an unnecessary expansion on a building no-one will use? Pointless.

"Those who lost in round three will be lifters. Heavy crates or material will be carried by them and dropped off at their necessary spots. They will work closely with the builders, working from eight until six for six pounds an hour. Those who lost in round four will be supervisors, working from eight until four for seven pounds an hour."

"This is ridiculous!" a boy near the front screams.

"Finally, the dragons who finished in the top ten will work as guards, working from ten until six for ten pounds an hour. They are, in no particular order: Winter, Asteroid, Indigo, Bumble, Drea, Katana, Kilo, Holly, Feather and Spider."

Ten pounds an hour? That's insane!

Of course, Ray's companion is in the top ranks. He'll be rolling in money.

"How stupid," Tyson mutters. "Most of those dragons are premier ones, of course; money goes to money."

Marco squirms uncomfortably beside me at Tyson's comment. He didn't know. Surely it's not his fault?

"Meeting dismissed. I will not be taking questions. But, if your dragon wishes to work overtime, they will get paid one pound for each extra hour they work."

Ray rushes into the back room with his cronies as an army of angry Cindaraans start hurling abuse at him. They have a right to be angry; our companions are *not* slaves.

"I'm guessing work starts tomorrow?" Tyson says to no-one in particular.

"I suppose."

I turn to my companion, who looks up at me guiltily. Why is he feeling guilty? He hasn't done anything wrong. *I* should be the one feeling guilty, for allowing him to fight in the first place.

"Hey, Haze? Rocky's coming." Marco nudges me back to reality.

"Huh? Oh, I'll see you later, Ty."

"Later."

With one last kiss, I meet my brother half way with Aqueous slinking along behind me.

"Hey, hun. Are you and Aqueous okay? He's going to have to get up ridiculously early." He pulls me towards him in a tight hug, ignoring the people who squeeze past us in an angry fit.

"I dunno. What about Cerberus? Making her clean all day is stupid."

He scuffs his feet on the floor, mumbling: "At least she'll be earning money."

"I've booked a table at that Italian restaurant, if you want to eat there."

With a grin, he wraps his arm around my waist. "Sure. Let's go; there's an opening."

It's a nightmare to squeeze through the exit. People aren't too fond of being pushed out of the way, and neither are the dragons. Once we're out on the street, I shiver in the cold evening air.

"Why didn't you bring a jacket?" He quickly takes his grey jacket off and forces me to wear it.

"But now you'll be cold…"

"I'd prefer you to stay warm."

Picking up the pace, we leave Aqueous and Cerberus outside to play in the paddock as we order. As the waitress leaves, butterflies start fluttering in my stomach.

How will he react? He doesn't like me hanging around with Marco at the best of times, so me going out on dates behind his back won't please him too much. Have I made it worse by not telling him straight away?

"Are you okay? You've gone pale." He strokes my cheek softly.

"I need to tell you something. It's really important."

"Braith already told me about the Primordial Dragon hatching."

Wait, what?

216

"What are you talking about?"

His expression falls. "She didn't tell you?"

"No, when did this happen?"

Glancing around the near empty restaurant we lean in close over the table. "It hatched yesterday," he explains. "The scientists found some kid who connected with it, and so far, it's acting like any normal dragon would."

"So... We have nothing to worry about?"

He chuckles. "I don't think we're in the clear as long as that thing is alive. It might re-discover its instincts and fight back. Who knows?"

The worst part is that it hatched.

It's alive.

But I thought no dragons but the Avian species could connect with a partner, unless they genetically modified it in a way so that it does.

Maybe it won't be like Draca. Maybe it will be okay.

That's a big, fat maybe.

"What did you want to tell me?" He smiles at the waitress when she brings our water.

Take a deep breath, and then tell him.

Here goes nothing.

"Look, you have to promise not to freak out, okay?" I reach forward and grab one of his hands, squeezing it softly. It's more for my benefit than his.

His eyes widen in terror. "You're not...pregnant, are you? Tell me who the father is; I'll kill him!"

"No, Rocky! I'm not pregnant!"

Relaxing a bit, he whines: "Don't scare me like that!"

"You scared yourself!" I snap.

"Is Marco bothering you? I'll get rid of him for you."

Through gritted teeth, I mutter: "Would you let me speak?"

Stroking my hand, he finally nods. "Sorry."

"I've been… I mean, I *am* seeing someone."

"I thought you didn't like Braith?"

"Not Braith! He's called Tyson, and he's sweet. We've been dating for a few weeks now, and I really like him."

He goes scarily silent, staring emptily at the vase of colourful flowers on the table.

Is he okay?

"Rocky?" I shake his hand softly. "Rocky…?"

After a few more moments his head snaps up, scaring me out of my skin. "Tyson Howard? The guy from my cabin?"

"Yeah."

"That's… Great. I'm happy for you." He smiles slightly.

What?

No panicking? No anger? No cursing?

He's happy for me?

"Really?"

"Yeah, really. If you're happy with him, then I can't argue. Let's enjoy dinner, okay?"

"Yeah, I'd love to."

Thank fuck that went well.

25

Chapter Twenty-Five

That cheeky little fuck. Sneaking past me to steal my *baby sister!*

Rocky had just walked Hazel home. She had talked to him about school and Aqueous, but he hadn't really listened. He was too busy devising a plan in his head. He needed to get rid of Tyson, before it was too late.

His little sister was his world. He didn't want to see her broken, like Mum.

It constantly haunted him. The memory of his father leaving them when Hazel was just a year old. It wasn't her fault she cried a lot; she had stomach problems. It wasn't his fault either that he was a bit rough with the other kids; he hadn't meant to push Marco down the stairs. But his father didn't care; he'd had enough. Mum was devastated when he came around with his new girlfriend. A pregnant girlfriend to boot.. His parents had argued and argued while his father packed his bags. Then, he was gone. He didn't look twice at him or Hazel, just left with his girlfriend in tow.

They never saw him again.

Rocky always wondered why his father left in such a hurry, and why his suitcase was filled to the brim with money the family never had.

He and Mum always told Hazel her father had left shortly after she was born. He didn't want her to know she'd played a part in why he left.

Mum moped for weeks, caring for him and Hazel like a robot, and crying when she thought neither of them could hear her. Shortly after the government announced their scheme to seize all children and take them away from their parents. Mum didn't seem surprised, it was like she knew it was going to happen, despite the protests from parents across the country.

"Look after your sister," she'd always told him. *"This will be hard for you two, but as long as you have each other you will be fine. You're both special, always remember that. You don't need a father, not one like yours anyway. Look after her, she's younger than you are."*

For months she made him promise, over and over. And now, he'd broken it. Hazel had already started to become attached, so he needed to cut the bond before it could get any stronger. It would be for her own good, to save her from future heartbreak.

I'm sorry, Hazel. But this will be for your own good, I swear.

The cabin was bustling as he walked in. Marco and Braith were chatting on her bed, constantly glancing at Tyson, who was sat up on his bed and laughing with his friends.

It would break his heart to see his sister as upset as his mother was, so he had to do something quickly, something to drive Tyson away.

"Hey, Rocky! Did Hazel tell you about...?" Braith pats an empty space on the bed, wanting him to sit down.

"Yeah, she did." He slowly sat down on the bed, stealing one last glare at Tyson.

"And...?"

"And what? I'm fine with it."

Marco and Braith swap a disbelieving glance. For a few moments, they don't know what to say, but then Marco finds his voice.

"Are you ill?"

"No."

"When you thought she was going out with Braith, you flipped."

"I know. But I've seen how happy she is."

"Aww!" Braith puts her arm around his shoulders. "That's so sweet! I wish I had a brother now!"

Get off me.

"Have you talked to him yet?" Marco asks.

"No. Why, what's he like?"

He shrugs, his face scrunching up in distaste. "He's alright. Nothing special."

"Ignore him. He's just jealous." Braith hits Marco in the face as he tries to retort. "I think he's really nice. I wasn't fond of him at first because Hazy is *mine,* but, now that I've got to know him, he's a sweet guy."

"Looks like he's going to the bathroom if you want to talk to him," Marco points out, watching the brown-haired boy leave his friends and enter the bathroom.

"Yeah, I will, thanks."

They make no comment as he leaves, one hand balled into a tight fist. Tyson turns to look at him as he enters, a wide smile on his face.

"You're Rocky, right? Hazel's brother? I'm Tyson, I don't think we've formally met yet."

I'll protect you, Hazel.

I'll always protect you.

* * *

"Uh, should we have let him go?" Braith watches him leave, her mind coming up with all the bad scenarios that could spring out of this.

Marco shrugs. "I think so. For once he's being very mature; give

221

him the benefit of the doubt."

Braith sighs and falls back onto her pillow, her eyes locked on the bathroom door.

Give him the benefit of the doubt.

"How do you feel getting eighty quid a day?" She starts a new conversation purposely to distract her thoughts.

Squirming uncomfortably, he shrugs once more. "I dunno. I don't think it's fair on the other dragons."

"It isn't. Poor Damayanti will be cleaning for hours on end. Ray conveniently didn't mention breaks, so I'm expecting her to get none."

"I think it's good for the commoners, like Rocky and Hazel. They don't have much money as it is; they can't treat themselves. Hazel felt really bad when she couldn't afford to buy me a birthday present. She still doesn't believe I don't want one from her."

"Oh, did you like mine, by the way?" she smiles teasingly.

"Very much so. It was awkward when Sadie found the magazine, though. Now every guy is squabbling over it."

"I try to please everyone," she laughs. "Oh, did Rocky tell you about the Primordial Dragon?"

"Yeah. Is it true?"

With a sigh, she nods solemnly. "Unfortunately. Guess what they named the damned thing too."

"I dunno. Dragon?"

Slapping his arm, she says: "Draca. The cheek of those people!"

"So… You think everything will play out as it went for the Original Elementals?"

"God no, we've lived separate lives. History can't repeat itself exactly the same. The markings are here for a different reason."

Marco plays with his thumbs awkwardly. "Do you think the situation is better or worse than the Original Elementals'?"

"I dunno. At the moment, definitely worse."

"I don't want Hazel to get hurt." He bows his head, but Braith could already see his face reddening.

"I appreciate the concern for everyone else," she teases, shuffling closer to him and leaning her head against his shoulder. "We're all fine, by the way."

"You know what I mean," he mutters, not meeting her gaze.

"I do… So, when are you going to tell her?"

His head snaps up. "Tell her what?"

"Oh, you know… That you dream about her every night, constantly stare at her whenever she's around and not looking, absolutely hating Tyson for no reason…" She wiggles her eyebrows knowingly.

"I don't know what you're talking about," he answers a little too quickly and defensively.

Feeling his heartbeat quickening and his face heat up more, Braith giggles and pushes him playfully. "You're a huge pussy, ya know that?"

26

Chapter Twenty-Six

First day of work for Aqueous.

I got up to see him at quarter to eight. He didn't look impressed at having to get up to go to work. I wasn't the only person up; two others had met their dragons on the way out as well.

"Here; I want you to be warm." Gently I wrap my blue scarf around his neck.

At first, he looks annoyed, but then his gaze softens upon seeing my sad expression. He's a heavy builder, so he'll most likely be working on the building itself. I hope it isn't too taxing for him. So far, we haven't heard anything about breaks or meals, so we have no idea what to do. If I give him food to take, they might take it away.

"Be good and don't hurt yourself. Drink lots of water, and if gets too cold just-"

He cuts me off by nosing my cheek softly. I'm nervous, and I'm not even the one working.

"Do you want me to walk you over?"

Shaking his head softly, he licks my hand before joining the other dragons as they leave. He casts one last glance at me and waves his tail in goodbye before disappearing around the corner.

Don't work yourself sick.

Once he leaves I remember that I'm stood outside in nothing but my pyjamas, so I quickly hurry back inside to the warm. Most people are still asleep; alarms are usually set for eight to get up for school.

I can't go back to sleep now.

I decide to get a head start on everyone else and get ready. Once I'm done in my stall, alarms go off and people stir.

He'll be working now.

Wes stretches and rolls out of bed as I return to get Normie his breakfast.

"Is Aqueous gone?" he asks.

"Yes. I waved him off."

"I'm sure he'll be fine. He's quite stubborn; he won't allow other dragons to boss him around."

"That's not necessarily a good thing." I pour the food in Normie's bowl and stand by the door to the stables, holding it open slightly with my foot.

At the sound of food, a furry ball comes bounding over the few sleeping bodies left and sits on my foot expectantly.

"Better than nothing."

"I suppose. Asteroid doesn't start until ten, does she?"

He laughs and shakes his head. "Nope. She was quite excited about being able to sleep in."

Normie meows impatiently so I put his food bowl on the floor by the bed. He looks down at it, then at me, to show his distaste at another day of dry kibble.

"It's that or nothing," I sigh, sifting through my drawer for today's textbooks.

When it's time to leave, I'm pleasantly surprised to see Tyson waiting outside for me. He must want to walk to school with me.

"Hey." Once he turns towards me, I freeze. His face is covered in bruises, and his eyes are wide and unfocused. "What happened?"

"I-I got into a fight..." He ducks away when I go to hug him.

It looks nasty. Who did he fight? A bear?

"Are you okay?" Wes comes up behind me, his mouth open in shock.

"We can't see each other anymore," he blurts out, backing away slowly. "It's not you, it's me. I'm just... I'm sorry."

"What do you mean?" I cry out as he starts running down the street.

Wes holds me back as I got to follow. "Leave him alone. He might change his mind."

It's not you, it's me.

It is definitely me then. Did I do something wrong? It wasn't like we were officially 'together' or anything. He looked happy enough yesterday...

I must have done something.

Maybe I was too clingy? Maybe I embarrassed him in front of his friends?

"Hazel, we need to go to school now." Wes tugs my arm, pulling me forward in a slow walk.

The walk to school is silent. My mind is buzzing as to what I could have done to upset him, and Wes has no idea how to console me. Once we reach the playground he quickly scans the area, trying to spot a friendly face to help him. He looks even more panicked when he can't find anyone. All morning he still can't find the right words to say.

I try hard to concentrate on my schoolwork, but my mind keeps flicking back to Tyson, and how upset he looked. It's just seems *too* convenient that he got into a fight the day after I told Rocky about him.

It has to be him.

As much as I don't want to believe it.

I should have known that he wouldn't be okay with it.

Why can't he treat me like a sister rather than a daughter?

* * *

I watch the dragons work from a safe distance, trying to spot my companion. It doesn't take long. A black dragon with a blue scarf appears on the roof of the building, holding a large wooden beam in his mouth.

Aqueous.

Even though I'm quite far away I can see he's tired. The wooden beam is at least three times his length, and he's carrying it on his own. He holds it in place while two other dragons nail it down, pushing a black and white dragon back with his tail when it gets too close.

Damayanti is with him.

She's holding a mop in her mouth, cleaning the one part of the roof that's already been built. My partner's legs wobble as he starts to weaken, but then the two other dragons step back, and he drops it, the beam staying solidly in place.

I'm proud of him.

He's working hard even though I don't agree with his ten-hour shift.

"Haze, are you just gonna sit there all day?" Marco plonks himself on the bench next to me, looking up at the dragons who are hard at work.

"Dragon training isn't for an hour. How am I supposed to do it without him?"

My friend smiles slightly. "We'll concentrate on you for the next few weeks, until this stupid expansion is done."

This is stupid. I don't see why Ray can't just hire extra builders to expand the building.

Probably because dragons will work longer hours for less pay. Asshole.

"Have they had a break yet?" I wince as my companion carries another wooden beam, only to get it wedged in the roof and bang his jaw.

"I… I don't think they're getting one," he admits, playing with his fingers. "Ray wants this done as soon as possible. I don't think breaks are part of the agenda."

I hadn't realized I had jumped to my feet until Marco pulls me back, his hand clamped around my wrist. We share the same expression. Both of us hate this. We hate what we've dragged ourselves into. But, because of my markings, Ray has a hold on us. It's my fault Marco's involved. I should never have dragged him into this mess. He's more expendable than I am. If he loses his use, Ray won't be kind to him.

How could I have been so selfish?

My best friend would jump in front of a bus if I told him to. Why didn't I tell him no? Why didn't I shoo him away when he first saw my markings?

Why did I tell Ray that Marco knew?

And now all of us are already on his radar thanks to hitting dead end after dead end trying to find out about the markings. He's already hurt me; Aqueous or Marco or Rocky could be next, and I have no idea what to do to prevent that.

"What's-"

"I'm sorry," I bury my face into his chest, clinging to him as if he might disappear before my eyes. "I'm so sorry."

"What for?" My friend chuckles softly. "You haven't done anything wrong."

"I dragged you into the whole markings thing…"

With an eye roll, he pulls away, holding my face up to his. "*I* dragged myself. *I* offered to help. Stop worrying about it. You always worry yourself sick over the tiniest of things. It *doesn't* matter. We're both in the same position, and I'm planning on sticking with you, okay? Now, stop crying. It isn't a good look for you."

"What can we do? Ray's got a firm grasp on us, he won't let go willingly."

Wiping tears off my cheek, his eyes narrow in determination. "Maybe so. But as long as I have you, and you have me, he can't control us."

"But-"

"No, he can't. He can't control what we think or do, so what does he have? Yes, he has leverage over the whole markings situation but he doesn't know the full story on the Primordial Dragon."

Mulling this over, I realize he's right. Ray can't control *everything*, no matter how hard he tries. I'll always have my friends beside me; he can't take them away.

"Okay." I whisper.

Grinning, he says: "Good."

He allows me to hug him again, but this time I feel more comfortable knowing that there are positives to our situation, despite what Ray does to us.

He can't trap us forever.

He will *not* keep Aqueous doing hard labour for ten hours every day for the rest of his life either.

"Hey, Wes told me about Tyson... Are you okay?" For a moment, I think I see a glimmer of happiness in his eyes, but it's quickly replaced by concern.

It's not you, it's me.

"I don't understand why," I admit, letting him run his fingers through my hair.

"Me neither," he shuffles uncomfortably. "It's just that... Rocky talked to him last night. You don't think he would have done something, do you?"

Rocky was just *too* accepting. He flipped when he thought I was going out with Braith, yet he's completely fine with Tyson? I don't think so.

As much as I hate to admit it, I think he's done something.

"I think he has. I just don't want to accept the fact that he ruined it for me."

Marco shrugs. "You could ask him."

"I don't think I'll like the answer."

We're both silent for a few seconds, before Marco stiffens and squints at the dragons. "What's that?"

I follow his gaze to a large red dragon carrying a thin glass tube in its mouth with royal purple liquid sloshing around inside. Two guards flank it on each side, pushing the workers out of the way. Carefully, the dragon places the tube into a small metal hole in the floor, fitting into place with its head tilted at an awkward angle. The guards snort in satisfaction and point the dragon to several other glass tubes with different coloured liquids inside.

That doesn't look like furniture for the new Headquarters.

"What are they building now?" I ask.

"No idea, it looks strange though. Why would Ray want that built? It makes no sense. Could it be acid or something?"

"I dunno, but I don't like the look of it."

* * *

"Aqueous!"

At quarter past six, dragons start returning from work. My companion is near the back, his tail trailing in the dirt. A thin layer of sawdust drapes his entire body, making his usually pitch-black scales look dark grey. As he reaches me, I look into his eyes and see pure exhaustion. A patch of crusted blood is stuck at the base of one of his claws and a thin trail of crimson on his shoulder drips droplets onto the floor.

For a second I don't know what to do. Then I decide to test how powerful my element has become by giving him a shower.

CHAPTER TWENTY-SIX

"Come on, get under the tree."

With a sigh, he lumbers over to the gnarled oak tree a few yards away and collapses underneath it. I unwrap the scarf from around his neck and throw it over a low branch. He gives me a puzzled look until I raise my hands and point them at him.

With a loud 'whoosh', water comes spraying out of my hands. For a second my companion stiffens, before grunting happily and clambering to his feet. He spins around in the cold streams, making sure every scale is clean. Once I'm satisfied that he's clean enough, I drop my hands, making him whine sadly.

"You'll get another one tomorrow," I promise.

He stands upright and closes his eyes, drops of water streaming off him. Once he's dry enough, he opens his eyes and looks down at his stomach before looking at me with a hope-filled gaze.

"I know."

My companion noses my hands as I produce a large clump of tinfoil from my bag. He yelps excitedly when I unwrap it and place it on the ground, watching him eat the beef greedily. As he's eating, I study his claw. It doesn't look too bad; he probably caught it on something while he was lifting, or stepped on a loose nail. Happy that it's not serious, I lean against his side and sink to the ground, watching the orange sky fill with light pinks and yellows as the sun begins its descent down the empty horizon.

I'm happy that he's okay. He hasn't got any serious injuries, although he acts like he hasn't eaten for a week and a half.

I don't know how much progress there is on the building, but I hope it doesn't take months upon months to build. After all, the dragons won't be able to keep up working like this if they have to do it non-stop for weeks on end. My companion is exhausted after one day of work; how is he supposed to last weeks without getting ill?

Aqueous licks his lips after he's finished eating and wraps his tail around me lovingly. I make a sphere of water appear in my hand, and he laps at the cold water eagerly.

He can pretend that he's a tough guy, but I know he's just a huge softie.

After he's finished we lie on the grass together, watching the sun set. Secretly I hope it never does, so Aqueous can stay with me under this tree forever, where we can keep each other safe. I must have dozed off, because when I open my eyes, the sky is pitch black and littered with stars. The half-moon glows brightly in the sky, with not one grey cloud hovering around to block out the glowing sphere.

"Oh," I rouse my partner, who has fallen asleep with his feet in the air. "Aqueous, we fell asleep! Let's go to bed before we catch a cold, okay?"

Groggily, my companion groans before stretching and rolling onto his feet. As I go to get up, it feels as if I've been glued to the ground. I tug at my arm to break free but it is encased in rock. I panic as rocks form around my neck, threatening to choke me.

Seeing me panic, Aqueous leans down and clamps his jaws on the rock around my neck, huffing with effort until it crumbles in his mouth. It makes no difference, however, as another forms in its place.

"Tch tch. I thought you two were smarter than that?"

My heart beats uncontrollably as Ray steps into view, a dark smile on his handsome face.

Fuck.

A roar hits my ears and something is dropped beside me. I can just about see Marco, in the same predicament as I am.

"You two should know better. First of all, watching the dragons work. Second of all, talking shit about me next to a *fucking* security camera!"

He's heard everything.

"Now, tell me about the Primordial Dragon, and what it has to do with the markings. Marco, you seem to know what to say, you tell me."

"Why should I?" Marco tries to kick out at Ray, but the blond boy steps back and clicks his fingers.

I gasp as the rocks tighten around my neck, blocking off my breath. Aqueous panics above me, attempting to bite through the rocks once more.

"What are you doing? You'll kill her!" Marco shouts, panic-stricken.

"You better hurry up then," Ray says coolly.

My companion's jaws are too weak from work all day. He starts to whimper and cry out as he can't think of anything else to do.

"Okay! A team of scientists have created a Primordial Dragon. It's what the Original Elementals had to defeat."

"Go on."

Black dots dance in front of my eyes and my head pounds painfully. My companion cries out in fear as my struggling weakens.

"We think the markings sprang up again because of the creation of the Primordial Dragon. It hatched a few days ago and connected with someone. That's all I know! I swear! Let her go!"

Ray taps his chin with his finger. "You had better not be keeping anything else from me."

The rocks clamped around my neck and hands crumble, and I twist onto my side, coughing violently and breathing heavily. My companion stands over me protectively as Ray paces around, his eyes locked on me with a smirk on his face.

"Winter, I think we are done here." Ray pats his companion's head, who nods quickly. "Good. Both of you expect your dragon's wages for today docked in half. I do *not* want to see you two watching them work ever again."

My friend sighs in relief as the rocks around him crumble into dust. He quickly crawls behind Drea, who is watching the duo with blazing eyes. If looks could kill, they would have dropped dead that instant.

"What was that stuff in the tubes?" Marco calls put defiantly.

"None of your concern. Do not watch them work again."

As Ray walks away, Winter hesitates for a second. She looks at Aqueous, guilt clouding her vision. My companion grunts something to her, but her gaze quickly hardens and she gallops after her partner, not looking back.

"Haze!" Marco throws his arms around me, patting my back as I have another coughing fit.

"Wha... Why..."

"I didn't know there was a camera there! Did you see it? I bloody didn't!"

"I... We... Need to tell the others."

"Tomorrow." He gives me a stern look as I open my mouth to argue. "Rest. You've just been strangled, let yourself recover."

Fuck, he's right.

I don't have the energy to tell Wes right now. The world is still spinning for me. I really should go to sleep...

"You'll have to sleep in the stables with Aqueous," Marco mumbles. "I don't think people will appreciate us waking them up, and I'm sure he'll keep you warm."

Aqueous grunts in approval and lets Marco lift me onto his back. My friend turns to leave but I grab his arm and manage to whisper: "Please don't go."

Marco smiles slightly and brushes his finger against my cheek. "Are you sure you want me to stay?"

I nod mutely and reach down to grab his hand. Aqueous grunts and nudges open the large wooden door to the stables. Some dragons raise their heads as they enter. It must be late, as the stables are completely full. My companion gently nudges me onto his blanket before curling up around me protectively. Marco squeezes in the little space left between Aqueous and I, curling his arms around my waist. The other dragons start probing Aqueous for answers, and look shocked as he starts to grunt agitatedly, swinging his tail back and forth wildly. Some growl and hiss in shock when he's finished, but others don't look surprised.

A beige ball of fluff rubs himself against me, purring loudly and happily about the possible late-night attention. I reach out to stroke him, and he headbutts my hand and licks it, his tongue rough against my sore skin. With a loud meow, he curls up against my chest and rests his head on his paws, sighing contently.

"Night," I mumble to the half-asleep cat.

Marco sighs contently and breathes a 'good night' before quickly falling asleep.

Aqueous curls up fully around Marco and I, resting his head on his pillow. Drea grunts and settles down in a crowded corner, keeping one eye on Marco. Aqueous lets me rest my head on his foot, and even folds a wing over my body to keep me warm.

It feels nice to be able to be so close to him again. I have missed waking up to his cheeky grin in the mornings. With one last yawn, I close my eyes and quickly drift into sleep.

It feels like only a few minutes have passed when I open my eyes, and Aqueous rises to his feet beside me, gently lowering my head to the floor. Marco must have left earlier because it's only me in the makeshift bed now. When I open my mouth to speak to my companion, only a small rasp comes out. My throat aches.

Spotting that I'm awake, he leans down and nuzzles me before stepping around the sleeping bodies of the other dragons and quietly slipping out the door.

Be good. Once the building is done, it's done. No more work.

27

Chapter Twenty-Seven

"Cindaraans! Now that you have all gathered, I wish to unveil our new expansion! It is free for all of you to use at any time!" Ray motions for his companion to cut the red tape.

Winter quickly obeys, biting the thin tape until it falls in two pieces to the floor. People cheer hysterically as the grey building with blacked-out windows is viewed for the first time. It doesn't look like anything special.

The damn thing took long enough to build.

After four months, it's finally finished.

But, due to the money Aqueous brought home, I've been able to treat him and Normie. Wes and I decided to buy the little fluffball new toys and a proper bed, which he largely ignores. Aqueous also got a comfier pillow for his bed. I don't know how long the money will last though, because I have to buy new textbooks and another dragon kit for the start of Year Two in August.

"How did Ray pay for all of this?" Rocky wonders, staring at the building in a mixture of disgust and awe. "The materials and wages must have cost a shit ton."

I've asked Rocky about Tyson multiple times, and he swore he knew nothing of it. He told me his injuries were from Kyle, for saying something sleazy about his mother. I don't believe him.

"Ray docked daily wages when dragons stopped working, remember?" I nudge his arm playfully, and he does the same.

However, I can sense a lot of hostility in the air, as some kids are still upset over a loss of pay. If a dragon was caught resting, even for a few seconds, it would lose an hour of pay. After the first month, I don't think anyone got the full day's pay they were promised.

"Unfortunately, I do. I got warned about Cerberus dropping a mop, which meant they docked her pay by an hour. It's ridiculous." Cerberus grunts her agreement, busy sizing herself up to my partner.

He's slightly bigger than her now, and Rocky said he's stopped growing. Next year all he's got to worry about is his wing strength increasing, so by Year Three I'll be able to fly him.

We walk away as Ray dismisses us. I don't want to spend any more time around him than I must.

Rocky nudges me back to reality, concerned by how quiet I'm being. "You're not worried about your exam, are you? It's just to test your element and your bond with Aqueous; you'll have no problem passing."

"I know. But it's with Mr Reedman! What if he fails me?"

"Then you take it again next year...?"

"But I'll have enough on my plate next year as it is; there are academic exams thrown on top of the Elemental one. It'd be hard work to keep up."

My brother nods slowly, his gaze locked on the ground. "Yeah," he mutters.

"I know you're worried," I murmur, resting my head against his arm. "But just keep calm and you'll be able to see the words."

"I won't though. It doesn't work! They still jumble up!" He wipes his nose on the back of his hand.

School is so hard for him. The teachers aren't too helpful; they only care for the smart kids. Or the ones who try to help have no idea how to deal with dyslexia. It's one of the reasons he tries so hard in art; it's the only academic subject that requires minimal reading and writing. He excels in it.

His art *is* beautiful.

"I know. Try your best, okay? I'll be proud of you no matter what you get."

He smiles slightly at that, but it doesn't quite reach his eyes. "I know you will."

"I've gotta go see Marco; he's giving me one last lesson before the exam."

With a small smile, he mutters: "Your hair is growing well."

My hair now reaches my shoulders, but only just. They cover up my markings though, which is one good thing, I suppose.

"I know. It'll be long again in no time. I'll see you later."

"Later." He hugs me once before allowing me to jog down the street, Aqueous flying high above me doing back flips to show off.

It doesn't take long to reach the field, but I don't spot Marco anywhere. I guess I'm early. Aqueous jumps into the river, swimming through the water like an otter. Despite the narrow banks, he loves swimming under the water and exploring the riverbed.

I see Drea before Marco. I sit down as they approach, and he quickly sits next to me.

"Hey, ready for your last lesson with me?" He punches my arm softly.

"Yeah. Can't say I'll be sad to see you go," I joke.

With an eye roll, he tackles me and pins me to the ground. "Take that back and I'll let you up."

I kick out wildly for a few seconds before huffing in defeat. "Fine. You're the best teacher ever. Happy?"

"Yep." He grins and allows me to sit up.

Aqueous slithers out of the river and shakes his foot over Marco, covering my friend's face in dirt. My friend whines childishly and rubs his eyes, making his hands brown with dirt and bits of leaves. Other kids have started gathering on the field with their mentors for their last lesson at this point. I spot Rocky and Ciara sitting underneath a tree, laughing and holding hands. Marco groans as Mr Reedman comes into view, wandering around and eyeing everyone's progress.

"Come on, before he starts screaming at us for not doing anything."

He holds out his hand to help me up and I take it, only for Mr Knight to walk past and roll his eyes in disgust. "I remember the days when poor people were separated from the rich," he mutters under his breath.

Shut up.

Mr Knight has been weird with me all year. He's been teaching me to the best of his ability, but I know he secretly looks down on me for not having much money. He was never happy with Marco mentoring me; I think he saw it as a waste of time. Marco seemingly ignores his comment, but studies my face to see my reaction.

"What do you want me to do?" My words snap my friend out of his daydream.

"Nothing. You've worked hard enough. This is the last lesson we have together, and I want you to relax before your exam. What time is it anyway? Aren't you one of the first ones?"

"Wind and ice are before me, because they have the smallest classes. My time is twenty past six."

"You'll do great, I know you will." Nudging my elbow playfully, he jumps back as I try to do the same to him.

"But Mr Reedman is the examiner. He'll fail me for sure."

"*All* of the dragon training teachers are there. They each say whether you've passed or failed, and the majority wins."

The fact that it won't just be Mr Reedman has calmed my nerves a bit. Surely they can't *all* fail me just because Mr Reedman says so.

"That sounds a little better," I smile.

"Good. Have you been told about the mentoring qualification?"

"Huh?"

He rolls his eyes and unfolds a piece of paper in his pocket. "You need to fill out a form on how well I taught you. I'll get a grade for teaching you, basically."

With a sigh of mock irritation, I take the form from him. "I *guess* I'll fill it out…"

"You'd better! Otherwise I'll put spiders in your bed!"

"Fuck off!"

He reaches into his pocket again and gives me a pen. "Fill it out now. Mr Knight has to collect them in a few minutes."

"Alright, calm down. I'm going."

The form is only ten questions, and I have to rate each from excellent to unsatisfactory. It shouldn't take long to fill out.

"Are you struggling with the questions?" he mocks.

"*What would you rate your mentor's attitude to your learning?* Oh, this is easy! Unsatisfactory…" I tick 'excellent' and pull away when he tries to grab the form.

"Haze!" he whines.

"*What would you rate your mentor's attendance?* Unsatisfactory again…"

"Come on! Stop teasing!" Snatching the form out of my hands he relaxes upon realizing that I'm joking.

"You wanted me to fill out the damn thing and now you're snatching it away – make up your mind!"

I fill out the rest of the form with little joking, and once I'm done I sign the bottom. Gratefully, he takes the form from me and hugs me quickly. We spot Mr Reedman approaching, so Marco quickly straightens up and stops grinning.

"You and Aqueous need to be sharper; one of you is creating more water than the other, which could be perceived as a sign of a weak bond between you."

"What would you suggest?" My gaze flicks to Mr Reedman, who is watching us with an amused smile on his face.

My friend hesitates for a second, making Mr Reedman smirk. "Watch each other carefully. Your body language gives away how powerful you want your element to be."

Thankfully, Mr Reedman starts to walk away. Eruption, however, hangs back a second to hiss at my partner, his mouth glowing orange in a warning. Aqueous says nothing, just ignores the threat and turns to me, his eyes lit up in excitement. This makes Eruption snort and lumber away, his tail swinging back and forth as a sign for everyone to stay away.

My friend sighs as Eruption moves out of earshot. "Fucking hell, they are scary."

"Everyone knows that at this point, I'd hope."

Sinking to his knees, he pats the ground next to him. "Come on, we look like idiots just standing around and doing fuck all."

As I sit next to him, his arm snakes around my waist. "You'll do fine, Haze. I'll take you out to dinner beforehand, okay? It'll calm your nerves."

"Fine. But I'm paying for myself."

"Fuck off. *I'm* paying. I'm a gentleman."

"You're not even remotely a gentleman. The last time we went to dinner you called me fat." I wriggle out of his grip and cross my arms.

"Rocky got me back for that. I couldn't walk for hours."

"Maybe if you didn't make stupid comments he wouldn't have had to kick you in the balls."

"It really hurt! You just laughed!"

"I found it hilarious. Highlight of my night."

His arm wraps around my waist again and he pulls me close to him.

"So… I'll see you at five? Preferably without Rocky? My balls can't take another kick."

"Fine. *I'm* paying for myself."

* * *

"Fourth and final ice Elemental: Isabella Hughes." The invigilator calls for the last ice Elemental, who walks in fearfully with her partner.

I'm next.

It's unnerving to be sat out in the hall just outside of the classroom. My leg is bouncing wildly because I'm so scared of what will happen. The questions are fired at us at random. The exercises we have to do change each year. They can be either hard or easy, and I heard last year had the easy questions. This just means there's more chance of my Year getting the difficult questions and exercises.

Aqueous places his foot on my knee again until it stops bouncing. He then nuzzles me softly, though his wide eyes give away his nervousness.

This could go horribly wrong.

The other water Elementals are also panicking, so at least I'm not the only one. My stomach churns as loud noises erupt from the classroom; the girl must be onto the exercise portion of the exam now. I stroke Aqueous' neck to calm myself down, but it does little to help as he has gone rigid, listening carefully to what's happening inside.

The room goes silent as the girl walks out, standing proudly and handing the invigilator a certificate. It is quickly signed and the girl is dismissed, beaming as she and her partner trot down the hall.

Deep breaths. No crying, no panicking.

"First water Elemental: Hazel Adams," the invigilator calls, holding the door open for me.

Here we go.

The classroom is tiny. Chairs and tables have been pushed against the walls. The only piece of furniture left in its actual place is the desk, which all eight dragon training instructors are huddled behind. Their faces are expressionless. They seem bored.

"Miss Adams," Mr Reedman passes sheets of paper down the line of instructors. "Before you perform the physical aspect of the test, we need to ask you a few questions about your relationship with Aqueous."

I nod quickly, sitting down in the seat in front of the desk. Aqueous stands behind me, his head resting on my shoulder to make me feel calmer.

"Don't worry," the Electricity Instructor, Mrs Butala smiles. "They won't take long. We've got the right answers here, you just need to say the right one."

Mr Reedman glares at her before clearing his throat. "How long did Aqueous stay in the cabin with you?"

"Um, seven months." I quickly re-count in my head, relieved that I came up with the right number.

"Has your bond decreased with him since you've been separated?"

"No." Aqueous grunts his approval behind me, making some of the instructors smile.

"How much, in total, did Aqueous earn while working on the expansion to the Cindaraan headquarters?"

Fuck.

Where did that question come from?

My head starts to fill with numbers as I try to think. I got the bank statement last week, but I didn't realize I had to memorize the stupid number!

"You obviously don't know, so we'll move on." Mr Reedman crosses something out on his sheet. "The next few questions are for Aqueous."

At least I get some time to clear my head.

My companion follows Mr Reedman to the board, staring at three coloured sheets of paper: one red, one yellow, and one green.

"Green means excellent, yellow means satisfactory, red means awful," the short man says. "First question: how would you rate Hazel's care for you? Be honest."

Without hesitation, Aqueous touches the green paper with his nose.

The short man rolls his eyes before continuing. "Second question: how would you rate Mr Knight's teaching of you and Hazel this year?"

Oh fuck.

Don't be cheeky!

My companion looks Mr Knight up and down before touching the red paper. The teachers look astonished, and I feel like sinking through the floor.

"Care to explain, Hazel?" Mr Knight glares at me, his fingers tapping on the table impatiently.

"Um…"

"Don't 'um' me. Dragons learn from their partners! So, come on, tell me about how *awful* my teaching was."

"That's *enough*, Mr Knight!" Mr Stirling intervenes, slamming his hand on the table and making everybody jump. "This is an exam. Try to be professional."

The room goes dead silent, before Mr Reedman clears his throat. "Last question: how would you rate Hazel's relationship with her mentor?"

My companion again touches excellent, and then trots back behind me, licking my face to seek my praise.

"Now, the physical examination." Mr Reedman sinks into his seat, his cold eyes locked on me. "Both of you take a few steps back and spread out."

My heart pounds once more as I stand there, waiting for further instructions. Aqueous obviously left his nerves outside; his eyes are now cold and determined.

"First of all, both of you create a ball of water," Mr Knight asks coldly.

I do as he says, the sphere hovering just above my hand. The instructors quickly scribble notes, before telling us to stop.

"Next, create an air bubble around your heads."

I remember when I used to struggle with this in the river; thankfully, those days are long gone. The bubble forms perfectly around my head, and I pop it with my finger when they finish their notes.

"Finally, a defensive water armour."

I sink to the floor and allow a layer of water to shield me. Marco and I worked for weeks to perfect this; I knew it would come up. The instructors whisper to each other as Aqueous and I stand up. He noses my hand softly as they stop talking and face us again.

"All those in favour of Aqueous and Hazel failing?" Mr Reedman asks, putting his hand up.

Mr Knight and the Earth Instructor, Mrs Farmer, put their hands up, but I can't help grinning when everyone else keeps their hands down, passing me.

Mr Reedman sighs. "Well done. Here is your certificate." He pushes it onto the floor, making some of the instructors tut. "Go get it signed and leave."

28

Chapter Twenty-Eight

"Yay! Celebratory kiss!" Braith screeches, throwing her arms around me and puckering her lips.

"I'd rather not." Giggling, I push her face away softly, making her pout.

"I knew you would pass." Marco wraps his arms around my shoulders and ruffles my hair.

"I just need to go home and feed Normie; he's probably hungry by now." I duck out of his grip and they both follow me down the street.

Damayanti trots beside Aqueous, smiling and trying her hardest to keep up a conversation. My companion doesn't realize her affection towards him. I'm afraid he sees her as nothing more than a friend. I think he's still hung up on Winter.

Marco chooses to stay outside as Braith and I go inside to feed Normie. My friend jumps on my back playfully, giggling and stroking my hair. When I open the door, our mouths hit the floor.

Someone's vandalized my stuff.

My duvet lays in tatters and the stuffing of my pillow is scattered across the floor. My old textbooks are torn and thrown across the room, with my clothes cut up and hanging off the bed.

"Oh my…" Braith jogs up to my bed and starts picking up my clothes. For a few seconds, I just stand there. What am I supposed to do?

"Hey, what are you…?" Marco notices my stuff and his lips purse into a tight line. "Who would do *this?*"

My feet finally work again, and I walk slowly over to Braith and start helping her. Everything is ruined; even the painting of Aqueous is covered in pen and has been slashed. With shaking hands, I start sorting through anything that might have survived. Even Normie's toys have been destroyed. I spot my furry friend huddled under Wes' bed, his bright blue eyes widened in fear and his claws digging into the floor.

"Here…" I hold my hand out to him, and he sniffs it cautiously before slinking out and clinging to my body, his ears pressed flat against his head.

"Haze? Are you okay?" Braith rubs my back softly.

Cuddling Normie close, I mutter: "No."

"Look at this," Marco kneels beside me, holding a scrunched-up note in his hand. "'*Commoners don't deserve to pass exams*'."

"So, whoever did this is a little shit?" Braith strokes Normie in my arms, one hand balled into a fist.

"Obviously," he snorts. "We need to find out who did this."

"I *need* to replace my stuff," I retort.

My friends help me get to my feet and lead me towards the door. Our partners look surprised as we approach them, but Aqueous is the first to notice Normie clinging to me. He noses his friend and starts muttering to him, so I let the cat climb onto my companion's back, meowing and hissing in distress.

"There she is!"

We swing round as a group of people carrying sharp sticks and pipes surround us. I back into my partner, who is swinging his head back and forth, growling at each person. I grab Braith and we cling to each other, our hearts beating wildly as we scramble to think of a plan. One person grabs Marco and drags him out of the circle, throwing him onto the ground behind them.

"Don't hurt him!" I cry as one of their dragons pins him to the ground.

Drea roars and swipes at one of the strangers, sending him flying into a wall. Instantly she's swarmed by the remaining dragons, buried underneath their scaly bodies.

"Shut up, bitch," one of the boys says. "We're here for you, not them."

"What do you want?" I squeak as the circle becomes tighter.

"Stop trying to climb the social hierarchy. You're *poor*. Deal with it. Don't take *our* jobs and *our* money and then throw it all in our faces! The hierarchy is in place for a reason, and you obviously needed reminding of yours!"

"Consider this a warning," another person says. "Pass any of your exams next year, and you won't live to your eighteenth birthday."

All of them back off, throwing insults and waving their weapons in front of my face as they leave. The dragons let Drea and Marco up, before launching into the air and screeching loudly, twirling and darting around in the wind.

* * *

"It's okay, you can stay in the hotel until we can get you new bedding," Rocky whispers, kissing my cheek softly and stroking my hair.

"Maybe it would be better to stay with us," Marco suggests, not meeting Rocky's glare of disapproval. "Then we can keep her safe."

I haven't got over what just happened. All that over a stupid exam. They have no right to trash my stuff over it. Marco called the Head Instructor and explained what happened, but they refused to pay for the damages. Instead, they said they would pay the strangers for any distress my exam caused them.

Cheeky shits.

"We can go shopping!" Braith exclaims. "You need new clothes; nothing escaped unscathed."

I'm barely listening to her. Next year, if I don't fail everything, they'll kill me. The trouble is that I want to do well; I want to leave this place at nineteen with good qualifications so I can get a decent job and earn a good wage. I don't want to have to struggle to feed myself for the rest of my life.

"Haze?" Marco nudges me softly, but I can't look up at him. "I know you're scared, but we won't let anything happen to you or Aqueous, okay?"

"They'll kill me next year," I sniffle.

"No, they won't." My brother pushes my friend away when he gets too close. "They'll have to kill me first."

"They probably will."

"Gee, thanks. I'm glad you have so much faith in me."

Braith sighs. "It's stupid that people in your own Year are throwing their weight around just because you passed a minimal test. They're so up themselves."

"I agree." I smile slightly as she starts tickling my stomach, only to have Rocky gently push her away.

"What are you doing?" my brother asks.

"Huh?" I look up at him, only to realize he's talking to Marco.

My friend is rummaging through my bag, pulling out various notes and chucking them on the floor. "They were shoving notes in Hazel's bag as they left; she dropped it on the floor."

The certificate.

Mr Reedman won't give any proof of me passing if it's been damaged.

Panicked, I crawl up to my friend and start throwing stuff out of my bag, looking for the yellow piece of card. He gently tilts my head up, and I'm relieved to see it's already in his hand.

"What are these?" Braith starts reading through the notes, chucking them away in disgust. "Oh fuck!" She jumps back at one, her hand over her mouth in shock.

"What? What is it?" Rocky peers at it, ripping it up angrily. "Stupid idiot."

"What is wrong with that guy?" she screeches. "He's *sick*! It's tiny! At least let it grow a little first!"

Marco groans. "That's not going to start up again, is it?"

"*What?*" Rocky and Braith shout in unison, the same disgusted look on their faces.

"I can't use my locker anymore. Great." I sigh and let my friend hug me from behind.

"Hey, I'll clear it out for you," Marco rubs my back gently.

My brother's expression quickly returns to anger. "This has happened before?"

Uncomfortable under his gaze, I duck my head. "Yeah, after Sadie… You know."

My brother opens his mouth, but Braith cuts him off. "*Anyway*, Haze. Come on, we need to get you some new clothes. What you're wearing is literally all you have, including your underwear." She yanks me to my feet. "I'll get her to the hotel by eight. If you're scared of her being alone, then Haze and I will have a sleepover."

"Naked pillow fights?" Marco asks hopefully.

Braith winks at me flirtatiously, making me blush. "I hope so."

Rocky doesn't look impressed at all, with his arms crossed and his lips set in a thin, tight line. "I'll go shopping with her. She's my sister."

"Oh? So, you'll help her get fitted for new bras, will you? And help her pick out new underwear? And help her get into dresses?" Braith's words make his face go bright red. "She's developed *a lot* since you last saw her naked at five years old. Let the girls take this one, Rocky."

CHAPTER TWENTY-EIGHT

This shuts him up, and even makes Marco snicker at how uncomfortable he is.

"Come on, we'll see them later."

* * *

"You look super hot in *all* of this," Braith reaches into a bag and waves a bra around her head. "Your boobs are growing, Hazy, I'm impressed."

Embarrassed as people stare, I sigh: "Braith, put that away."

"Killjoy," she mumbles, but puts it back anyway.

My companion is carrying Normie's new bed in his mouth, while said cat snoozes on his back, enjoying the free ride. Thankfully, after hours of shopping we're finally done. It's just bedding I need to get now, but that can wait until tomorrow.

As we walk into the hotel reception, I'm intercepted by Rocky, who has gone deathly pale. He looks like he's seen a ghost.

"Are you okay?" I murmur, putting the bags down to hug him.

"Those people were hanging around. I was scared they'd got you…"

"No, we're fine. I didn't even see them."

Marco stands awkwardly behind him, scuffing his feet on the floor. I hug my best friend next, but it doesn't last long as Rocky quickly rips us apart. Throughout this Braith has been rummaging through the bags again, sorting through the underwear.

"Braith, out," I sigh.

"Aww…" She stands up and crosses her arms sulkily as I pick up the bags once more.

"Did you get everything you needed?" my brother asks, taking a few of the bags off me, which I'm grateful for.

"Yep."

"Her boobs are fucking great," Braith giggles, turning to Marco and winking at him. "Bet you're jealous you weren't there to see."

Rocky shoots Marco a glare, but chooses to ignore Braith's comment. "Let's go book you a room now then, yeah?"

We all lean against the empty desk and wait to be served. I spot Marco staring at my chest, so I jab him in the ribs. His face goes red and he mumbles a quick: "Sorry."

A receptionist finally arrives, smiling at us. "What can I do for you?"

"A room for two for one night please," my brother says.

"Okay. Are there any commoners staying in the room?"

Rocky is caught off guard for a few seconds before answering: "Yes, my sister. She's sixteen."

"Okay. That's one hundred pounds in total with breakfast included. Because a commoner is staying she has to pay seventy."

"That's ridiculous!" Marco taps his hand on the table. "Why is she more expensive?"

The receptionist shoots Rocky and me a glare as if she hoped we would drop dead. "Too many undesirables were staying here, so we increased the price."

That's why Mum hasn't come to see us...

My friend sighs irritably and throws her the money. "Here. That room better be in good condition."

I knew it wouldn't be.

As far as I'm aware, Braith and I got the shittiest room in the hotel. Despite asking for two beds, we got one tiny bed squeezed into a small space. The only other piece of furniture is a small table next to the bed with a lamp and a phone on it. The bathroom only contains a dirty toilet and a sink..

"We'll make it work, Hazy." Braith falls onto the bed, making it moan loudly. "Fucking hell, is this made of rocks?"

"How are Aqueous and Damayanti supposed to stay?"

We look at our companions, who are peering inside and looking concerned by the lack of room. Normie wastes no time in claiming the bed as his own, kneading the covers before deliberately stretching as far as he can to push Braith off the bed.

"Does the hotel know you've brought your pet?" She sends the little furball a glare when he rolls onto his back with his feet in the air. At least someone is comfortable.

"They charged double for me to stay," I push the shopping bags under the bed to give us a bit more room. "So, they'll have to deal with it." Scanning the small space available, I sigh again. "Where can our partners stay, anyway? There's barely enough room for us."

"They can sleep on the floor, there's room under the bed!" She ushers our companions inside, as if it wasn't enough of a squash already.

My partner squeezes himself up between the wall and the bed, trying to offer more room. He looks at me sadly, his eyes dull and tired. Braith and I are pushed onto the bed, the room blocked by our companions.

This is a disaster.

"Braith-"

"Uh, uh!" She presses her finger against my lips. "It's *fine*. It's only for one night anyway!"

"Does the hotel not have stables?"

For a second she hesitates before nodding slowly. "No common dragons allowed."

How mature.

Why is everyone acting as if I have some sort of disease? It's just money!

Crossing my arms, I say through gritted teeth: "I should have guessed."

Scratching underneath the door makes everyone go silent. Even Normie shoots up into a sitting position, his ears swivelling. Just over Damayanti's tail I can see things being pushed under the door.

What now?

"Uh, sorry." With a lot of effort and shuffling, I clamber over

Damayanti, whose gaze is also locked on the door.

It's a tiny brown envelope. It's handwritten, with my name scrawled neatly on the front.

Who sent me this?

Or more importantly, how did they know where I was?

I open the letter, and a tiny, flat silver brooch falls into my hand. There's no pattern on; it's just plain. Curious, I read the letter to myself as Braith struggles to climb over her companion.

Dear Miss Adams,

Yet again, there has been a communication error with the school. We would like to apologise for this, as it has hindered your progress in education.

From now on, all commoners must wear this brooch to show their status. It makes it easier for teachers and instructors to mark work and see what trips are available to you. This brooch must be worn at all times when outside of your cabin: school, dragon training and even socialising.

We are very sorry if this late change has affected you, but we are trying our best to rectify it now. This change was introduced at the beginning of the academic year after complaints from teachers and instructors that records had to be sorted through to find any commoners and fit lessons around them.

You will still be able to approach teachers and instructors for advice or help as you used to, but if a student who is not a commoner asks for help at the same time, you will be seen to last.

Sorry for any inconvenience caused.

Thank you.

This is crap.

I roll the brooch around in my palm, staring it in disgust. I'm advertising my low status so everyone will find it easier to pick on me.

How did this letter even get to me? Surely it should have gone to my cabin?

"Is it a love letter?" Braith snatches the letter from me, quickly scanning the neat writing. It's obvious when she's finished, as her nose wrinkles in disgust. "This is bollocks!"

"I know."

"How is this even fair? I think they just want you to be a target!"

"That's the point. Commoners are undesirable, remember?"

"I disagree," she smiles sweetly, wrapping her arm around my shoulders. "I think you're pretty hot."

"Braith..."

"Fine." She drops her arm and screws up the letter. "Just wear the stupid thing and if anyone gives you shit for it, tell Rocky. You know he'll make them wish they were never born."

If all commoners must wear them, then so will Rocky.

I wonder how he's reacting to this.

"I'm aware. But he's probably got one too."

"Phst! He won't care! As long as sweet *baby* sister is alright!" she teases in a high, child-like voice.

With a reddening face, I snap: "Shut up!" I climb over Damayanti again and lie on the bed, my blood boiling.

She doesn't understand. I don't want him to get hurt over me.

"Hazy?" She murmurs, sliding onto the bed next to me. "I'm sorry if I hurt your feelings. It was only a joke..."

"It wasn't funny. I don't want my brother ending up in hospital because he was defending me!"

"He's not stupid-"

"Yes! He is *that* stupid! Fuck off, I don't want to talk to you!"

Recoiling as if she's been stung, hurt crosses her face before being replaced by anger. "Fine! *You* can sleep on the floor!"

Before her words can sink in, she's pushed me off the bed. On the way down I hit my head on the edge of the small table, making a sickening thud. My head aches as I sit up, and it stings horribly when I touch it. Blood covers my fingers, and spasms wrack my body as I start crying.

The evening just gets worse and worse.

"Shut up! Stop being such a-" Braith freezes as she peers down at me, and her eyes quickly widen in panic. "Oh, I'm so sorry!" Cradling me like a child, tears start running down her face too. "It was an accident. I'm so sorry..."

Between sniffles, I manage to mutter: "I'm sorry for snapping at you."

"I know, I know. Let's get you fixed up, yeah? I'm sure the hotel has a nurse."

"Be careful. She might charge extra when she finds out I'm dirt poor," I joke half-heartedly.

"We'll charge it to Marco. He won't care."

29

Chapter Twenty-Nine

It turns out Rocky was sent a brooch too. He got the letter when he went home, we're still not sure who delivered it to my hotel room. Apparently, Wes had been worried sick; he was terrified that Normie and I had been kidnapped. Why anyone would want to kidnap that furball is beyond me. Of course, my brother was unimpressed when I explained what happened with my injury; he gave Braith the worst death glare I've ever seen.

"You were supposed to be looking after her, not hurting her yourself!" my brother fumes.

"Rocky, please." I grab his face to make him look at me. "It was an *accident*. The whole room was a safety hazard. It wasn't her fault." He tries to glare at Braith again, so I use a harsher tone. *"Rocky."*

For a few seconds he says nothing, but then finally gives in. "Fine."

"Good." I let go of his face, and he starts rubbing one cheek painfully, trying to hide the red fingerprints.

He goes back to pawing at his breakfast, too unhappy with Braith to continue eating. Not that the food here is great anyway.

"How are you getting on with the brooch?" Braith asks timidly.

Rocky rolls his eyes. "Awful. Ciara teased me about it in front of her friends. They're trying to convince her to dump me now."

"Don't listen to them," I sigh, taking a bite of toast. "If she really loves you, she'll ignore them."

With a sigh, he smiles. "You're right."

It's bad that a part of me wants them to break up. I still don't think Ciara's good enough for him. Whenever Marco's around she forgets about Rocky and can't stop flirting with him. He never flirts back, but just the thought is enough to piss my brother off. It isn't helping him to be more civil with my best friend.

"Hey." Speaking of Marco, my best friend wraps his arms around my neck from behind, squeezing me softly and brushing my hair out of my face.

"You finally crawled out of bed, huh?" I tease.

"Mm-hm. I wanted to get a lie-in before my exams."

Now that school has finished for everyone, exams have officially started for the older Years. However, because I don't have any academic exams, I just get an extra week off.

"Which ones?"

"I've got chemistry and physics back to back at one."

"Ouch."

He smirks. "I know. But to top that off, I've also got English at four."

Rocky squirms uncomfortably in his seat. English must be his first exam. I really hope he does okay; it's his worst subject.

My friend finally sits down opposite me, eyeing everyone up. "Why are you all so quiet?" His gaze moves down to my brooch. "Why are you wearing that?"

"You haven't heard?" I sigh. "All commoners have to wear these from now on."

"Bullshit!"

"It's true," Braith swirls her cereal around in the bowl. "I read the letter myself."

"Well, if it makes you feel better I have to wear this-" he points to a gold brooch on his jacket "-to show that I'm a premier."

What is the plan with this?

They are pointing out the commoners and the premiers, but for what reason? Is it so that people look up to the premiers and down upon the commoners?

I don't really see the point in any of this.

"I guess it's so that they can easily separate commoners from the premiers," my friend leans back in his seat.

"What makes you say that?" I take another bite of toast.

"The guys in suits by the door."

Everyone whips around to the door, where three people in grey suits stand, scanning the area. They know what they're looking for.

And I'm sat right next to him.

My body stiffens as their gazes land on our table. They start making their way over, their companions moving to block the exit.

"Look what you've done!" Rocky pinches the bridge of his nose in annoyance.

"What? What did I do?" Marco snaps.

"You've led them right to us!" my brother snaps. "Everyone knows about how you're best friends with Hazel! So, who do you think they're coming *for* exactly?"

Realization dawns on my friend's face, and he goes pale. "Haze, I didn't know-"

Quickly I grab his hand and squeeze it as they get closer, more for my comfort than his. "I know. Just... Don't let go of my hand, okay?"

"Rocky and Hazel Adams, I presume?" one says, smiling at us sweetly. "We've been hired by the school to protect the premiers. I know your letter didn't go into detail, but I'll explain this to you two now. Under no circumstances are commoners allowed to interact with the premiers. There's a fine associated with it. Now you two-" He looks down at my hand locked in Marco's "-have broken that rule."

"She's my *friend*," Marco growls. "I've known her since she popped out of the womb."

"That's a lovely image, Marco," Rocky sighs sarcastically, rubbing his eyes tiredly.

"We understand that, Mr White," the second one says. "But it's the rules."

"Now." The first man pulls a white ticket out of his pocket. "This is the fine: two hundred pounds."

What?

For *talking* to Marco?

I can feel my friend's grip tighten. "That's ridiculous! She didn't even know!"

The last one, a woman, sighs irritably. "We understand that. But we need to set an example."

This is shit. But I can't cause trouble when everyone has exams; they're stressed enough. Rocky has enough on his plate without having to worry about some stupid fine.

"Who do I pay?" I ask venomously.

The second guy smirks victoriously. "The school reception. In cash."

"Alright. If we're done here you need to leave Mr White alone immediately." The first guy shoots my brother, who has been unusually quiet, a suspicious glare. "Either return to your room or leave the premises. You are not to communicate with him, or any other premier, again. Do you understand?"

Yeah, like that'll happen.

"Loud and clear. Come on, Braith, we need to check out anyway."

Braith looks astonished at how easily I'm giving up. Everyone does. Aqueous gets up as I do, his mouth open in shock.

"No, don't..." Marco yanks me back, his voice soft and pained.

Can't you see what I'm doing?

My eyes sting as I stare into his wide eyes; I don't want to give up and leave him like this. I try to pull my hand out of his grip, but he's stubborn. At this point the three suited people look annoyed. One grabs my arm and yanks it out of his grip herself. Despite my head reeling over what's happened and my arm aching, I manage to get around the corner with Braith before dropping my calm demeanour. Leaning back against the peeling wall, the tears finally flow. Aqueous nuzzles my hand softly and looks up at me with understanding eyes.

"We'll get past this," she murmurs, wiping a tear away from my eye. "We'll find a way. I know for sure Marco won't give up; he looked heartbroken."

"This is shit," is all I can think to say.

With a small laugh, she replies: "Everything is shit now. But we'll get past it, all of it."

* * *

"I hate English. Do I have to go?" Rocky whines.

"*Yes.* You'll do fine, honestly. I believe in you."

My words seem to have a tiny impact as his shoulders relax a bit. "What are you going to do now?"

"I'm going to go home. I haven't seen Wes yet; he's probably worried sick about me."

My gaze travels to Marco, who is leaning on the reception desk, his eyes dull and distant. Suited people are everywhere; I think there's one for each premier present. I couldn't go over to him if I'd wanted to.

"Haze?" He follows my gaze, and his face quickly hardens. "*Don't.*"

"Rocky, I'm not stupid." I sigh, averting my gaze as my friend looks up at me.

"You are around *him.* I remember when he thought it would be a hilarious idea to climb onto the school roof. You both fell through and into the classroom below, he broke his wrist and your head almost cracked open; you still have the bloody scar. I think that's quite stupid, don't you think?"

"Alright, I get it," I reply, self-consciously rubbing the large angry line stretching from my nose to my eye.

"No, you don't." He grabs me by the shoulders and shakes me slightly. "Being away from him could be good for you. You could make some new friends."

"Oh? I'm sorry, who introduced you to Braith and Wes?"

"Apart from them. Some proper friends, ones who will actually be there for you."

My heart thumps wildly at what he's saying. How can he question my friends? Braith has been extremely supportive through the really bad times, and although Wes is grumpy I know he still cares about me and would be there if I ever needed him. They're all there for me!

"Marco would dive off a cliff if I told him to," I snap, pushing him back, but he barely stumbles. "And Braith is always around. So, you have no right to say I don't have 'proper' friends."

He scratches the back of his head sheepishly. "I just meant that... I want you to make some new friends. People who will be good for you. Marco's a dick, Braith is unnaturally obsessed with you and Wes is a grumpy little shit. Make some *good* friends. Promise me you'll try?"

He won't back down.

Just because I say I will doesn't mean I have to, anyway.

"Fine." I don't meet his gaze as I speak. He knows I won't keep my word.

"All students line up in your seat numbers outside the hall for the English exam!" The invigilator calls, opening the large double doors to the freezing cold hall inside.

"Good luck. Try your best, I'll be rooting for you." I quickly kiss him on the cheek before he's swept off in the wave of students making their way to the lines.

He'll do fine.

After leaving Rocky to it, I briefly saw Braith and said good luck before I went home. Surprisingly, a lot of people were hanging around, chatting and laughing loudly amongst each other. Wes sees me before I see him, and he flies into my arms.

"I saw the mess and thought something horrible had happened," he says. "I'm glad you're okay."

"I'm sorry I didn't leave a note or something."

"It's no problem. I heard about that brooch thing. Are you okay with it?" He pulls away carefully, concern written all over his face.

"No. I'm not allowed to go near Marco anymore." My voice trails off as a lump forms in my throat. "It's not fair."

"You can't, but Braith and I can. We'll be your messengers, you know? You write notes to him and he'll write notes to you."

"Have you been coming up with this all day?"

He smooths his hair back sheepishly. "Kinda."

Softly, I smile and whisper: "Thank you."

"Do you need help with those?" Before I can protest he's taken a bag out of my hands.

"Yeah, th-"

"What is *she* doing here? This is a poverty-free zone!"

What the fuck?

All eyes are on the door at this point. A tall girl with ginger hair stares straight at me with utter distaste.

"I live here," I snap back, before remembering that she's a premier.

Smirking at my mistake, she skips outside and starts screaming at the top of her lungs.

Another fine for me.

Wes groans and rolls his eyes. "She provoked you!"

"That's another two hundred quid down the drain." I drop my bags and collapse on Wes' bed, awaiting my punishment.

A moment later a man in a grey suit strides in, his cold gaze immediately locking on me. "Hazel Adams?"

"Yes. Cut the crap and give me the fine," I reply venomously, crossing my arms as the man stops inches from me.

He pulls a pink ticket out of his pocket. "The standard two hundred pounds fine, but with an extra fifty added due to verbal harassment."

Bullshit! That girl is deliberately doing this!

"That's not fair!"

"We're doing our job to protect the premiers." He places the ticket onto my lap. "Have a good day, Miss Adams. Your markings are actually well hidden today, good job."

How does he...?

How much does he know?

I'm tempted to call him back. Did someone tell him?

The premier peeks her head around the corner, and bursts out laughing with her friends as they crowd around the door, clearly satisfied with their little joke.

I've lost four hundred and fifty pounds today. I'm just going to keep quiet, and ignore all the premiers from now on. Some of them obviously have ulterior motives.

"Wes?"

My friend's gaze flicks back to me, his eyes are round and scared. "Yes?"

"I need you to deliver something to Marco for me."

30

Chapter Thirty

Dear Marco,

This is the only way we can talk, okay? If we even look at each other on the street I'll be drowned in fines. Wes has agreed to be our messenger, so expect loads of letters.

The suited guys have it in for me, I know it. You need to look after yourself, mingle with the other premiers, make stupid jokes about commoners and all that. The other kids aren't stupid; they'll start singling you out if you continue moping.

And, yes, you have been moping.

I got another fine, which is stupid, I know. But the guy said that I've covered up my markings well today...

They know something. I don't know what it is yet, or how much they know, but this isn't good.

We'll have to designate a meeting place or something pretty soon; I don't want to have to send letters to you for the rest of my life.

This is stupid. We've only been apart a few hours and I'm acting as if we haven't seen each other for a year and a half.

See you soon,

Hazel.

PS, you owe me two hundred quid. I'm not paying your fine.

Braith gives the letter back to Marco, who looks confused about whether to feel troubled or happy. But this is bad. If they know about Hazel, surely they'll know about her? Or Wes? Or Rocky?

Maybe they know the other Original Elementals?

"What do we do?" she asks.

Marco folds the letter up and puts it in his pocket. "I need to write back, for starters."

"Not that!" Angrily, she whacks him over the head. "He called her out on her markings!"

"They must know something, maybe something we don't." He cranes his neck to look at Rocky, who is staring at them with a quizzical expression. "He really should be discussing this with us."

"He'll be fined if he does. Sadie deliberately bumped into him an hour ago, then she ran off screaming about his 'sexual intentions' and now he's got an extra five hundred quid to pay. I think he's got enough on his mind."

Marco leans back on the bed post, his eyes narrowed. "This is shit. I hate it. And I hate those stupid guys. They follow me around everywhere."

"I know. I watched that guy follow you into the bathroom," she smirks.

"It was creepy!" he whines. "It put me off."

"Do you think that's how they found out about the markings?"

He raises an eyebrow. "Huh?"

"Well, we don't know how long these guys have been around for."

"I *think* I would have noticed a group of people in suits following me around." He rolls his eyes.

"*Shut up.* I've recognized one or two of them; they probably disguised themselves as visitors. They might have been listening in on us."

Taking this into account, he shrugs doubtfully. "Possibly. It would explain why they want to keep me away from Hazel and Rocky, seeing as they have markings. But I can still speak with you and Wes."

"Maybe… You can ask some questions," she says slowly.

Surely if Marco could try to ask some questions, it might shed some light on their motives? It might give them more answers too.

"They might play dumb."

"Try! What have you got to lose? They've separated you from Hazel, they follow you around like hunting dogs and they're limiting what you can do! *Try!*"

"Calm down, I will." He puts his hands up in defeat.

"You'd better. Now, what do you want to write to Hazy then, huh? Are you gonna get a boner whilst writing it?"

* * *

"Are you serious? How old are you, five? I'm not a babysitter!"

"If this backfires, you're taking full responsibility!" Marco hisses, making Braith recoil.

How does Hazy put up with you?

She guessed he was still upset. Three days have passed since he last spoke to Hazel face to face, so she put up with his behaviour because she knew he was cranky about it. Despite this, it wasn't her fault. He didn't have to take his anger out on her.

"Are you sure you're ready? You've said this twice now and you-"

"That's because they keep running off to fine any commoners who even glance at me," he argues.

"Are you alright, Mr White?" The suited guy finally approaches, looking Braith up and down suspiciously.

"You know about the markings, right?" Marco asks him coldly.

He really does get straight to the point.

For a second the man looks unsure of what to say, before realization dawns on his face. "You know about Miss Adams' markings."

"Of course, I do."

This isn't staying on the down low...

"And the others?"

"Wes, Braith and Rocky. We want to know what you know."

Braith shuffles uncomfortably next to Marco, stepping behind him a little so all the focus is on him. This guy could do anything, and she didn't want to be in his line of fire.

The guy laughs manically. "And why... Should I tell you?"

"As my new protector, you have no right to keep anything from me. So, in your own time."

The man's face falls as he contemplates what Marco is saying. It's true, that rule was passed on the day the protectors were introduced, to try to make the students feel a little less restricted and more trusting of their new bodyguards. Braith saw it as a bunch of shit, but Marco mentioning it certainly made things easier.

"Fine," the man sighs, curling and uncurling his fingers, as if he wanted nothing more than to punch Marco in the face. "The Primordial Dragon won't stay in captivity for long. The markings are beacons, nothing special. Basically, your little friends are targets, prey for the dragon to hunt down once it breaks free."

Braith gulps and opens her mouth to speak, but can't find the right question.

Once the dragon breaks free and grows strong enough, it'll come for all of them first. It knows what will happen.

I'm only seventeen, for fuck's sake! Why should I be worrying about death now?

"They can only defeat it by using the methods their ancestors used. But, it looks as if the dragon has been created too early, so it's going up against children. And, they don't even know every person with markings, let alone their leader." The guy finally takes a breath, a smug look on his face. "Any questions?"

Marco looks back at Braith, waiting expectantly for her answer. Shaking her head vigorously, she ducks back even further behind Marco as the guy laughs again.

"Well, I'll back off again now. Have a nice day, Mr White." The man then walks backwards into the crowd, but hangs around close enough so that Marco is still in plain sight.

We were way *off with the whole 'stalking for months' thing.*

Marco clears his throat at the awkward silence. "Looks like I'm writing to Hazel."

"No, I'll go tell her myself," she mutters.

I'm sure Wes will love to hear this.

31

Chapter Thirty-One

Braith's news is horrifying, we're all in danger now. Well, more so than before. Rocky, Wes, Braith and I have sat here arguing about it for an hour now. No-one knows what we should do.

"We need to tell Ray," Wes pleads. "He'll know what to do."

"No!" Rocky fumes, moving in front of me protectively. "He's horrible! I don't want him hurting my sister again!"

Braith looks torn. She hates Ray as much as I do, but would it be a good idea to tell him? Could he point us in some direction?

I have to take that chance.

"Go tell him, Wes," I murmur.

"No!" My brother strokes my cheek softly, whispering: "I don't want him to hurt you anymore."

"I know. But if we keep this from him he will anyway." I look back at Wes, who looks smug that I've taken his side. "Now, before I change my mind."

He nods and jogs outside, taking his phone out of his pocket. My cabin is empty. Everyone is out enjoying a rare day of warmth and sunshine. It's usually pouring with rain or dull and grey around here.

Braith smiles slightly, though it doesn't reach her eyes. "It's the right thing."

I slither onto Wes' bed and let her lean against me. "I know."

My brother is enraged, but I know that he knows this is the right choice. He can't hurt anyone if we tell him straight away.

At least, I hope he won't.

He's unpredictable, and that's what scares me most about him.

After a few minutes, the door swings open and Ray speed-walks down the aisle, beaming. "So? Tell me!" he demands excitedly.

All eyes are on Wes, who clears his throat uncomfortably. "The protectors know about the markings and the Primordial Dragon."

"How did they find out?"

My friend shrugs, unable to meet Ray's intense gaze. "They didn't say. All they told Marco and Braith was that the markings are beacons. Once the dragon is strong enough, its instincts will take over and it will come straight to us."

The blond boy nods slowly, then straightens up and claps his hands together. "Good work. Can Marco get any more out of them?"

For a moment, I don't realize that the question is aimed at me. I want to answer, but I don't know what the truthful answer would be. He hasn't had the chance to write to me about it yet. For all I know he could be dead-set on never trying again.

"The protector didn't seem as if he was giving us the full story," Braith jumps in. "I don't think any of them plan to tell us anyway. I think [we've exhausted that option already;] we're lucky the guy told us anything."

What more can he possibly want? Nothing we do will be good enough for him.

"Give us the night to think it over," Wes chirps in as Ray takes a threatening step towards Braith. "We might come up with a better plan."

Thank fuck Wes has finally grown some balls.

The shorter boy stands his ground, his unwavering gaze challenging Ray to disregard his judgement. To everyone's surprise, Ray silently walks away. He throws Wes an angry glare as he opens the door, but my friend wasn't about to receive *any* repercussions.

"Yeah, he was a great help. Great plan, guys." Rocky finally speaks once he's sure Ray is out of earshot.

Okay, it wasn't the best idea in the world, but it was worth a shot.

At least that will shut Ray up for a few days. But now we need to devise a new plan. We can't just keep sending Marco out to ask questions; I don't want him *too* involved in all of this. The only other thing to do would be to wait for Olwen to contact us. Braith sent her a letter yesterday.

This is becoming more complicated by the minute. We could be going in the complete opposite direction for all I know.

Well, I hope not. It would be a huge waste of time otherwise.

* * *

"All the new First Years will be arriving tomorrow. This place will be packed," Braith mumbles through her sandwich, looking around the near empty café. "The kids get shorter every year. Next year they'll be the size of ants." Imitating squashing ants underneath her foot, she giggles at my unamused expression.

"I heard that it's one of the largest Years in school." Rocky fiddles with the food left on his plate, pushing it around in circles aimlessly. "There will be screaming kids everywhere."

"I know, but it's so sweet! Seeing all of them run around with their eggs reminds me of when Damayanti was newly hatched." She sighs blissfully.

"Cerberus hatched and immediately chewed my duvet," my brother huffs, though a hint of a smile appears on his face.

Remembering Mr Reedman and the egg fiasco makes me shiver. I hope none of the new kids have to experience that. I've heard that their Head of Instructors is Mr Stirling though, so I'm sure they'll be fine.

"I wonder if I'll get to mentor another kid this year," Braith says.

"Maybe you could, Haze." My brother nudges my arm playfully. "It'll be good for you. It's really rewarding."

I don't know any of the kids coming up, but if I'm able to it would be a good opportunity. Marco taught me well, so it could be cool to help some kid to master their element.

"Maybe. It would be cool to teach someone everything Marco taught me. Despite what you think of him, he was a great mentor." My gaze travels to Aqueous, who is happily playing with Cerberus and Damayanti, batting at a bouncy yellow ball. All dragons need friends, so helping a new kid could build their dragon's confidence.

"Um, Hazel?"

I'm brought back to reality as Lilac Samuels, a girl from water dragon training, taps me on the shoulder.

"Oh, hey," I say awkwardly.

"Can I talk to you for a sec? Privately?" Her blank expression gives nothing away.

Casting my brother a confused glance, I follow her to edge of the café where a large rosebush is planted, poking out the white fence at all angles. Her companion, a black dragon with purple splotches, sniffs Aqueous cautiously, before the two quickly trap each other in a friendly headlock. The dragon's horns are long and straight, so my partner struggles to get out of its grip when its horns become entangled in his curved ones.

"Midnight, no." Lilac scolds her companion, who frees itself from Aqueous and plonks itself down sulkily and swings its tail around.

"Is something up...?" I ask carefully.

The ginger girl shakes her head. "No, no. It's just, I overheard your conversation with your friends and…I was wondering if you'd maybe mentor my sister when she arrives?"

This is unexpected. I hadn't thought about becoming a mentor that much, but it would be a good distraction from everything else going on. Plus, I'll get a qualification at the end of it, so I really should accept…

"Sure."

She smiles gratefully. "Thank you, really. My sisters are triplets, you see, and I can only mentor one. I think Violet would really benefit from learning from you. You and Marco had such a great relationship at dragon training, and I'd like her to experience that."

Fuck, now I've got to fill Marco's shoes.

"No problem." I giggle as Aqueous and Midnight start wrestling again, with my companion puffing his chest out in pride at pinning the other dragon down.

"After she's got her egg you can meet her, if you want. She's very, very quiet and shy, but maybe you and your friends can get her out of her shell."

She's got high expectations of me. What have I got myself into?

"Of course. We'll be at Flamethrower's."

"The burger place?"

"Yeah."

"Okay, I'll take her over. Thank you, really. I owe you one."

I smile sheepishly. "It's fine, really."

"I'll let you get back to lunch now." She backs away in embarrassment, calling her companion to follow. "See you tomorrow."

That was awkward, but I'm a mentor now. I just need to be laid-back and gentle like Marco was; that helped me when I was learning. There's nothing worse than having a mentor who will push you too hard. I don't want to overwhelm the poor girl.

"Hey, what was that about?" Rocky glances at Lilac as she returns to her friends.

"Oh, she asked me to mentor her sister. She's a triplet, so Lilac could only mentor one."

My brother beams with pride. "Well done! You'll do great!"

"Is the sister hot?" Braith leans closer over the table.

"Braith!"

She holds her hands up with a shocked expression. "I can't wait forever for ya, Hazy. I've got needs. But, I'm always here whenever you decide to switch teams."

Rocky and I decide to ignore her comment, as he pulls me close to him in a hug. "Haze, you'll do fantastic. It's a huge responsibility, though."

"I know. I don't need the lecture, okay?" I giggle playfully, squirming in his arms.

"You're not going to tell her about the markings, are you?" Braith's tone turns serious, and her signature grin has been wiped from her face as she anxiously awaits my answer.

I can't burden Violet with what's happening. She is not involved, and I intend to keep it that way. If she were to see my markings, however, I'll come clean. I wouldn't be comfortable lying to her and breaking her trust so early on.

"No. She doesn't need to know."

Rocky nods his approval, while Braith sighs: "Good. We don't need to drag more people into this mess. But, if you're going to be a mentor, I want you to know that you can ask me for advice any time."

"Thanks," I mumble, smiling half-heartedly as she grins excitedly.

I really should be asking Marco for advice. He was my mentor, after all, but this stupid separation thing is still crap. If I need anything, I guess I'll just write to him. But I know that Braith reads anything she delivers, so I'm not sure that's a good idea.

Oh well.

I guess I'll just wait and see.

* * *

"What time do you think she'll be here?" Braith asks again.

"I dunno. Give her a chance."

I've invited Rocky, Braith and Wes to meet the girl that I'll be teaching. She might see them occasionally and I want to minimize the number of awkward encounters.

"Oh, great," Rocky sighs irritably and puts his face in his hands.

Braith looks towards the door and points excitedly. I follow her gaze and I'm pleasantly surprised to see Marco come in with Mason and Sadie. A few others follow who I don't recognize, but I don't care about them.

He's finally cut his hair. It's now short and tufty like Mason's, but it suits him better than looking like a surfer. My face heats up at the thought of him looking more handsome than usual. As they all sit down, I see how miserable he looks. Previously he told me how he didn't like any of his old 'friends'. He doesn't want to hang out with them. But I realize that he has no choice, as I'm always with Braith or Wes, so I suppose he doesn't really get the chance to hang out with the group anymore.

"What's he doing here?" Rocky groans.

"He's got a face like a smacked ass." Braith waves her hand in Rocky's face to silence him. "I don't think he's happy with them."

"I wouldn't be," I say.

I find myself staring at him, half-hoping he would notice me. His eyes are locked on the table, although he isn't engaging in any of the conversations.

"When is this chick coming again?" Braith whines, with her chin resting on the table.

"Braith, I still don't know," I slap her hand away as she tries to poke me with a fork. "I need the toilet."

"You know where it is?" my brother asks.

"Yes. The eagle bush, I remember." Before they can follow me, I rush into the bathroom to give myself a minute to think.

I can't just leave him.

I can't believe money is standing between me and my best friend. Surely I should ignore it and pretend everything is normal? I may be in debt for the rest of my life but maybe it will be worth it?

What am I thinking?

It's horrible. Either way, the outcome won't be good.

With a heavy heart, I go to re-join the others, but I'm yanked inside the boys' toilet when I pass by the door. With my heart racing, I panic as the person's grip tightens.

What do I do? A cold stream of water shoots out of my hands and at the person's feet, making them jump back in surprise.

"Haze, stop!"

How can I not recognize that voice?

Squealing happily, I jump into Marco's arms and snuggle into his chest. For a moment he tenses up, before relaxing and muttering in my ear: "I just wanted to talk to you."

"In the toilet? How did you know no-one was in here?"

"I took a chance."

"Ew."

"Whatever; just be glad I didn't hide in the girls' toilets."

Without letting me go, he starts fiddling around in his pocket and shoves paper in my hand. Money, to be exact – a lot of it. "What is-" He cuts me off as someone knocks on the door from the outside.

"Mr White? Is everything okay in there?" a man's voice rings out.

"Yeah. I'll be out in a minute."

"A commoner wants to come in, so you'd better hurry up."

"My protector," he whispers, seeing my confused expression. "I just needed to talk to you; letters aren't the same."

"I know. But we haven't found a safe area to meet yet. Either protectors or other students go to the places we've already scouted."

Braith and I have looked around, behind shops or secluded areas, but each is visited too often to use. It's getting frustrating; we may never find a place.

"It's okay." He rests his head on top of mine. "We'll work around this, I swear."

"So, the money...?" I don't feel comfortable putting it away; I don't want it. It makes feel like I'm using him for his money.

"For the fines. Both of them. I don't want Aqueous' working funds to run dry."

"No, don't-"

Messing my hair up with his chin, he sighs: "Hey, in that first letter you told me it was my fine, and it's true. If I didn't have a protector it wouldn't have happened. As for the second one, I'm just being nice."

"No, please..." I try to shove the notes back in his pocket, but he holds my arm back. "I won't be able to pay you back..."

Smiling widely, he strokes my back softly. "Talking to you is payment enough."

"Mr White!" The protector bangs continuously on the door.

"I've got to go." His eyes glaze over as he backs away. "I hope I can see you again soon."

"Please, another minute..." I bolt to block the door stubbornly, my hand practically glued to the handle.

He rolls his eyes at me, amused. "No. You'll get in trouble."

"If you won't come out, I'll come in!" the protector warns.

Effortlessly, he pushes me out the way and kisses my cheek softly, staying a second too long, making my skin burn in embarrassment. "I'll write to you tonight, I swear." He turns to leave before swinging back around and brushing my fringe back gently. "Stop hiding behind your hair. How am I going to see your pretty face if your hair is constantly blocking it?"

Before I can object, he's gone. I can hear his protector scolding him outside, and Marco brushing him off. It was nice to talk to him again, even though we talked about crap. I didn't even ask him for mentoring advice.

"I knew you were in here!"

My head snaps up as Rocky enters the bathroom, slamming the door behind him.

Oh crap.

"Rocky, I-"

"No, *I'll* talk," he warns, his face contorted into anger. "You and Marco are not one person, I don't know why, after every opportunity you have to get away, you go running back to him!"

"He's my-"

"Look, Violet is sat outside waiting for you! You're just standing around in here, wasting yet more of your life talking to that prick!"

Violet's outside?

Why am I still in here then?

I side-step around him to get out the door; he follows me out, his eyes narrowed and waiting for my answer. "I need to see her. We'll talk later." As he opens his mouth to retort, I kiss him on the cheek before rushing outside.

Violet is the first person I spot at the table. A smaller version of Lilac, she has chin-length curly ginger hair and dull grey eyes. Her face is small and covered in freckles, and she is a lot shorter than my friends, who practically swamp her in size. Her skin is pale and her frame is quite chubby.

"There she is!" Braith points at me excitedly, making Violet look up timidly.

"Hey." I greet the new girl, but she just smiles back shyly.

"Can she talk?" Wes asks, eyeing her up suspiciously.

Lilac did say that her sister was quiet and shy, so we need to be patient with her; she might open up if we give her time. Rocky sits down looking sour. He won't meet my gaze, instead crossing his arms stubbornly.

"Can we see your egg?" I ask her softly.

With a sharp nod, she lifts a large cream egg with brown splotches onto the table, making my heart sink slightly. It's a rare dragon, so how am I supposed to attend her higher training sessions as a commoner? All the premiers in her Year are bound to attend too, so I could get swamped in fines each lesson.

"Woah," Braith picks up the egg, handling it with great care. "This one is *huge*. It might beat Asteroid in the size department."

"Our dragons will be happy to have a new friend," Wes comments.

"Can I see them?" Violet speaks up for the first time, but her voice is a barely a whisper.

"Yeah, sure. They're outside."

Rocky stays sulking at the table as we go outside, not excited in the slightest for her to meet our companions. Cerberus is the first to spot us, yelping and jumping around as we approach. Surprisingly, Violet runs towards her and starts fussing over the brown dragon, who can't get enough of the attention.

"Aw! It's so cute!" Braith coos as Aqueous and Asteroid join in.

In fact, *all* the dragons in the paddock want to be touched by Violet, trying to squeeze as close to the fence as possible to join in on the fun. Drea is also vying for a chance to join in, as well as Fortune and Exquisite.

This is...unusual.

"What is going on?" Wes murmurs. "This never happens!"

"I guess she's just really good with dragons?" I throw in unhelpfully, still trying to wrap my head around the scene before me.

Violet beams at us, petting Fortune with one hand and an unknown dragon in the other. "What are their names?"

Wes pats Asteroid on the neck, who noses the unknown dragon out the way to be petted. "This is my companion, Asteroid."

"This is Damayanti!" Braith squeals, her arms locked around her companion's neck.

Aqueous' concentration breaks off when I stroke his nose, and he looks at me with over-excitable eyes. "My partner is Aqueous."

Violet ignores the other dragons to stroke my partner; he practically melts in her eyes. "A black common dragon," she breathes. "You're lucky."

"Yeah, I know."

The ginger girl glances at her little pink flowery handbag, out of which her egg pokes. "I hope mine is as funny as these guys," she murmurs, mostly to herself.

This girl is mysterious. She's as quiet as Lilac said she would be, but she seems comfortable around dragons, which is understandable I guess if she doesn't really like people. She will have a great companion at this rate; maybe that's what will bring her out of her shell.

"Can we go to the shops quickly?" Wes suddenly asks, opening the gate to let our companions out of the paddock.

"How come? Are you bored already?" Braith clambers onto Damayanti's back, swinging her legs like a child.

"No; we need to get our textbooks for the year and our dragon amateur kits. Not to mention Violet needs her starter kit," Wes says, matter-of-factly.

Fuck, I forgot about that. The shops only sell them today, otherwise we have to pay double to get the textbooks from school.

"Yeah, we have time." I glance at Rocky through the restaurant window, and motion him over as he looks up with a quizzical glare.

As he lumbers outside he raises an eyebrow when he sees Violet playing with the dragons in the paddock, but makes no comment about it. "Yes?" he mutters through gritted teeth.

"We're going to the shops to get our dragon kits and textbooks. Are you coming?" I play with my fingers sheepishly.

"Fine. Whatever."

I'm going to have to do a lot to make things up to him. I don't even know why I should anyway; he's the one making a huge fuss out of nothing. Marco is my best friend; how can he expect me to just drop him with no notice? I refuse to do what Maya did.

I won't drop Marco for some idiotic reason.

Rocky will just have to live with that.

32

Chapter Thirty-Two

"You'll need to explain again; I'm still not getting it," Rocky says, tapping the table impatiently.

Braith sighs, opening Bonfire's book again, the Original fire elemental. *"Before Bonfire bravely investigated Draca's lair in the mountains, the Original Elementals had no idea why Draca would attack them with such ferocity and hatred. His discovery was that Draca wanted the Original Elementals for their elements, which the dragon thought could be obtained by swallowing the Original Elementals whole."*

"How did he find that out from looking at the damned thing?" Rocky tries to take the book from Braith, only for her to yank it back protectively.

"Let me finish!" she whines, kicking her feet against the table childishly.

My brother puts his hands up apologetically. "Fine, fine, continue."

Before continuing, Braith takes a deep breath, probably for effect. *"However, due to the markings on the Original Elementals' backs, Draca struggled to swallow them, as Bonfire found out, because the markings would heat up and burn its throat until it coughed them back up."*

"Bonfire got swallowed?" Wes' eyes widen in amazement.

"Yes, shh!" Braith puts her finger against his lips, making him move his chair back in disgust. "Anyway, if I *may*," she clears her throat, glaring at all three of us around the table. "I will finish. *Bonfire managed to escape, leaving an enraged Draca behind him.*"

For a few seconds no-one speaks, until Rocky sighs and squeezes the bridge of his nose irritably.

"Are you done now?" he asks.

Braith closes the book excitedly. "Mm-hm! Whaddaya think?"

"At least that clears up why Draca wants us," I chip in before Rocky or Wes can start asking questions. "Good job, Braith."

Her eyes light up like a Christmas tree, and she leaps across the table to sit on my lap. "Thanks, Hazy! Your approval means the most to me, let's kiss it out!"

As she leans down to kiss me, Rocky yanks her off and pushes her lightly back into her seat, his eyes burning with fury.

"Braith, you'll tell Marco, won't you?" Wes asks sheepishly.

"Yeah, sure, I'll tell 'im, although I'm sure he'd prefer Hazy telling him."

My eyes burn slightly, but I quickly blink any forming tears away. I miss Marco, but we still have the letters; he's even started spraying his cologne so they smell like him. Every letter reminds me of when he kissed me in the bathroom, which makes me squirm with embarrassment. He's kissed me like that before and it's been no problem, so I don't understand what's different this time.

My brother snaps me out of my daydream by huffing irritably. "He'll have to deal with you instead; I'm sure he doesn't care that much."

"He does, believe me," Braith shoots back, glaring at Rocky to keep silent.

"So..." Wes leans on the table, obviously trying to change the subject. "Draca..."

"The solution is easy, dude. Don't get swallowed."

"Braith, that's not a solution. How am I supposed to prevent that?" Wes sighs irritably.

Tapping her chin lightly in thought, she suddenly jumps up and bangs her hand on the table. "We eat loads of hot stuff, then it'll be even more unpleasant for Draca!"

"That's beyond stupid." Rocky rolls his eyes, leaning back in his chair and staring blankly at the table.

Braith's lip quivers slightly in mock hurt. "You come up with an idea then, jackass."

"You're a jackass."

"No, you!"

"I'm not arguing about this-"

"You're a huge jackass, I bet you're only like that to compensate for something." She shoots a quick glance at his crotch.

My brother goes bright red, his mouth open in shock. "That is not true and you know it!"

"Maybe that's why Ciara-"

Before Braith can finish her sentence, Rocky shoots up and flips the table on her. *"Fuck you!"*

Damayanti rushes over, nosing the table off a shivering Braith. The girl snuggles into her companion's chest, her brown eyes wide with fear.

"Rocky!" I ignore Aqueous as he starts nosing me to test if I'm okay. "What is wrong with you?"

Wordlessly, Rocky walks away, his hands balled into fists. Cerberus looks between everyone for a few seconds before letting out a sheepish whine and galloping after her angry companion.

"Are you okay?" I ignore Rocky and tend to my scared friend. If he wants to sulk then so be it.

She nods slowly, holding her arms out for a hug. Aqueous headbutts me into her arms, making Damayanti whine happily and nuzzle the top of our heads.

Rocky was out of order.

Does this mean the group is falling apart? First the separation from Marco and now little squabbles turning into huge arguments. This isn't good.

* * *

I giggle as Aqueous leaps on Damayanti, making the black and white dragon squeal in excitement as she puts him in a headlock. The two dragons continue to wrestle on the grass, growling and screeching as they pin each other.

After the argument earlier I thought it would be best to spend some time alone with Braith; she was pretty shaken up.

"They're such cuties!" Braith coos as Damayanti jumps into the air, soaring above Aqueous' head.

"You'll be flying her soon," I murmur enviously, watching the bright dragon tease my companion by swooping just above his head, while he's trying to nip her long tail.

"I know! I'll be the best, you know it."

"Yeah, yeah, you say that about everything."

"'Cause I am!" she argues, crossing her arms sulkily.

"You're the best at whining," I tease.

"I'll take it!"

"You're so weird!"

"Nuh-uh! You're the weird one!" She pushes my shoulder playfully. Flicking her arm, I huff: "Whatever!"

"Hey, Hazy?"

"Yeah?"

"Can you promise me something?" She turns towards me, taking my hand slowly.

CHAPTER THIRTY-TWO

"I'm not marrying you," I giggle.

She rolls her eyes. "Another day. I want you to promise that you'll be my friend."

"I am your friend, and you know that."

"Forever?"

"If we live that long."

She pushes me playfully. "Thanks, Hazy. We'll get married one day."

"Sorry, I'm not interested in marriage."

She prods my side a few times, trying to tickle me. "You'll change your mind! And when you do, I'll be here, in a bright white dress, waiting."

"I'd pay to see that!"

We both laugh and continue to watch our companions in a comfortable silence. I am glad I met Braith; she is one of the best friends I've ever had, second to Marco.

I can see us being friends for a long time.

33

Chapter Thirty-Three

"This is stupid. Can't we do something else?"

Braith shushes me and continues messing around with my hair. About an hour ago she came to me bored because Marco and Rocky were out, and Olwen had sent her some hair straighteners, which she wants to try out on me seeing as her hair isn't long enough.

"You're going to look outrageously sexy when I'm done with you!" She yanks at my hair once more, making me hiss in pain.

"Why did your sister send you hair straighteners when you barely have any hair anyway?"

"She's a big fan of make-up and shopping and all that crap. I'm only interested in it when I get to do it for other people. Mainly hot girls, though."

"Right…"

Pushing my head forward, she squeals in glee. "I'm done! It looks perfect!"

A small mirror is shoved in my face, allowing me to see the complete mess on top of my head. Strands of blonde hair stick out at weird angles and some parts aren't even straight at all. Braith needs practice, obviously.

"Perfect, huh?" I take the mirror from her and unsuccessfully try to comb it down with my fingers.

"To me. I'm wiping out all the competition, you see. No-one will go near you with hair like that, so I'm instantly your girlfriend." She leans in close and nuzzles my neck softly. "Let's make it official."

"I'd rather not." Her lip quivers in hurt as I push her away.

"Hazel?" Wes' voice makes me jump, I hadn't realized he'd come back from helping Ray sort through Cindaraan files.

"Hm?" I stop brushing my hair to glance at my friend, who looks horrified. "What's wrong?

"It's Draca. It's growing."

"What do you mean?" Braith puts the mirror down to stare at him quizzically.

With shaking hands, Wes crouches down next to us and plays a video on his phone. A woman in a black dress with a lanyard around her neck steps into view, clutching a microphone.

"Now we will speak to Dr Gard, who has been caring for the Primordial Dragon since its conception."

The camera pans over to an older man in a white lab coat. He glances uncomfortably at the camera. "We have named this specimen Draca after the legends of the infamous Primordial Dragon. It has far surpassed our expectations with its growth and intelligence. We are now working towards seeing if we can re-introduce it back into our ecosystem, with suitable safeguards in place of course."

"Isn't that dragon a little too big for our ecosystem?" The woman chuckles, flashing a fake smile to the camera. "How do we know this dragon won't just destroy like its ancestors did?"

"Ah, that is where these guys come in," He holds up a vial with a small wriggling grey shape in it. "These parasites lived off the Primordial Dragons, if we can harness their power, we can control Draca."

The woman scrunches her nose as the parasite leaps to the top of the vial, it's tail curling around itself. "What is that?"

"It's a Wyrm. The previously extinct ruler of the Wyrm family. This little guy may look small," he shakes the vial, and the Wyrm thrashes wildly. "but they have abilities that we hope to harness to control Draca. Let me show you."

"No, that's quite okay Dr-"

Before the woman can protest further, Dr Gard pops the lid off the vial, allowing the Wyrm to crawl onto his finger. It coils around his thumb, looking straight at the camera.

"Listen carefully." He says, raising his finger closer.

The camera zooms in on the Wyrm, sharpening its image. It has the body of a snake, but is covered in dull grey scales. It looks straight at the camera with its beady eyes, almost entranced.

"Why not listen to me?"

The woman and the cameraman gasp as the Wyrm speaks without moving its lips.

"I thought this was about-" Braith tries to interrupt.

"It's coming." Wes assures her.

Dr Gard nudges the Wyrm back into the vial as the woman composes herself. "Dr Gard, what was that?"

"Our way of controlling Draca. Manipulating its mind. Come, my colleagues have finished setting up."

"Setting up for what?"

Dr Gard points behind him, and a roar makes the camera shake.

"My God, it's-!"

"Beautiful." Dr Gard finishes.

The camera turns towards the noise, showing a blurry image of a giant amber dragon before swiftly cutting off. My arm starts to burn and Marine's bracelet glows brightly, as if reacting to Draca's roar. It glows brighter and brighter, turning my wrist a sickly shade of red.

It's going to come for us.

Want to find out more about Draca and the markings it follows? Read the next part of Hazel's adventure in *Venom and Earth*

About the Author

I am an author who mainly writes Young Adult Fantasy. However, I am hoping to branch into Sci-Fi, Horror and New Adult. Books got me through my darkest years as a teenager, and I hope that one day mine will inspire young people to keep going. I live in the UK with my two cats, Rocky and Mishka.

You can connect with me on:
- https://www.jessicaturnbull.com
- https://twitter.com/jess_a_turnbull
- https://m.facebook.com/jessicaturnbullauthor/?ref=bookmarks

Subscribe to my newsletter:
- https://www.subscribepage.com/jessicaturnbull

Also by Jessica Turnbull

Get a free eBook when you sign up to my mailing list!

Short Story Collection

https://www.subscribepage.com/jessicaturnbull

Read four short stories from the Elemental Dragons universe:

Circles - Russet dreams of being free, but will this ever become a reality again?

Hesitation - Hercules has an opportunity for escape, but is it entering the same world it left?

Passion - Ophelia paints to remind herself of her companion, can she find her inspiration?

Purpose - Moon has been alone ever since his companion died, can four younglings cheer him up?

You will also receive my monthly newsletter, which will contain: announcements, cover reveals, my book of the month, writing excerpts and more!